The People of the Broken Neck

The People

of the

Broken Neck

SILAS DENT ZOBAL

unbridled books

UNBRIDLED BOOKS

Library of Congress Cataloging-in-Publication Data
Library of Congress Cataloging-in-Publication Data
Names: Zobal, Silas Dent, author.
Title: The people of the broken neck / by Silas Dent Zobal.
Description: Lakewood, CO : Unbridled Books, [2016]
Identifiers: LCCN 2016011035 | ISBN 9781609531348 (alk. paper)
Subjects: | BISAC: FICTION / Action & Adventure. | GSAFD: Adventure fiction.
| Suspense fiction.
Classification: LCC PS3626.O236 P46 2016 | DDC 813/.6--dc23

LC record available at https://lccn.loc.gov/2016011035

1 3 5 7 9 10 8 6 4 2

For my kids, Emerson and Lake

We men are wretched things,

and the gods, who have no cares

themselves, have woven sorrow

into the very pattern of our lives.

HOMER, *THE ILIAD*

AT NIGHT THE TILLED EARTH looked like a black lake. A stand of trees sheltered on the near side of the field and on the far side was a log cabin. The long branches of the trees leaned against the ground and something as dark as oil dripped from their tips. When the halogen lights began to sweep the inside of the cabin, the father did not rise from where he hunkered between his daughter and his son beneath the hollow pine. On each of them he rested one of his hands. The ground beneath them was still stiff with late-March cold and the scent of wood smoke drifting from their cabin smelled like his children's sleeping skins.

Down the hill, past the line of willows and the hollow pine and the plum tree, the Susquehanna River coiled like a black rope. Above them something moved in the branches. Something that moved quickly with unseen claws scraping against unseen bark. The wind brushed dead leaves off the ground, and the moon came and went, and the blossoms of the plum tree lifted and settled again like a thousand shushing tongues.

The cabin's screen door opened and closed with a metallic crack and two man-shaped shadows stumbled forward as though tethered to the narrow ends of their beams of light. A crackle of static on a handheld radio. The distance between the father's ear and the log cabin stripped away the particulars of enunciation, the likely raised vowels of easterners, and what was left was pared down to the bark of anger in a man's voice. Bootfall against stone. Headlamps appeared and a guttural engine sparked to life as if it was inside his chest, and then the gravel lane pattered and cracked behind the wheels and the headlamps circled back toward the dark, flat line of the road.

The father said the names of his children to himself under his breath. A kind of incantation to keep them safe. The older, the boy, he called "Clarke." The younger, the girl, "King," short for Kingsley. The cuneiform of his two kids in their downy sleeping bags looked sunken in rather than risen up. Like impressions in the ground.

NOTHING HERE. THE first man into the cabin had known it from the start. Empty. He swung his halogen flashlight back and forth. There was nothing. He lightfooted through the dining room. A table and four chairs. A clock on the wall that did not keep time. A second man shadowed the first like an obedient dog. They rifled the medicine cabinet, then the first man stopped in the center of the living room and listened. Again, nothing. It was a small house. A cabin. He touched the black woodstove. Still warm. He wiped the sweat from his lips. He was tired of hunting men who'd mucked up their lives, who'd done things wrong. He played the light around the children's room. Unmade bunks. Baseball gloves. Sock monkeys. A worn doll. Spine-snapped books on a shelf of cement block and pine two-by-sixes. The first man put one hand to his neck. His skin felt hot enough to mold into a new shape. He wanted to go home to his wife and their cool sheets and their new bed. He opened the refrigerator in the kitchen. The second man leaned over him, breathing heavily. Two hot dogs. Leftover macaroni and cheese, no mold. No hot dog buns. His nylon jacket swished as he turned. The second man scrambled back, his shoe slipping on the vinyl floor. The second man fell sideways until the first man reached out to catch him by his forearm. Still, the second man's upper lip caught the corner of the countertop. The flesh split. When the second man straightened, the first man shook his head. One drop of dark blood fell. Two drops of blood. The first man stepped out on the porch and looked out. His flashlight petered into the darkness. The night was like a foreign sound. He put his hands in the pockets of his nylon jacket. "Let's go," he said to the second man. "There's nothing here."

THE NIGHT NOISES startled the children from sleep. The turn of an engine. The pad of some quick dark feet. A rock falling distantly into the river. When they half woke and slit their adapted eyes through the narrow aperture of the cloth cinched around their faces, they would see him. A great shadow with broad wide-set legs. A breadth of shoulder that they knew as intuitively as their own smaller shapes. A woody smell to the air and a sense of immovability. Their eyes would close again. Their breath would even out. On the ground, they slept well, so long as their father, silent and impassable and granitic, guarded against the night.

He waited in the dark with his hands cupped before his face. His name was Dominick Clarke Sawyer. His kids' faces were like points of light circled by the dark fabric of their mummy bags. Dominick did not think of who had been inside his house. He did not think of how the lights had swept back and forth systematically looking, looking. He did not think about whom the lights had looked for. He did not think about his past or about the weight of the pistol in the waistband holster beneath his belt. He did not think about where his boot prints could be seen crossing the mud of the field or how a barred owl had hooh-hoohed in alarm because he and his kids had lain down near the nest. He did not consider why he had disconnected the cabin's main line from the electrical box.

What he thought about was his children. The deep mysterious ache of his love for them hurt like something huge he'd swallowed. Where to take them now? How to keep them safe from what had come for them? How to keep them as they were, quietly at rest, wrapped and warm and cocooned in the dark? Where? His sister's house in Illinois? North? South?

His daughter, King, turned inside her mummy bag. Then her eyes opened. She whispered, "Hi."

"Hello," Dominick said.

"Where are we?"

"Out behind our house. Camping out. Remember?"

"Oh. Okay."

"Go back to sleep now."

"Have you been here with us all night?"

"Yes, right here."

"You didn't go anywhere?"

"Where else would I go?"

She went to sleep again, and then both his children slept side by side. He sat next to them and waited. He felt something welling up in him, maybe the past or the thought of the flashlights in his house, lighting up his kids' things, and he clamped down on his thoughts hard, held them to the moment. He sat quietly and waited. He held his mind still, the effort as physical as holding back a leashed dog. Until, in the last minute before the ground broke with light, Dominick saw it. A hovering something for which he knew no adequate terms. A dark cloud that rose from the log cabin and hovered and pulsed with menace and swung a part of itself, a great insubstantial head, back and forth as though searching all of them out. Dominick's heart beat like two sheets of steel clapped together. He let himself slowly sink between his two children. He held his breath. His eyes squinted the cabin into a narrow line. The edge of the sky broke into crepuscular rays and, as light began to color the cabin's cedar-shake roof, the dark cloud winked out of existence as though it had never been a possibility at all. But it left Dominick's heart stuttering and the chimney smoke crooked, like a thin finger, toward the north.

ON THE ROAD to the hotel the second man shook the first man awake. The Chevrolet Suburban's huge lights arched over the macadam. The first man's chin felt wet. His eyes struggled open. "What?" the first man said. "What?"

The second man said, "You were making noises." His hands held the steering wheel loosely. Where his lip had caught against the counter, it looked swollen and dark.

"What kind of noises?" the first man said.

"You were whimpering."

"Come off it."

"I'm not kidding. You got problems at home?"

The first man's name was Charlie Basin. He didn't speak. He wouldn't be home for a few days. An early riser, his wife was long asleep. His youngest child, his daughter, was away at college, which was a relief, and two days ago his wife had said she was worried again. His wife was always worried about their daughter. Whenever his daughter came home she avoided looking at him, left the kitchen whenever he walked in. Had something gone wrong? How long ago? Charlie Basin stared at the road long enough that it looked bifurcated and stitched together with white thread. "You know what?" he said.

"What?" said the second man.

"Did you see any photographs?"

"Pictures?"

"Just one in the whole house. Of the father. What kind of people don't keep photos of themselves?"

"Ugly people?"

KING'S MOTHER CAME back to her in her dreams. Her mother crawled from inside the hollow pine. Her skin was pale. Brown leaves caught in her hair and bits of bark and honeycomb clung to her skin. She wore no clothes and her nipples looked like prunes. She pulled herself forward through the grass with her arms. Half awake and half asleep, King struggled but her limbs met some soft resistance. Her hands hurt. She tried to call her brother's name but the nameless fabric of the mummy bag wadded against her lips. This was the way her dreams had been for years. Half real. Half confused. Often she sleepwalked.

Her mother dragged her way toward King. Her skin tore open near her neck. There was a light rain that dimpled the earth at King's feet. Bees landed on her mother's neck and chest. The red buds on the trees lifted and stood on the ends of their branches as though trying to flee. Her mother's face moved toward hers and her eyes looked as soft and sad as King remembered them, and, when her mother's mouth began to open, small black legs scrambled against her lips.

By morning, King's sleeping bag had moved so that it overlapped with Clarke's. Clarke woke but did not open his eyes. The fish-mouth of his mummy bag haloed his eyes and nose. A circle of cold against his face. Clarke was fifteen years old but already the size of a fully grown man. Because he hadn't opened his eyes, he listened. A few dead leaves fluttered against branches. His sister lay beside him, asleep, breathing in a faint rasp like a faraway mosquito. Heavy footsteps approached. Plodding. His father's gait. When Clarke's eyelids cracked, the sky above him was slate blue. Top branches reached like thin fingers. His breath was a cloud rising from his mouth. The moon looked like a hangnail.

He unzipped the mummy bag and the cold knifed inward. He stood and rubbed his eyes and he felt the collision of his father's boots against the ground. He said, "Dad?" His father put his hand on Clarke's shoulder and squeezed. "I don't want to be out here," Clarke said. "I'm cold." He shivered and his father stepped from behind him.

"Somebody broke in," his father said. His hair hung in his eyes. He wore tan canvas pants and an insulated shirt and a vest.

"Broke in where?" Clarke said.

"Our house," his father said.

"Why didn't you wake me?"

"They're after me, I think."

"Who?" Clarke said. "What for? What did you do?"

"I'm not sure," his father said.

Clarke said, "That doesn't make any sense." He spat on the ground and the spit steamed. He said, "Somebody's after you? That's why we slept outside last night?"

His father said, "You didn't like it?"

"It was fun," Clarke said. Birds chattered and warbled from the trees. King rolled over in her sleeping bag.

"I seen other things last night," his father said.

"Like what?"

"A ghost, I think."

"I don't believe in ghosts," Clarke said.

His father said, "I don't, either."

"What kind of ghost?" said Clarke.

"A dark thing that hovered above the roof and waited," his father said. "It came out of our house."

"That's bullshit," Clarke said. "Maybe you're losing your mind." He paused and his father did not respond. "What was the ghost waiting for?" Clarke asked.

"It wanted us to run."

The yellow grass bent beneath a cold wind. Clarke shivered. Dominick turned and walked back into the old orchard and gathered fallen wood. He made separate piles for logs and for kindling. He pulled the lint from his pockets to use as tinder. He glanced at Clarke sitting on the earth but he didn't ask for help. King looked so small in her sleeping bag. Dominick piled the wood and pulled a lighter from his worn leather satchel. He lit the tinder. When the fire caught, he rifled through his satchel for the binoculars and, as the warmth began to rise, he scanned the ground around his house. The hulk of the wood-pile. The screen door standing open. The thin blur of heat rising from the chimney. Heel prints in the mud of the driveway.

Clarke asked, "Why don't we just go inside?"

"We'll head in after your sister wakes," Dominick said.

Clarke said, "What are you looking for?"

"I'm not sure yet." He raised the binoculars to glass the empty road.

"What're you scared of?" Clarke said.

From the leather satchel, Dominick took a small yellow notepad, a jar filled with ground coffee beans, his Wharncliffe knife, a thermos, a can of black beans, an avocado, three heels of bread, and a tin cup. He put coffee grounds in the tin cup, filled it with cold water from the thermos, put it on the ground next to the can of beans, and nudged both into the fire with his boot.

Behind him, not moving in her sleeping bag, King whispered, "I'm up." She put her arm through the small cinched hole. She said, "This is great." Her hand acted like it was grabbing hunks of air.

Dominick sliced the avocado with the knife. He said, "Clarke, pull the beans out of the fire."

"Beans?" King said. She was still in the mummy bag, her hands making circles. "Is there anything else?"

THE SECOND MAN drove the dark Suburban down the county roads. They had risen early from the bland hotel room to canvas the neighbors. The neighbors' eyes widened when they heard that the suited men were with the Federal Bureau of Investigation. Each neighbor stood outside a front door without offering an invitation to come inside. None of them knew a thing. From the Suburban, Charlie Basin tried to call his wife. He wanted to ask about his daughter. Between house visits, he made three attempts, but each time he got only a recording of his wife's voice.

The navy-suited FBI men worked their way down Flint Valley Road. None of the neighbors lived very close to the Sawyers' A-frame cabin. The closest house sat a mile from the cabin they had searched the night before. When they pulled up outside the nearest house, Charlie Basin said, "You getting the sense that these people don't like us?" His voice was wry.

"What's wrong with them?" asked the second man.

"Wrong with them?"

"Yeah, they're rude."

"They don't trust us," Charlie said. "They don't want to give up one of their own." He gestured toward the clipboard in the second FBI man's hands. "Who's this last one?"

"Jon Howland," the second FBI man read from the clipboard. "Former member of the Central Pennsylvania Militia."

"He ought to be a lot of help then."

"Right, he ought to."

KING WALKED INTO the stand of trees to pee. The willow branches whispered against one another. Light filtered through pine needles. The lemony scent tickled her nose. She walked fast and farther than she needed to. She rubbed at her eyes to free herself from the whip of her dreams. The unseen creek made a noise that sounded like it came from the back of a throat. She followed the crumbling rock wall to the stacks of reddish stones that rose upward in broken flues. She picked up an arm-length branch of oak and stopped to snap off the leaves and twigs. She swung her staff at low-hanging branches and a few yellowed leaves tumbled. She began to hum under her breath. She skipped. A gyrfalcon flashed downward, the light making its white feathers burn.

When she got back, Dominick pointed toward the A-frame. "I need you to pack up whatever food you can," he said. They walked toward the cabin, their shadows stretched out in long thin lines before them. They passed through the tilled field into the long grass that roughed against their pant legs. They walked in a line. Dominick passed the thermos of water, and he and Clarke took two conservative mouthfuls. King drank the rest with rivulets at the sides of her mouth.

Bark peeled like burned skin from the logs of the cabin.

King ran and the porch cracked under her feet. Clarke hurried after her. Dominick dragged his feet. He stopped five full steps behind his children. He looked up. No smoke rose from the chimney. Under his breath, he said, "The fire is out."

Dominick stood like a stranger at the door to his own house. His head crooked on his neck, his white face and brown hair looking just like his children's. The morning air was as colorless as wet ash.

Clarke reached out for the doorknob and the front door wheezed open. Near the deadbolt, splintered bark exposed a pale sapwood. Clarke fingered the broken wood. He turned to look back at his father and said, "What the hell have you done?"

Dominick took a slow step forward. Only the left side of his lips moved when he spoke. "Watch your mouth." With a sweeping gesture he motioned toward the front door and his kids crept forward as though time had slowed.

The cabin that Dominick had built had four rooms. The great room with a cathedral ceiling, the open kitchen with a bathroom tucked into a small space at the front, and, at the back of the house, the master bedroom and the kids' shared room. A bearskin rug sat by the woodstove. Dominick's boots knocked against the hand-planed walnut floors. Inside, the kids began to live again, their faces to flush, their legs to scamper beneath them. Quick to their bedroom and then still as two pillars of stone. Quick to the pie safe. Quick to the photograph of their father in the desert wearing his combat uniform and tactical vest and carrying an M4 carbine. Quick to the kitchen. There King said, "Hurry, Dad, come here!" She gestured with her hands. She pointed at the floor.

Dominick's boots tracked mud. Their mother never would have let him past the low shoe rack to the west of the door. He said, "What is it?" but his children did not speak. They pointed. On the linoleum by the sink, two bright red drops of blood.

Clarke said, "Are you responsible for that?" His father's head, all hard angles, searched back and forth, but King had turned away from the house's confusion. She touched her father's elbow and Clarke could see the blush of need rising, the child's hope for answers that he distantly recognized as his own, too. He reached up and pushed at the tender place behind his ear until thought disappeared.

"What's it from, Dad?" King said.

"Don't know," Dominick said. "Nosebleed?" He walked backward through the great room, looking. Past the deer antlers, the collection of ten-points. Past the coatrack hung with a woman's red scarf. He stopped by the rough-hewn table. He spent a long time studying the surface.

Clarke called, "What'd you find?"

Dominick pointed. "Come here," he said.

The three of them stood together looking down. Their faces edged with light from the window. King reached out and touched the side of the table with a single finger. The shaker was overturned. Thin trails of salt scrolled in alphabetic shapes. Whorls and straight lines.

Wasp, read the words in salt, *Neck, Broken.*

Outside the house, their father's knees pressed into the mud and the rotting bulkhead doors to the basement opened. Warm mildewed air rose and entered their noses and lungs and was pushed back out of their mouths.

King asked, "What's happening?"

Clarke asked, "Whose blood was that on the floor?"

Their father used an old blue rag to clean a Beretta pistol and a scoped Springfield Armory M1A rifle. He cocked the pistol and held it out and sighted into the distance, then he pointed the gun toward the ground and pulled the trigger. His pupils were bright and feverish and the beginning of sun-wrinkles tightened at the corners of his eyes. His head bowed. His children looked at the small Latin words, SUA SPONTE, coarsely tattooed into the dark skin of his neck.

"Why don't you answer my question?" Clarke said. "Whose blood was on the floor?"

"I'm not sure," their father said.

"You have a guess?" Clarke said.

"I do."

"What is it?"

"I'm not going to tell you," said Dominick.

"Why not?"

"What you might think of me."

Dominick sent the kids back to the camp under the hollow tree. He made trips back and forth between them and the house. He gathered things and put them in piles around his children. Green military duffels made of canvas. Pistol cases.

Bolt cutters. A small set of tools. Cans of tuna and peaches. Rope. Bullets. An electric drill. A loaf of bread. A tent. A slim-jim. Sinkers and hooks and fishing line. A tarpaulin. A machete. He didn't say a word. His face looked like a plank of wood and both kids waited without asking questions. They sat in their sleeping bags as the day passed and night began to gather in front of their eyes like a linen veil. They looked into the dark hollow of the tree where they'd hidden in games of hide-and-seek and where their mother had left clues inside plastic eggs for treasure hunts that led them to the woodpile and the window well and the forked trunk of the plum tree to find chocolate and peanut-butter eggs wrapped in gold foil.

While their father gathered things and paced and talked to himself, they whispered to one another. "You remember how Mom used to make whoopie pies?" King asked.

"Sure," Clarke said. "Pumpkin. Chocolate."

"She made them for my birthdays," King said.

"Mine, too, sometimes."

"How long has it been?" said King.

"Since when?"

"Since she's been gone."

"Less than a year," Clarke said.

"Is she coming back?"

"I don't know."

"My birthday is coming up," King said.

Dark winged shapes flitted above their heads. Night had set in fast. Their father covered packed duffel bags with brush and stropped his Wharncliffe knife until his kids fell asleep to the soft repetitive rasp. The moon had risen like a silver dollar and when Dominick stood he heard the ungreased creak of his knees. He set off quickly, up between the low Pennsylvanian mountains to the green saddle. There he breathed hard but smoothly and looked out over the pieced farmland, and the radiant church steeple, and the dead black of the Susquehanna River snaking through the valley. He moved his head slowly back and forth, searching as far as he could see for any moving light.

Below the saddle between low mountains, King pushed Clarke awake.

"What?" Clarke said.

"Dad's not here," she said.

"He'll be back."

There was a long period of quiet. Branches clattered overhead. The mummy bags rustled. "If Mom was going to come home," King asked, "when do you think it would be?"

"Once I heard her telling Dad that she was going to leave," Clarke said.

"When?" King asked.

"They were arguing," Clarke said. "I think she wanted to get away from him." He looked down. "I think they hate each other."

"No, they don't," King said.

"I don't think she's coming back," Clarke said

"Why don't we ask Dad again?" asked King.

"I've asked him. He won't answer. There's something wrong with him."

LONG AGO BY the covered bridge, the cold had turned their breath to rime. Snow lay thick over the flat yellowed grass. The sun rose like an orange. Dominick and Sarah had stood under the bridge, not a mile from where, in a few months, Dominick would use his enlistment bonus to buy a plot of land on which he dreamed of building them a cabin. They stood under giant hewn beams supporting an old slate roof. Boards bowed beneath their feet. Icicles stretched from the eaves. She held his arm and leaned. She was as young as he was and dressed densely enough that the skin of her face looked reddened and warm. She tightened her fur collar. She was pregnant and she hadn't yet taken his surname. Her name was still Sarah Tower.

"You shouldn't go," she said. "This baby will need you." Wisps of dark hair escaped the hood of her woolen coat. She had eyes of dark rock.

"I don't know." His gloves felt tight as he moved his hands.

"I don't want you to go," she said.

Beside the bridge, the creek water had been diverted into a small channel that fed a pond. It was round as a hand mirror and frozen solid. They walked gingerly across the ice. He swiveled his leather satchel from his back to his front. He unhooked the ice auger and opened the satchel for the collapsible rod and wax worms and hooks and line and bobbers. Sarah Tower put her hand up to shield her eyes from the light. He augered a hole in the ice. He took off his gloves to assemble the pole and to fish the line through the hook's eye. The cold stiffened his fingers. He lowered a worm and sat to watch the bobber in the shrinking hole in the ice.

She said, "You'll barely ever get to see him. Or me."

"You can come with. After basic training, I'll be at Fort Benning. You can live there, too."

"I'm not leaving here," she said. "This is what I know."

"Then I'll be home whenever I can."

"It won't be enough," she said.

"Jesus," he said, "we've talked this through already."

"I know." She turned away from him. "We ought to name him Clarke," she said. "I want him to know you really well."

Light trammeled the ice. The field to the south was dotted with snowy hummocks.

"We don't know it's a boy yet."

"I *do* know," she said.

"It's not like I want to leave," he said.

"Can't you listen to me?" she said. "I don't want you to, either."

THE SECOND FBI man lay down on the beige bed-cover at the Days Inn near Lewisburg, Pennsylvania. Yellowish flower-print curtains hung over two windows. The second FBI man still wore his smooth brown shoes. He sniffed. The air smelled like disinfectant. "This place is the fucking pits," the second FBI man called toward the bathroom. The door was open. The water ran in the sink. A dark shadow roiled in the mirror attached to the back side of the door. On the bed, the second FBI man put his arms behind his head.

"Clean towels anyway." Charlie Basin appeared in the doorway holding a hand towel. He was thin and dark-haired. He looked at the second FBI man on the bed. He thought of his wife at home, asleep under their down comforter. He glanced at his watch and pulled his phone from the pocket of the jacket hung over the back of a desk chair. She answered at the first ring.

"Rosamund," he said, "I'm going to be stuck up here a few days."

"I miss you," she said. "Stuck up where?" Her voice sounded clotted and unused.

"Central Pennsylvania," he said. "You in bed?"

"I am," Rosamund said. "Charlie, did I tell you that I've been worried about Charlene?"

"Sure," he said, "you did."

"I haven't been able to get her on the phone in three days."

"That's what you've been worried about?"

"She's drinking," Rosamund said. "She's skipping class. I think she's depressed."

"She'll be fine," he said. "She's always fine. I've got to go, Ros."

When Charlie Basin got off the phone, he hesitated. Their daughter was a junior at Duke. On the lacrosse team. President of a pre-law society, the Bench and Bar. A good kid who didn't want to talk to her father much. Charlie sat in the chair by the desk and dialed his boss. Andrew C. Fry, the assistant director of the Criminal Investigative Division of the FBI. When Fry answered the phone, Charlie said, "I think this guy's gone underground, Andy." He paused a moment and pulled Dominick Sawyer's file from his briefcase.

"Underground or flown the coop?" Andy asked.

"Hard to tell. Neighbors aren't cooperative."

"You want to pull out of there? Put out the APB, come home, and wait for something to come in?"

"Maybe better to stick around a day or two."

"No more than two," Andy said. "Let me know when you learn anything."

"Will do," Charlie said. He hung up the phone.

The second man moved his elbow backward so that it knocked against the headboard. "This is a fucking waste of time, Charlie," he said. "This place is a backwater." He took out his gun and laid it on the nightstand. "This guy isn't here. He's split. Maybe he killed his kids."

"He's not the kind," Charlie said. "He's been back and forth from Iraq for years."

"You think he's lingering?"

"He's still here." Charlie turned and tossed the hand towel into the bathtub.

"What makes you say so?"

"He's here but he's readying to leave," Charlie said. "He won't bolt, he'll depart. So we hang around. See what pans out. Wait and see if the local police find anything."

"What's taking him so long?"

"He's got two kids. Kids slow you down. Maybe he needs time to think."

"He's going to take them with him? What for?"

"Let's hope he does, because those kids are our way to find him. You look at his military records? Without the kids, we'll never catch him. He'll flee the country. He'll disappear."

THE NEXT MORNING Dominick roused the kids with a cold boot. They ate out of tin cans. Then he marched them past the plum tree and through the soft light of the fields. Ruffed grouse startled in front of them, their wings thumping like giant hearts. They traveled by deer trail and derelict rail-road track. King said, "Where we going, Dad?"

Her father asked a question in return. "What way we heading?"

"West," King said.

"What's to the west?"

"Mr. Howland's place," King said.

They walked along a small brown path to a short-grass field spotted with budding jonquils. Clarke straggled behind, his feet scuffling against the ground. Reluctant to follow, afraid to be left behind. Near the middle of the clearing, a tiny covered bridge, no wider than Dominick's broad shoulders, split a creek in half. Ivy lumped at the bridge's base and moved too slowly for their time-sharpened eyes to see. Beyond the ivy sat a stone cottage. Smoke rose from the chimney.

Dominick knocked on the plank-and-iron-batten door. The door cracked and Jon Howland's long beard appeared first, then the whites of his eyes. The walls of the house behind him were lined with heart pine.

Howland looked out toward the clearing. His head swung back and forth. His lips twisted as though touched by something gone sour. He said, "Come on then, get inside."

The children filed in and Dominick followed, heavy on their heels. They stopped by a long table. Howland lifted his chin at the kids. "In the basket on the table," he said, "there's the last of my Gala apples. Eat."

Clarke stepped slowly toward the basket and King grabbed an apple in each hand. Howland reached beneath his horseman's duster to wipe his hands on his jeans. Then he shifted the pot on top of the woodstove. Heat rose and brought the smell of celery and bay leaves and ham hock. He lifted an eyebrow toward Dominick. The eye beneath the eyebrow was brown as a stirred puddle. His cheeks were reddened with work. "Lentil soup?" he said.

"Howland?" Dominick said.

Both kids stopped moving, Clarke with an apple in his hand and King with one in her teeth. They looked at Jon Howland. They'd known him for their whole lives. He paid them well to split wood. He'd helped their mother when their father had been gone. He'd given them pocketknives with handles whittled from pear wood.

"Jon?" said Dominick.

Howland picked up a shallow wooden spoon. He turned his back on Dominick. He picked up a gray rag and pulled the top from the Dutch oven.

Dominick said, "Whose side you on in this?"

Howland turned to face Dominick and looked at him with his mouth pursed. "I'm on your kids' side," he said. He stirred the pot and the children's appetites rose with the thin steam. "I think they're coming after you hard."

"Who's coming?"

"Not just Dallas Pope."

King stared at Jon Howland, her eyes dark and sightless, her mind tunneling through a coin thrown into the air and the dank rotten smell of the ginkgo berries, and she was sitting in the car again, the old Plymouth. Her mother walked toward her. Dallas Pope leaned into the window well, his weight on his elbows, his tan uniform and his sheriff's badge a costume that King would tell her father, in a letter, that she'd like for Christmas, and Sheriff Pope's mouth kindly turned downward as he pulled a silver dollar from behind King's ear and juggled it in his hand.

"More than Pope?" Dominick said. "Who else?"

"Feds."

"You remember the names?"

"Nope," Howland said. "But they wore city shoes. Slipped in the mud. Walked about high-stepping like my rooster."

"What'd you tell them?"

"Didn't tell them that the wind was from the east this morning. Or that I could smell peach wood burning in your fire."

"Thank you, Howland," Dominick said.

"No thanks needed."

"Can the kids sleep here while I gather our things?"

Jon Howland looked at Clarke and King. "The couch is theirs," he said. He took in the shadows under their eyes, their greasy hair. "You got anything else to ask?"

"It's a big one."

"Shoot."

"I need a car," Dominick said.

"Don't have a car to spare," Howland said, "but you can take the F-150."

Dominick cupped one of his hands with the other and looked down into the well of his palms. He nodded toward the kids and stepped toward the door. "All right then, I'll be back before morning."

Howland caught Dominick lightly. "Hold your horses," he said. Both children watched the arthritic curve of the thick hand on their father's shoulder. "The truck," Jon Howland said, "you'd better thank me for that."

When their father had gone, Clarke and King did chores until the day was nearly over. Washed clothes, swept floors, chopped wood. For supper they had soup. Then they sat side by side on the couch, their legs hidden underneath an afghan. Howland stooped over the sink, wiping bowls clean with a rag. A lentil hid in his beard. The electric lights flickered off and on, leaving an impression of the constant darkness to come. The children's eyes stuck to Howland's back. He turned his head to one side and called, "I feel you staring."

"Can you tell us what's going on, Mr. Howland?" Clarke said.

Howland turned, wiped his wet hands against his shirt, and sat in a wooden chair across from the couch. "I only know a little," he said.

"Dad said he saw a ghost," said King. She held her arms up.

"I've no faith in such things," said Jon Howland. There was

a wry turn to his mouth and his tongue pushed at a tooth as though it ached.

"What's happened?" Clarke said. "Why're they after him?"

"Here's the thing, boyo," Jon Howland said. "A deputy's maybe been killed."

"Killed where?"

"Sheriff said there's no body yet. They only found blood down by the river."

"Why do they think it was my dad?" Clarke asked.

"They didn't say."

Air pushed against the windows and the heavy curtains shifted. A dog bayed at some distance. Clarke said, "You're giving Dad your truck?"

"I'm giving you kids that truck."

"I'm not going with him," Clarke said. Just to say it, this half-truth, he felt like his spleen had torn inside him. Howland offered no opinion. "He's not telling me anything," Clarke said. "He's not making any sense."

King stood up and placed her palm on Howland's arm. "If we leave our house," she asked, "how will Mom find us?"

"I don't know," Howland said. "She's been gone how long?"

"Almost a year," Clarke said.

King said, "What's my dad done wrong?"

"Depends on the way you see it," Howland said. "He's not precisely law-abiding. There's hooch in the back field. All those guns. No belief in taxes. But then a lot of us got those problems."

Clarke said, "Did he kill that deputy?"

"You're asking the wrong man."

"What *do* you know?" Clarke said. His face tightened like a clenched fist.

"I know your daddy doesn't want to lose you," Howland said. A small lamp disgorged a disproportionate quantity of light. The shadows of Jon Howland and Clarke and King held still on the walls. Half-moon-shaped mice debouched from the room's corners.

"What do we do?" King asked Clarke.

"I don't know," Clarke said.

King turned to Howland. "Do you know what we should do?"

"Nope," Howland said. "But you stay around here, they'll take you from him."

When night fell and they wearied of talk, the children went to sleep on the couch. King dreamed. In her dream, not everything was as it should be. Her eyes were open and she was alone. Her skin crawled as though someone was watching her from a distance. The house, Jon Howland's house, was a shadow made solid. The air smelled of damp honeysuckle. Something dark and soft and small crawled beneath her shirt, and she held still. Where was everyone who should have stood beside her? Had they left? Would they come back? One of her eyes began to tremble. She called out for them, first for her mother and then for her father and brother. Her mouth was so wide and loud that her lips tore at the edges. She called again and again.

Someone came. Someone dark and calm stood over her, and a sense of peace swirled like ink in water, and she knew that everything she had lost would be returned.

When Dominick came back, he found his kids asleep on the couch, one head on a cushion at either end. He stood above them and the fire crackled and darkness hummed all around. He leaned in and the floor creaked beneath his feet as though complaining about his weight. Clarke rolled his face toward the back of the couch. When had he gotten so big? He lay still and breathed deeply. He smelled like a boy should, of sweat and grass and something citrusy. King shook. Dark lank hair trembled as though it had come fearfully to life. Her eyes rolled behind her lids. Her legs twitched back and forth in mimicry of walking or running.

Dominick felt a tightness like steel bands wrapped around his chest. He gently laid his hand on his daughter's shoulder. Before him his children were dark possibilities, the night like a great breath drawn in. His vision blurred, his hand against his daughter's drumming heart. Why was this pleasure always entwined with sharp pain? Was he mistaken in his understanding that this was love?

Under the hand on her shoulder, King woke. The deep gulch in her eyes looked so old. Old in the way that belonged only to the young and tender. Old in the way that ancient visions rise only from infants' eyes, and Dominick knew that his daughter was a child in the dark and not yet narrowed to a woman.

King's head rose inches off the couch. Her lips parted like a broken seam. Her breath smelled strange and forlorn. "Daddy," she said, "I dreamed a great dream."

IN THE MORNING at the Days Inn, the second FBI man said, "There's not been a goddamned word. There're out of here. We've got to broaden the search."

"Might be," Charlie Basin said. In adjacent hotel rooms they could hear two women's voices speaking softly in Spanish, high-pitched giddy laughter, the long indrawn breath of a vacuum cleaner.

Charlie lowered himself to the floor. He began the push-up routine that he followed every morning. He believed that the human body must be stunned awake, that left to follow physiological desire our muscles curl toward sleep. His arms levered him up and down. It was not without effort. He sweat. He had been doing five hundred pushups each morning for the last thirty years. It calmed his mind. Gave him space to think. To think, on this particular occasion, about his daughter, Charlene. Had his wife spoken to her? Would she want to speak with him? Then Charlie thought of Dominick Clarke Sawyer. About post-traumatic stress disorder. About what a man would do to keep his children at his side.

"Let's get out of here, Charlie," said the second FBI man. "A coffee. A burger. I don't care."

When they left the hotel, the two suited figures drew many

eyes. The sallow pinched clerk pointed at them with the business end of his pen. In the hotel windows, curtains shuffled slightly so that dark hollows were exposed, cloth held back by the tips of pale fingers. Stools swiveled in the donut shop across the road and older men with oiled hair shaded their eyes in detached accidental salutes. When the dark SUV drove onto the road, the hotel seemed to open up, to let in light, to take a long shallow breath.

JUST BEFORE FIRST light, they drove the Ford pickup out of Jon Howland's old barn. Dark hulking hay bales and bleating sheep, the huge stump of wood past the threshold, the indignant rooster and the old blood and the ax and the smell of slaughtered things. The truck bumped over wheel ruts. King opened the window and leaned her head outward and the wind blew over them, traveling from nowhere to quiet nowhere. Not one of them said a word while the cottage shrank behind them and the road lumped ahead. The slow hills were lined with budding vegetation. Out the windows, the children saw only what they were leaving behind. Cow-spotted mountains, and the safety of a cabin that their father had built with his hands, and thick deciduous woods they could navigate blind, and the easy way they had often sat together by the honeysuckle beneath the plum tree in the back field, and the cast of the fishing line beside their father on the bank of the river. And the wait, too; they remembered the wait that had both hurt and saved them, the wait for winter to turn into spring, or for their father to light the woodstove in the morning so that they could stop shivering, or for the last of the snow to melt, or for the tulips to rise like the undead from the earth, or to turn twelve and sixteen years old, or, most pressingly, for their mother to come home.

Their father told them to shut the window by spiraling his finger. Then his hand took the steering wheel where it fixed and became part of the wheel and the wheel gave itself over to the column, and the column to the steel beneath. He opened his mouth as though he was about to speak. He closed his mouth again. He leaned across King, rifled through the glove compartment, and balanced a pair of dusty wire-rim sunglasses on his nose. He tugged on his bottom lip. Even now he wanted them happy. He smiled awkwardly.

They rode past dark woods and past a stream that cut through rock. Gray-and-white water gullied around a bolus of melting ice and then spilled downward into the great open mouth of a steel pipe that ran beneath the road and poured, faucetlike and tamed, over a short cliff. They rode past dynamite-blasted red rock that rose steeply to either side and betrayed thousands of years. They rode over hills covered with trees reddening with spring growth. They rode past curtained windows and past a man in a trapper's hat waving at them with both arms. They rode past a skeletal peach orchard and past topped apple trunks and branches aborted into reachable spheres. They rode with their own thoughts past a bonneted woman hanging clothes on a thin wire. They rode behind two women on bicycles, an ancient tractor, a team of six pale horses. They rode without speaking. They rode without fear. They rode through a countryside that they felt was their own. They rode together as they'd done a hundred times before over a short barren mountaintop, beside a dry round-stoned creek, through a crease of a valley lined with violet crocuses.

When the boxy sheriff's car pulled behind them, the spin of tires cast stones into the woods. A siren sounded once in a short strain. Lights flashed. Dominick's eyes were hard and narrow. He said, "It's Dallas Pope." He gunned the Ford and then gently braked. He pulled halfway onto the shoulder and then accelerated back onto the road. The tires squealed. The brakes clutched like the arms of a nervous parent before the truck shot forward again and they skimmed across the county on a road bordered by no houses. Parallel to the road, a line of reddish-gray rock rose up into occasional cliffs. The sun glared down painfully, the sky was a baked late-winter blue, and everyone in the Ford F-150 squinted at the squad car behind them.

"Dad," Clarke said, "are you going to pull over?"

Their father failed to answer. His eyes shifted back and forth. His foot rose above the pedals, poised in indecision. Then the truck pulled to a stop on the side of the road. The sheriff's car angled to a stop just behind.

"Kids," their father said. He turned and leaned halfway over the seat toward them. The red and blue lights altered his face. A thin film of moisture veiled his lips. "Kids," he said, "I need you to trust me."

"I do," King said.

Clarke's leg jumped against the floor mat.

"Listen," their father said, "I'm headed back to talk to him."

"What about?" Clarke asked.

"I need you to listen to me," their father said. "Especially you, Clarke. Right now I need you to do what I ask. You stay right here."

"Okay," King said.

"And you close your eyes."

the people of the broken neck

Clarke and King looked at one another. Clarke shivered and the tremor brought the far-back memory of his father shaking him gently awake in the dark. Clarke had sat up in his bed and the quilt pooled around his waist and the air was night cold. His father, rucksack over his shoulder and fishing pole curved in his hand, told him to get up, to put some pants on. Clarke trusted his father. He reached over the side of the bed toward the pile of clothes on the floor. Like always, he did as he was told. Where had they gone? A pool deep in the woods where trout seemed to jump onto their lines.

In the cab of the truck, Clarke swept the goose bumps on his forearm with a hand. He looked at King again. The decision he had to make felt bigger than he, out of his control. There was no way he was going to do as his father asked. Not this time. Not with the lights of the sheriff's car flashing behind.

His sister nodded and put her hands over her eyes. When his father opened the door, Clarke refused to close his eyes but he looked straight at the road in front of them and didn't glance toward the wing mirror. Wouldn't it be okay, this one last time, to choose to be a child?

With their eyes turned away, their ears opened to receding bootsteps. A muffled voice. The honeybee that circled the truck round and round. A low voice followed by a period of quiet. The knocking of a woodpecker against a hollow tree. A whisper and a thud and a metallic scrape. A lull. A grating sound. Heavy thumps as things were tossed into the truck bed. The bounce of the shocks. The crinkle and pop of unfolding plastic.

The whisper of their father's hand on the handle of the door. The concussive closure. The engine choking into a semblance of life. Wheels spinning against earth.

They drove for less than ten minutes before Clarke broke. He felt split wide open with the twinned impulses to question and to obey. He couldn't hold his tongue anymore. He looked over at his father. He said, "What happened?"

"What happened where?" asked Dominick.

"Give me a break, Dad."

"We worked it out," Dominick said. "He let me go."

"That's it?" Clarke said.

"Uh-huh."

"What did Sheriff Pope say? Why did he pull us over? Is he on your side? Is he helping you get away from here?"

"I said that's it," Dominick said. "That's *it*."

They drove for half an hour, then encamped in a roadside hotel outside Lewisburg. A Days Inn. Their father parked to the rear of the hotel, the only other car in the back lot a battered red coupe. The man behind the desk had no hair and gray skin and deep uneven lines on his face. His eyes looked as near death as the orbs of a strung fish. Their father wrote Jon Howland's name in a broad flourish and the hairless man handed them a key while he looked at the clock fixed above their heads. They gathered ice and Styrofoam cups and packaged food from vending machines and ate around a small round table in a plain clean room. Fake roses stood in a vase at the center of the table. The children were quiet. They avoided looking directly at one another. Finally, Clarke spoke. "Dad, what're we doing here?"

"We can't just drive," his father said. "We've got to know where we're going."

"Aunt Annie's?" King suggested.

"Too predictable," their father said. "I've got to think." He sat at the table in his peacoat and watch cap. The kids were tired.

"I have a question," Clarke said. He sat on the floor. King sat down and leaned against him.

"Go ahead, Clarke," Dominick said.

"Why should we go with you?"

"What do you mean 'why'?"

"Maybe we should stay here. King and me."

"You're children," Dominick said. "We've got to stick together. I need to keep you safe."

King slumped against Clarke. He had gotten so big already, but not as big as her father. Her eyes were closed. Clarke could hear a slight hitch in her breathing. Her head rocked against Clarke's shoulder and he felt her weight, light in pounds yet heavy with responsibility. When she spoke, her eyes stayed closed. "I want to be with Dad," she said.

Clarke lifted King quietly into the bed. He picked her up, set her in the bed, and then got in beside her. Their father pulled the bedcovers over them. The children's eyes closed. They slept like the dead.

When they woke the room stood empty. A Styrofoam cup of coffee steamed on the table. Father-sized scuff marks in the carpet. The kids lay in bed looking at one another. Clarke said, "Let's go look in the back of the pickup."

"What for?" King asked.

"You know what for."

"I don't want to," King said. The bedcovers slid off them like shed skins and they cracked the door to the room and looked out. The front parking lot was empty.

"I'm going," Clarke said. He slipped out the door and around to the rear lot. The Ford sat near a line of trees and a sycamore limb curled over it like a finger. The sky had grayed into a vortex of clouds. There was no one around. At the front of the truck bed lay their father's green duffels. Behind the bags, a blue grommeted tarpaulin folded over a lumpen mass. Clarke froze. He went pale. King walked across the lot and stood beside him. Clark held up his hand and moved it, glacially, toward the tarpaulin.

King called, "Don't!" and the word hung as Clarke's hand pinched onto a grommet and pulled slowly back. They found a green sleeping bag. Inside the sleeping bag were a police-issue shotgun, a bulletproof vest, speed cuffs and keys, a bivouac sack, a side-handle baton, a stun gun, a tactical flashlight, and three canisters of tear gas.

Relief shivered down Clarke's legs, and he touched King's shoulder where her hair tickled his hand, and they were joined together by a conflicted architecture of fear and love. They heard the scuff of rubber against cement and a cold shadow fell across them. They looked up and up until they could see their father upside down against the gray sky. He was breathing hard. "What're you doing?" he said.

"Where is he?" asked Clarke.

"Who?"

"Dallas Pope."

The breath left their father with a puncturing grunt and hiss. King turned her back on both of them. "What?" Dominick said. "You thought I put him in here?"

"How'd you get all this police stuff?" Clarke asked.

"He gave it to me," Dominick said. "How else?"

"I bet you stole it," Clarke said. He reached down to pick up the flashlight. "This is cool."

"You can have it," said Dominick.

On the way back to the room, their father stopped off at the hotel office to settle the bill. The kids went ahead.

In their room, a chair had been knocked to the ground. A wet, flowery smell hung in the air. King edged behind Clarke. The blankets had been stripped from the bed. Ragged slits in the pillows exposed stained foam. A ceramic lamp cracked open on a small square table. A head-sized hole in the plaster beside the bed.

Behind them sunlight broke through the clouds. As though they were in a museum, Clarke and King moved slowly through the room without touching. The white shower curtain spread across the floor. Bits of broken mirror caught the light and burned. Furrows the width of fingers marked the drywall. King touched one with her hand. "The ghost?" she whispered.

"No such thing," Clarke whispered back. The complimentary glasses had shattered into thousands of pieces atop the bureau. Artificial rose petals scattered across the carpet as wind rushed in the open door.

They stopped by the round table. Salt blew over the edge and onto the carpet. Still they could read what remained in thin scrolls.

Daughter, they read, *River, Ring.*

Behind them, their father cleared his throat. He stood by the window. Half his thick frame awash with light. He looked to them as he always looked, as oversized and solid as a landmass. He pointed a finger between the window's flower-print curtains. "Oh, crap," he whispered. "We'll go north."

"North?" King said. "What for?"

Clarke said, "I don't want to go."

"We've never been to Maine," Dominick whispered.

The kids' feet whisked across the carpet. They stood beside their father. In the lot, a dark boxy four-door spilled two men dressed in navy suits. Even from the window they could see the slick-bottomed city shoes. One of them younger and chest-heavy, accustomed to the punching bag. The other thin and dark-haired and kind-looking, the sort of man who might play a father on television.

"Howland's right," Dominick whispered. "Must be feds."

Clarke said, "I don't want to go."

Dominick had to keep Clarke with him, keep him safe, clear the path ahead of them. If his kids left, he'd have nothing worth protecting. He pulled a pistol from a green duffel bag and tucked it into the holster underneath his belt. His voice was low and quiet. "I don't want us to split up."

Clarke cursed. What if he walked away? Would King come with him? Where would they go? What would they be then?

"You want to go to Maine, don't you, King?" Dominick said.

"Okay," she said.

"She needs you, Clarke," Dominick said. "And she needs me."

"Fine," Clarke said, "I'll come."

the people of the broken neck

Dominick tossed his beaten leather satchel over his shoulder. He sniffed. The air smelled of diesel fumes. His chest beat hard. He began to sweat. He knelt down. The navy-suited men walked close to one another, talking casually, gesturing with their hands. They walked across the lot and into the squat bakery next door. Dominick's eyes blurred. He smelled tire fires and raw sewage. He blinked and blinked again and in the moments his eyes were closed, he was kneeling on top of a hot flat roof with his rifle, an M24. He forced himself to take a deep breath.

"Time to go," Dominick said. He gathered the bags. His movements were crafted and efficient. "Outside now. Walk quick. To the back of the hotel."

As they walked out onto the balcony and down the stairs and through the tunnel filled with vending machines, the children felt as if they were followed by hundreds of eyes. No one stopped them. No one put up a cry. No one pointed. The F-150 truck sputtered and the wheels turned against the cement lot and the neon bakery sign blinked at them in red and yellow.

Then they were on the road. Route 15. The feds had been left behind. The ghost, too. Driving as the darkness settled down from the north, the pickup's headlights battered the road. The countryside passed by in glimpses dimly lit by billboard lights. "We'll drive the night through," Dominick said. They were silent. Clarke and King sank into the old seat. King played with her fingers for a long time.

IN HIS ROOM at the Days Inn, Charlie Basin listened to the tinned voice coming from his phone. The local police had called. The air smelled of stale smoke. The ceiling was cracked.

With one hand, Charlie Basin closed his black suitcase. He returned his phone to his jacket pocket. Why had Dominick Clarke Sawyer gone on the run with his children when, in so many ways, it was easier to leave them behind? Why put himself so close to his kids that he'd have to talk to them? To explain himself? To have them there beside him to watch what he would have to do? To be asked what it was that he had done with his life? Charlie Basin turned to face the second FBI man. His eyes were small searchlights. He said, "Somebody found Dallas Pope's car."

"The sheriff's car? Who found it?"

"A farmer," Charlie Basin said. "On the side of a country road. Not far from the Sawyer place."

"What about Pope?"

"No sign of him yet."

"You think he's in the woods taking a long piss?"

"Let's go take a look."

THE TIRES OF the F-150 ground flyspeck pieces of themselves into the blacktop road. The oncoming cars drove with their sun visors lowered to block the falling light. Clarke and King rode alongside their father on the single broad seat. King had her knees pulled to her chest and her eyes closed.

"Why're those people after you?" Clarke asked. He was so tired. His father held the steering wheel in a firm hand. He filled the driver's seat with purpose. He surveyed the road ahead as though it belonged to him. If Clarke could understand what his father had done, he'd know what he should do now. If he could understand who and what his father was, he'd know what to measure himself against and in accordance with.

"I haven't always been a good father," Dominick said. He tapped his foot against the floor mat. "I made first sergeant in the Army, sure. I got the Distinguished Service Cross, and I've served in more than one war. But I also been in barracks confinement. The war took a lot away from me. Now they're trying to take you, too."

"Me and King?" Clarke asked. "What do they want us for?"

"Sometimes there's no simple what for, Clarke."

"Yes, there is."

"Not that I know about."

The distant flashing lights of airplanes dotted the sky. Something dark and furred ducked into the brush at the side of the road. Dominick reached over and put his hand on his son's shoulder.

"Dad," Clarke said, "I'm scared of you sometimes."

"There's nothing for you to be afraid of," Dominick said. The truck pushed against the night, bouncing on its worn struts. Dominick took his hand off Clarke's shoulder. "You don't want to go to Maine?"

"No," Clarke said.

"Listen, Clarke," Dominick said, "I don't think your mother's coming back."

Clarke said, "I know she's not."

King said, "I miss her." She didn't open her eyes. Through the windshield a rectangle of light washed over them from top to bottom.

"Me, too," said Dominick.

"They have lobsters in Maine?" King asked.

"They do," her father said.

"Can we get one?"

"You bet," said Dominick.

"Will we pass through a big city?" King asked.

"No."

"I'd like to see a city."

"You've been to a city."

"No, I haven't."

"You were pretty little. You don't remember?"

They drove on. The road glittered like chitin beneath the headlights. The children were quiet beside him on the seat. Dominick watched his fingers on the steering wheel.

CHARLIE BASIN CIRCLED Dallas Pope's police car and swept the ground with light. He wore plastic gloves. He opened the front door, surveyed the vinyl seats, the empty gun rack angling up from the floor, the sunglasses on the dash. "Shotgun's been lifted," he called as if he expected someone behind him to take note. He stood with the door open. The full moon silvered the roadside beeches. Half-lit clouds curled up like rolled carpets. Across the road rose a bank of reddish rock. Just past the road's shoulder trailed a drainage ditch. He rocked back and his heels crunched into the gravel beneath him. He walked ten paces in front of the police car and toed the tire marks in the mud. A second vehicle. "Well," he called, "they're in a truck." He put his hands in his pockets and squeezed his jacket around him.

As though without intention, he strayed to the side of the drainage ditch. Head-sized stones and dark gully weeds. A dry mud bottom etched in sinuous lines. A snakeskin. He hopped in and raised his light near his shoulder. A wet wind blew inside the neck of his coat and he shivered. He traced the light up the line of the ditch until it lit the round opening of a steel pipe running beneath a farming lane. "Oh, shit," he said. He began to walk up the line of the ditch. He shoved aside an evergreen branch with his foot. A ridge of crabgrass. The jut of rusted steel formed into a great impenetrable O.

He shouted, "Who's going to take a look in there?"

FOUR MONTHS BEFORE Clarke was born, Dominick and Sarah put on what finery they had and drove to Philadelphia. In a week Dominick would ship out for basic combat training at Fort Benning in Georgia. In Philadelphia, they stood across the street from City Hall. The winter air still had teeth, but the sky was a grand blue and, when they held still, the sun heated their clothes and skin. Dominick wore a wool jacket over the white shirt he'd pressed himself. Sarah had a long wool coat trimmed with fur over a cream-colored brocade dress. Their cheeks were reddened. They kept glancing at one another, shyly, from beneath their brows. They held hands. They looked away from each other and at City Hall. The gray-and-white stone of the building was at home in the snow. A bronze statue of William Penn stood on top of the clock tower.

"This is exciting," Sarah said. Traffic moved through the street. Cars blared horns. The sidewalk was battered by winter boots. She took off her gloves and reached up and put her warm fingers against his cold cheeks. "Let's go in," she said. "Let's go get our marriage license."

One of Dominick's gloved hands touched her stomach. "After basic, I should get to come home again," he said. "For the birth, anyway."

"Are you nervous?" she asked. She put on a brave face. "There's no war, there's nothing. You'll be fine. You'll sit around and get fat."

The piles of melting snow looked bluish in direct sunlight. They turned toward the massive building. The pillars bordering the doorways, and the pale stone, and the slate roof. They stepped off the curb together and their feet squelched in the slush.

At the entrance, Dominick stopped her by pulling on her hand. He said, "You ought to come with me. Don't you think?"

"I belong here," she said. "I'm not going to be the kind of woman who follows you around." People lined up behind them.

He looked into her quiet curious face. He asked, "Will you be okay alone?"

THEY WERE ON the road. As King fell asleep against her brother and Clarke's head began to nod and straighten, Dominick felt an unspeakable pressure mount inside him, some dark fermentation rising into his voice. Each word deep, missing the crispness of its edges, spoken as if around something lodged in his throat. "I love you both."

"Okay," Clarke said.

"They won't let me keep you."

"Okay."

"I've got to run, Clarke."

"Okay."

"I want you to come with me no matter what happens," Dominick said. "Will you come?"

Once, Clarke remembered, his father had arrived home unexpectedly, still in his camouflaged Army combat uniform and beret. He gathered the kids up and drove them to Penn's Cave. His dad had been promoted recently, to master sergeant. Clarke felt proud. Dominick knew the overly tanned guide at Penn's Cave who drove the boat on the cave's waterways. They left the cavern lights off and navigated by flashlight, the beams flashing down limestone corridors and across stalagmites and catching against the trout that leapt from the water for the pellets the guide tossed out. Another time Dominick took just Clarke on a weeklong trip to the bottom of Pennsylvania's grand canyon. Dominick packed for both of them. Rifles. Sleeping bags. Fishing line. Buck knives. Not nearly enough food: a bag of peanuts, a handful of granola bars, powdered milk. Clarke tried to ask a few questions about Iraq, but his father didn't answer. He said they would gather some of what they'd eat, but most they'd have to kill.

So many unannounced trips swelled into Clarke's mind like links of chain. But each of them ended in the same way. The excitement of the journey was followed by letdown. Back home, his father stepped into his combat uniform, hugged them all too quickly, and left again. Clarke had spent much of his life hoping his father would stay.

"Speak up, Clarke," Dominick said. "Will you stay with me?"

Clarke stretched out against the truck's seat, rolled his head toward the window, held his eyes closed and his tongue tight. Should he act like his father? Or should he act like what he'd always wished his father could be?

Dominick waited for an answer until he forgot what he was waiting for. Finally, he glanced beside him to see both his kids asleep. He was tired, too, but he held his eyes wide open and drove until he couldn't drive anymore. In New York State, he pulled into a rest stop. He nestled the Ford among the big rigs.

When the car stopped moving, the kids woke. They pulled the mummy bags from the rear. Almost immediately Dominick's breathing settled into the long even pull of sleep. The kids looked at one another. Each was wide-eyed. The sky had just begun to glow faintly to the east. Clarke pulled the door handle gently and they slipped out and ran up the hills covered with flat withered grass. They stopped at the edge of a stand of rotting elms. King pointed into the thicket toward a child in a hooded coat who had only half a face. They crept toward the kid until the hood turned into a fallen branch and the half face to peeling bark. The first salvo of light leapt over the horizon and landed about them so that their limbs and the landscape startled into certainty. Rabbits chased each other across the grass. King ran headlong back down the hill and Clarke sprinted after her, and though he could only see King's back he could feel the wide childish smile that split her face like an old dream rising into the living world.

In the truck their father slept hard. Clarke cracked the driver's door. He'd gotten so big that King peered through the slit between his ribs and arm. Her chin brushed Clarke's shirt and tickled. Clarke smelled yeasty, like something growing. Clarke pulled their father's beaten leather satchel from its position at his feet, then shut the door softly and waited. Dominick didn't stir.

King whispered up at him, "What're you doing?"

"Going through his things," Clarke said.

"What for?" King said.

"I want to know what's what." He put the satchel over his shoulder and moved toward a weathered gray picnic table and

King followed at his heels asking questions. Was he looking for candy? For chewing gum? What did he hope to find out? What if they were caught? What was in it for them?

They emptied the satchel onto the tabletop. Their hands sweat. The sun touched the windshield and as their father's hair fell across his face and his chest rose and fell slowly, they took inventory of the possessions spread out on the table.

The Wharncliffe knife. A roll of duct tape. A dozen loose bullets. A small metal President's Hundred tab. A photo of their mother in a two-piece swimsuit. Medicated Chapstick.

There was another photo, lined and frayed, of the two children from another time, Clarke holding an infant King awkwardly in his arms, a worn mountain behind them.

Their father's black-and-gold Ranger tab, dangling by loose black thread. His driver's license, which they spent a long time with, calculating that he was thirty-three years old. "Dad's that old?" King whispered, and Clarke nodded in the heavy-headed way his father would have used to acknowledge such a sad thing.

A penlight. A sheaf of bills in a silver money clip. A rattle made of apple wood. A half-filled canteen. A woman's golden ring.

Their father woke as they slipped into the truck. His leather satchel lay back at his feet. He put the truck in gear and the boredom of the road set in quickly. They were uncomfortable, squeezed together on the seat. King sat in the middle. They had odd conversations. For King's sake, Clarke talked about curiosities.

"I've seen a picture of a girl who was born with three legs," Clarke said. "Do you think she could walk?"

"Wow!" King said. "Three legs?" Her voice was hushed, almost reverent.

"She couldn't walk," Dominick said. "No way."

King asked, "How tall is the tallest person in the world?"

"I'm not sure," Dominick said.

"Eight foot something," Clarke said.

"Hey," Dominick said, "you think somebody could be eaten by bees?"

"I don't know," King said.

"They can't," Clarke said.

"Maybe they can," said Dominick. "I don't know."

"Come on, Dad."

"Remember all the bees around the house?"

"The mud daubers," Clarke said. "You had me clean nests off the porch."

King, whose eyes were closed, did not open them. She did not move her head. She said, "There are wasps down by the river."

"I mean the honeybees in the clover," Dominick said. "And the carpenter bees drilling perfect little holes in the wood? And the hive in the crotch of the plum tree?"

King's head rose from the back of the seat. "Mom hid things by the plum tree," she said. "And in the attic and the hollow pine and under the woodpile, too. That was fun."

The drive from New York to Maine took eight hours. The Ford hummed along the road like a hungry insect. The sun traveled in an arc overhead. Dominick turned the dial on the radio until he found news programs, or weather advisories, or bluegrass. The lines on the road spun out eternally before them, winking on and off in a kind of promise that movement might unite what had been broken. They drove through farmland, and wooded country, and small towns that hunched inward against time and decay. They drove alongside a river and startled herons and egrets into low desperate flight. They saw a dark plume of smoke circling into the sky, distant but blowing their way. They stopped and bought turkey sandwiches and boiled eggs from rundown convenience stores. They drove through entire states and read the signs aloud. Connecticut. Massachusetts. New Hampshire.

Clarke considered his father's profile, its hard and defined edges, and the way that his sister's body conformed against her father's shape, the way she looked up at their dad, the ancient need gathering like sand in her eyes.

They drove past suited firefighters running from an explosion in a cement fire-training house. They saw four men brace their feet against the recoil of a giant hose. Three of the men at the hose listened to the shouts of the fourth and Dominick remembered his sergeant stripes and the responsibility for others' lives, and the smell of goat flesh and tire fires. He felt again that he should go back to Afghanistan, back to his privates, Benny Ward and DeJesus and Floyd. Back to swapping MREs and the sun and the heat and all the privations like the long walks with pack mules and being tired and being sore and being shot at by snipers in low mud buildings until they all flopped and hid behind their dying mules, passing a canteen of hot water and shouting into the radio until the Apaches came riding in with their chain guns.

As they drove north, the early spring receded into late winter. The trees hardened into a dull gray-brown. The crocuses retreated back into bulbs in the earth. The temperature dropped. They began to pass remnants of heavy snows pushed into dark gray piles on the sides of roads and parking lots. Protean clouds swirled above. Though the road remained clear, the thinnest film of snow appeared on the ground and then thickened gradually as they progressed, as if ice grew like mold upon the ground. They pushed forward and Dominick kept his eye on the rearview mirror. He drove the speed limit. They passed a police car hidden behind an overpass and they all froze beneath the air that lashed like a giant tongue around the truck's cab. They rode on. They waited. But the police lights did not turn on. The chase, which they feared as they feared the inevitable, did not begin.

PULLING INTO HIS driveway in the D.C. suburbs, Charlie Basin leaned over the passenger seat to pull his gun from the glove compartment. It was late. Maybe he shouldn't have come home. In the front window, his wife stood in a white gown. Startlingly beautiful and eerily thin. Pale skin and dark lips looking down toward something that he could not see. Her nightgown was gauzy and her skin seemed pinkish and translucent. How could someone so important to him seem even momentarily insubstantial? He put a hand against the passenger seat to push himself back up. He wanted to trace the three lines that trailed from the corners of her eyes. He wanted to run his fingers over her lips. He wanted to take her chin in his hand but he sat in the car with the gun in his lap. The moon behind the roof caught at the edges of things. On the peak of his roof sat a nighthawk with its wings stretched open. It was large. Its head turned toward him and its neck moved in small increments, like something mechanical. Its beak was hooked at its tip.

Charlie Basin called his boss, Andrew C. Fry, who had clearly been deep asleep. "I'm back in D.C.," Charlie said. "Dominick Sawyer has split. He's likely out of Pennsylvania entirely. I put out the APB."

"You sure he's gone?"

Charlie shrugged. Then he said, "Sure enough."

"He killed the local sheriff?"

"Looks that way. He's driving a truck. I think he had his kids in the cab when he killed the cop."

"Jesus. You tell me what you need to go after him, Charlie."

The lights went out in the house and Charlie opened his car door. He felt like a stranger walking across his own lawn. He went inside, undressed, and stood on the chilly blue tile of the shower stall. He let the cold water run over his face. He hadn't lived the family life that he had once wanted to live. Did he care? How often did a father need to speak to his children? How close did he need to be? Charlie dried himself on a plush Turkish towel, folded it, and hung it back on the bronze warming rack. He put on no clothes, held the shivers off by force of will. He turned the doorknob gently and peeked in the bedroom at how his wife's dark hair was overwhelmed by the white down comforter. He slipped in beside her, tired but waiting. The blanket seemed to float above him. The bed worked on him like an oven. He held still, moving toward her only after the deep, aching cold had left his body alone.

JUST INTO MAINE they saw a sign advertising Wells Beach and pulled off the highway. Dominick directed the pickup toward an ocean they couldn't see. They cracked their windows and smelled bacteria and fish and salt and decay. The kids had their feet resting on the dash. Clarke breathed deeply. "It kind of stinks," he said. Dominick smiled, his hands tight against the wheel.

A small road ran parallel to the beach. On either side sat houses. Older square clapboard and cedar-shingle homes sat among out-sized modern renditions with more windows than walls. Visible between houses, a cement retaining wall and then a long stretch of wet sand and the gray water lapping at the beach. Ahead, distant rock faces topped by hunkered pines. The truck bumped along. A red fox, quick and furtive, ran from a saltspray rose shrub and stopped in the middle of the road and raised its head to stare them down. Dominick slowed the Ford and the fox's hair bristled; its eyes were huge and dark and wet. They all felt the great trapped wildness in its gaze, its curiosity about their naked skins. Its dark-lipped humor at their ungainly two-legged shapes. Each creature's perpetual foreignness to the next.

They pulled into an empty parking lot outside a small sewage-treatment plant, the low beige buildings lumped to-gether behind a chain-link fence. The Ford's doors squealed open and crashed shut. They all took their shoes off and rolled their pant legs. They followed a small sanded trail. The wet air pushed across their faces. Beyond the houses, the beach opened up on either side. A frail mist hung over the sand. A light winked on in the house just behind them but they didn't see another person anywhere on the beach. At the water's edge, King and Clarke stopped. King stripped off her shirt and pants and stood there in her panties and her thin, angular childhood. A door of the house behind them opened and two dark-coated women came to stand on the retaining wall. One of them raised a pair of binoculars to her eyes. Dominick stood behind his kids. "Go on," he said and King waded in and began to hop, first on one leg and then the other.

"It's so cold," King said. She hadn't ventured in past her knees but the reddening of her skin crept upward to her thighs. The water stretched out before them, pounding in and pulling back, and King felt the mixed signals of its desires. She asked, "Stuff really lives in here?" Clarke began to wade out toward her to make sure she'd stay safe and Dominick dug his toes into the cold sand. Clarke waded to his knees and stopped and crossed his arms over his chest and turned to look at his father on the sand. King's body shivered and goose-bumped, but she waded deeper. "Dad," she called, "come on!" She arched her skinny body in a diving posture. "Get in here, Dad!" Her voice did not shake when she yelled, "I'm going in."

When they got back in the truck, King's teeth chattered. They dried themselves with blankets. The cab felt tight with the three of them, but already it had become a kind of home. They sank into the seats. When they were warmed, Dominick turned the engine off so that the fan sputtered out and the blowing heat began to fade away. He said, "I need you to wait here." He adjusted the holstered pistol beneath his belt and covered it with his flannel shirt. He zipped his dark red vest.

King's arms were wrapped around her chest. She said, "I don't want you to leave us."

"I won't."

"Okay," King said.

"I'll be right back."

"You will?"

"We've got to take care of each other, King."

"All right."

Dominick opened the door and stepped out and walked out of the parking lot and onto the gray street. The wind began to blow, and the mercury dropped, and the warmth of the ocean rose up and lifted the clouds above them into dark castellated towers. Clarke opened a can of mandarin oranges with his Swiss army knife. Here he was again, sitting about while his father left him behind. The air loosed a long howl. They wrapped themselves in blankets. They waited.

"If I took off, would you come with me?" said Clarke.

"Took off where?" King asked. "What about Dad?"

"He's always been fine without us."

"No, he hasn't," King said.

They tightened the blankets around them. Cracks of frost began to grow on the windshield. Grains of sand skittered across the glass.

To make his way back to them, Dominick had to lean against the wind. His range of sight wasn't more than thirty feet. The children saw him slowly materialize. First a coalescing series of darker and lighter spots out in the blowing sand and mist. Then a single darkness. Then a shifting shape thickening and lengthening and thinning into the silhouette of a man. His head was wrapped in a black scarf. He leaned forward unnaturally against the wind. His hand reached out for the door.

"I got us something to eat," their father said. "A place to stay."

He drove the Ford to a two-story garage behind a beach house. At the top of the exterior staircase to the second floor, they stood outside the door of the garage apartment. Dominick set King down and fumbled in his pocket. The kids pulled their collars tight. The wind pushed them forward against a window to one side of the door. Their faces pressed against the glass and they looked inside at a soft light. A bed in white linens. A television. Walls that had been recently painted a sunflower yellow. A pile of split wood in a basket, a fireplace that glowed hotly with embers, a door open to a bathroom. A sink, a shower, a microwave. A tile-floored kitchen. A refrigerator. A hot plate. Flowered window curtains and a vase of daffodils on a nightstand.

In his hand their father held the silver key. "Can you feel it?" Dominick said.

"Feel what?" said Clarke.

"This is a good place."

After they dropped their bags on the floor, Dominick took Clarke to the main house to meet the owner, a woman named Clarisse Parish. They used the brass knocker to hammer at the door until it opened. A woman with a deeply creased face and white hair pulled them forward by their hands. She said, "Come in, come in." She wore a long velvet skirt and a pastel sweater and shoes soled with cork. Her smile deepened every crease in her face. "Sit down," she said. She pointed through them toward the garage and said, "That old place has been empty too long." Dominick and Clarke looked down at themselves, then around and back behind.

Alone in the apartment, King threw herself backward onto the white bed. She bounced a few times. She crossed her arms behind her head, leaned back, and stared at the long crack in the ceiling. The edges of her mouth lifted. She reached for the remote control on the nightstand.

She scrolled through the channels until her hand froze. On the glass was an image of her father in the desert, wearing fatigues and holding an M4 carbine. King knew this image of her dad in the way that her hand knew how to find her mouth in the dark. A black-haired newscaster announced that Dominick Clarke Sawyer was wanted for questioning in the murder of Sheriff Dallas Pope of Snyder County, Pennsylvania. The newscaster spoke with a man from the FBI. The FBI man said her father was armed. He said her father was dangerous.

King's body jumped like a wire running with electricity. She slapped at the remote until the screen fell dark. Her hands squeezed the white sheets and she held herself still until she decided what to do. She wouldn't tell anybody. Not a single soul. Not her father. Especially not Clarke.

CHARLIE BASIN SET out a white tablecloth and small blue plates that had belonged to his wife's grandmother. It was midmorning. He sliced two baguettes and placed them on a plate with a portion of brie. He cut the tomatoes on a bias. He bruised the basil with his fingers and laid it on the cheese. He pulled the seat out for Rosamund and gestured for her to sit.

Her dark hair had begun to gray at the temples. She had strangely long fingers. A slight wattle beneath her chin and strong cheekbones. A charming self-consciousness. "Something's happened with Charlene," she said. "It's pretty bad."

"What happened?" Charlie said.

"She's in the hospital."

"What for? What hospital?" He tensed in his chair and leaned forward.

"She's okay, Charlie." Rosamund put both of her hands in front of her on the tablecloth. Her head dipped and rose like something at sea. "She's at Duke University Hospital."

"'Okay'?" Charlie said. "What happened to her?"

Rosamund paused. She looked up at him. "She's in the psychiatric ward."

"What happened, Ros?" Charlie said.

"She cut herself."

"Cut herself where?"

"It wasn't that serious. One of the doctors called it deliberate self-harm."

"Jesus," Charlie said. "Why?" His mouth hung open, then closed, then opened again. He leaned back in his chair, tried to relax. "How long's she been in there?"

"Two days."

"I'm going to go see her," Charlie said.

"I don't know, Charlie. I didn't want to tell you this part."

"Tell me what?"

Rosamund straightened in her chair. "She said, pretty specifically, that she doesn't want to see you."

Charlie touched his fingers to his lips, then to the tablecloth. He put his hand around his glass of water, raised it halfway, then put it back down. They were quiet for a few minutes. Their seltzer water hissed against their glasses.

Rosamund said, "What is this?"

"What's what?" he said.

"This," she said, gesturing to the tablecloth and her grandmother's plates and the halved baguettes. "Is this *brunch*?" She spread a white napkin across her lap. "Why're you going in so late to work today?"

"Things got worse yesterday," Charlie Basin said. "It doesn't really matter much now."

"It still matters," Rosamund said. "Tell me about it."

"I crawled inside a corrugated drainage pipe," Charlie Basin said.

"What for?"

"I pulled out a body." Charlie Basin looked down at his palm in his lap. His hands had left deep prints in the silt as he had crawled. The pipe had barely accommodated his shoulders. The light had jerked forward in his hand until it hit a patch of brown greasy hair. Basin's elbow had come to rest in blood-wet mud. He'd recoiled. A folded body and a jumble of limbs. A head bent back too far. A snapped neck. A throat slit open like a great mouth.

"I'm sorry, Charlie," Rosamund said. Her voice was quiet. Her arms were folded on the table.

"What are we going to do about Charlene?" Charlie said.

"I don't know."

Rosamund picked up her bruschetta. Charlie Basin scooted his chair nearer to his wife's and they sat beside one another. He turned sideways so that he faced her. "Why didn't you tell me about this right away?" he asked.

"This is hard for me, too," Rosamund said. She set her baguette back down and pushed it across her plate. "You look tired," she said. "Can you skip going in today altogether?"

"No," he said, "I can't."

"Do you want to tell me about this case?"

"A father running with his two kids. An Iraq vet, an Army Ranger from a reconnaissance detachment."

"Two kids?"

"Uh-huh."

"One boy, one girl?"

"That's right."

"Just like us," Rosamund said.

"WHY DO YOU have a gold ring?" Clarke asked.

Dominick held up his hand. He lay in the bed. "This one?" he said.

"The woman's ring. In your satchel."

"You've been rifling through my stuff?" Dominick's knees cracked as he stood. He could hear King in the bathroom brushing her teeth.

"Whose ring is it?" Clarke said.

"Clarke," his father said. "What's mine is mine." He took a step forward.

"Is it Mom's?"

Dominick sat back down on the edge of the bed. He put his head against his hands. "We've got to take it easy on each other," he said.

"Is it?"

Dominick looked up at his son. He held the silence for a moment. "Of course it's your mother's."

"Why do you have it?"

"Who else'd have it?" his father said.

"Why didn't she take it with her?"

Dominick was quiet for a minute. He looked at his son. "Because," he said, "she didn't want it."

Later that afternoon, Clarisse Parish pulled bits of Styrofoam from her attic. She sat on the rag rug in her living room and pieced them together. When she knocked on the door to the garage apartment, her arms were filled with airplanes. Clarke and King opened the door. Behind them, she could see Dominick bending over the hot plate. She hefted the planes and said, "Kids, let's fly these things."

King reached out and took a plane from the crook of Clarisse's elbow. She handed it to Clarke.

Clarisse looked at Dominick. "Come on," she said. "There's enough for you to have one, too."

They stood in the wilted grass that ran from the front of Clarisse's home to the retaining wall. The tide was high and the surf crashed. They threw the planes back and forth at one another. The planes cut upward in curious curlicues. They described neat little curves. They nose-dived and ran into house windows. Clarisse's neighbor came out and stood on her back porch with her bathrobe pulled shut against the wind. Her mouth pursed tight. She smiled when the planes splintered against rocks. From the side of her mouth, Clarisse whispered, "Her name's Roseanne Small." Then she gestured them closer. "She's a witch." Clarke smiled but King stared at the neighbor's dark robe and long bony fingers and then she turned and threw her plane against the wind, and it caught an errant upward draft and rose with its wings tipping back and forth. It soared pretty far. Farther than it should have been able to from such an awkward throw. It lofted over the neighbor's roof and dived and

Roseanne Small began to smile until it rose and floated across the backyards. It turned in a great arc toward the swamped beach and floated over breaking waves to the quieter water. They all watched the plane descend with dry open mouths. It came in fast and low. Like a warplane.

◄ Some of their days in Maine took the shape of normal lives. Dominick slid the pistol under the bed. They bought bagels and yogurt at the Price Chopper. They bought and split a lobster from the Lobster Pound. A film of snow came and went on the beach. Bundled in a jacket, King pestered Clarke until he loaded sand into buckets for her sand castle. They waded in the cold salt marsh. They hunted up and down and found decayed kelp and rotting clams and hundreds of dead crabs no larger than silver dollars. They collected empty shells and brought back a blue mussel and a razor clam and a knobbed whelk that King held to her father's ear. "Listen," she said.

He listened. The noise washed back and forth in his head, moving from place to place. He could hear two oceans, one inside and one out. It made his mind feel like a hard place that he could turn around and get lost in, a place that contained places within other, darker places. Inside the sweep and dip of Pennsylvanian mountain roads was his memory of a brick alleyway in Philadelphia. The hilltop village of Maduu nestled inside Iraq like an eardrum inside the curled nautilus of an ear. With his free hand, he pushed at his temples as each place spiraled into another. He took the whelk shell and pressed it into the sand. He was here, right now, with his children. He didn't want to be anywhere else. He pointed at the shell. "Is there still a critter in there?" he asked.

"I don't know," King said.

Dominick took a deep breath, let himself feel the room inside his chest. They were safe here on the beach. King sat in the sand a foot away from him. Ten paces over, Clarke squatted by a tide pool, sullen, disturbing the water with a stick. Dominick felt the distance between them like a cold breeze tightening his skin. He let his held breath out. Wasn't this the way it was meant to be with a teenager? Couldn't distance signal growth? Couldn't it be a good thing to watch Clarke, who'd suddenly gotten large, grow even bigger? Couldn't Dominick relax into the strain? He let himself smile. He reached out and touched King's knee.

"I love it here," Dominick said.

"The ocean is so loud," said King. "Did you know it was so loud?"

"I'd forgotten about it," Dominick said. He stood, stretched his back, and brushed the sand from his pants. "Let's go see what Clarke's doing," he said.

"I know what he's doing," King said. "He's poking the water with a stick."

"What's he poking?" Dominick said. He pulled his daughter up by a hand, hard but slow, so that she floated up above the sand as though jumping in slow motion. Her mouth split wide. She laughed. When he set her back down, she said, "Do it again."

Dominick sat by Clarke's tide pool with King so close that her side touched his leg. He could feel her breath. The clouds in the sky had stretched out long and thin. Dominick didn't say anything to Clarke. He just sat. In the ocean water he watched dark seal heads bobbing and disappearing. On a jut of rock sat a cormorant with outstretched wings. A troop of pelicans took turns diving.

In a shallow tide pool, Clarke had discovered a juvenile lobster hiding beneath a rock. He had only a single claw. Dominick's kids poked at the lobster with a stick. They wanted it out in the open. They wanted to see how it would choose a path through the clear water. They wanted it to come out from beneath that stone shaped like a round of bread.

Finally, Clarke leaned back in the sand, resting on his elbows. He had been thinking things through. He watched King lean against their dad's leg. "If they're after us," he said to his father, "you better show us some things."

"What kind of things?"

"Like how to take care of ourselves."

"I'll take care of you, Clarke," he said.

"No, you won't."

Each day Clarisse invited the children to the main house for lunch. She set the table with pastel linens. On the giant butcher's block that served as a kitchen island, she laid out homemade bread and peanut butter and jelly and salami and bologna and mustard and mayonnaise and tomato and apples and pears and carrots. She said, "You go on. Fix it yourself."

When they were about set to eat, she said, "I think I'll have something, too. I like bologna and a lot of butter. Which one of you will make me a sandwich?"

Clarisse Parish was a kind woman. With her whole hand, she often touched King on the shoulders but she only touched Clarke on the forearm with her fingers. Her eyes, brown but bright, reminded King of kindled wood. Clarisse didn't any ask questions about their father. When King came to lunch with a hole in the knee of her jeans, Clarisse said, "Those pants are failing you."

"I fell," King said.

"Where?" said Clarisse.

"On the rocks by the beach."

"That'll do it," Clarisse said. "Take them off. We'll patch them." She took a sewing kit from a cupboard and found a square of denim and a needle and blue thread. King sat on a stool in her white underpants. Clarke chewed on his second salami sandwich. Clarisse pushed the thread through the eye of the needle. She glanced up. She said, "You think I'll get to meet your mother?" and the children's faces fell like the two halves of a split log. "Oh," she said, "what's happened?"

She said, "You don't want to talk about it?"

She said, "You know I'm a mother, too. A son and two daughters. But they've grown up and moved away."

She said, "I miss them fiercely."

That evening, King and her father sat on the sand too close to the water. Sea spray sprinkled their bare faces. Wind flapped the clothes around their limbs. Foamy orange scum collected along the surf line. There were a few birds. Seagulls, their wings folded behind them, bobbing in the waves.

"What is it, King?" Dominick asked. "You look worried."

"I don't know," she said.

"I'd like you to feel that you can talk to me," Dominick said. They lay back and an osprey rode an updraft overhead. Sand-pipers ran the shoreline in a frantic back-and-forth.

"I miss home," King said. "I miss school. I want to see my friends." They watched as a few terns skimmed the deep water.

"I miss home, too."

"I'm worried," King said.

"Worried about what?" Dominick asked.

"Mom disappeared," King said. "Are we going to disappear, too?"

FROM HIS OFFICE Charlie Basin dialed his son. Oswell. An assistant district attorney in Baltimore. Tall and stooped and too thoughtful for his own good. The secretary answered and Charlie asked to speak to his son. He hadn't talked to either of his children since Christmas.

"Dad," Oswell answered. "I'm due in court in half an hour."

"I've got you," Charlie said. "I'll be fast."

"What do you need? Is it about Charlene?"

"Yeah," Charlie said, "it's about Charlene." He paused. "Have you been talking to her? Has she been okay?"

"Before the hospital, you mean?"

"Yes."

"Well, she'd been seeing somebody."

"Dating somebody? That's a problem?"

"No, well, that, too. But I mean she'd been seeing a psychologist."

"What for?" Charlie said.

"Depression," said Oswell. "She'd missed classes. Some days she didn't get out of bed."

"Does your mom know about this?"

"I don't know. I presume so. I've only got a few minutes, Dad."

"Have you talked to her in the hospital, Oz?"

"Twice."

"How is she?"

"No good," Oswell said. "She sounds drugged."

"Your mom says she doesn't want to talk to me."

"Mom's not talking to you?" Oswell said. "What'd you do?"

"Charlene," Charlie said. "Charlene doesn't want to talk to me."

"Oh. I think she'll talk to you if you want her to."

"What's that supposed to mean?" Charlie said.

"It means that you can call her, Dad. Ask her. See what she says."

"I don't know," Charlie said. "You have time to talk about something else? Another subject?"

"What subject?"

"There's this case that's starting to get to me."

"I'm not a therapist."

"Good, 'cause I don't need a therapist."

"What kind of case is it?"

"A father running with his two kids. Killed a sheriff who got in his way."

"In front of his children?" Oswell said.

"I don't think so," Charlie said. "He's an Iraq vet. Decorated. Other Rangers I talk to say only good things. They ask if he's okay."

"Is he okay?"

"Doesn't look like it," Charlie said.

"What's he running from?"

"His wife left him about a year ago," Charlie said. "Then she called in to the local police office and said she believed the children were being abused."

"Were they?"

"Child Welfare didn't think so," Charlie said. "Then, a few months later, a deputy went out to ask him a few questions. That deputy disappeared."

"What happened to him?"

"I don't know. We still haven't found him."

"Why's this bother you, Dad?" Oswell said. "You've seen worse."

"I don't know," Charlie said. "Those two kids, I guess. It's my job to get him away from them."

"There's a lot of kids out there who need help," Oswell said.

"Yeah?" Charlie said. "What if somebody had tried to take you away from me?"

"You wouldn't have let them."

WHEN HIS SON was born, the valley between his wife's legs had been as hot as a blast furnace. He'd had to stand there in that frail V of flesh. Sarah Tower Sawyer. Her face like burled wood. He'd just come back home.

After he'd finished basic combat training, he'd gone straight to Ranger school, a brutal sixty-one-day combat course. He'd been so excited. The course had four stages: Benning, mountain, Florida, and desert, and he passed through without recycling, without being sent back to try again. He could do hundreds of push-ups. He could run five miles in under thirty minutes. His body adapted so easily. In a few weeks, he would go back to join the Third Ranger Battalion, Seventy-Fifth Ranger Regiment. He wasn't nervous. He could follow orders. His body never failed. He had never been this good at anything before.

But in the hospital with his wife, he didn't know whether to sit or to stand. The nurses bumped into him, their hips soft and broad. Sarah's gold wedding ring sat in the breast pocket of his shirt. Her fingers were too swollen to keep it on. The doctor, a squash-faced man dressed in white, leaned over her. "Push," he said, and she held her breath and strained and the veins rose against the skin of her neck and face. "That's good," the doctor said. Dominick looked at his sun-dark hands and the hooks of grease beneath the nails and he thought, What's good? He stood there and watched the whole world open up. He thought, We want things to be open? He thought, What comes next? He thought, How far do we want to see? That round of head slowly advanced and withdrew like the shuffle of heavy infantry or like a great bass struggling against the line. He saw the thatch of dark hair between her legs like river moss. A wrinkled face. A warbling mouth and bluish lips and then a long quivering wail. How could a young woman give birth to an old man? A thing as wrinkled as used linen. It was slick and bloody and sniveling and his wife was slick and bloody and sniveling, too. But Dominick was sweatless and unbloodied and fairly calm. He imagined it was just like this when you held someone while they died. When the doctor passed the child into his hands, he held it like he'd hold a fish and thought of gutting it or throwing it back.

"CLARKE," KING SAID, "you're going to stay with Dad and me, aren't you?"

"What do you mean?"

"You're not going to leave?"

"I don't believe the stuff he says," Clarke said. "Do you?"

"Some of it's true."

"I don't know, King," Clarke said. He paused, picking his words carefully. "Maybe he's done something bad."

"I don't care. I don't want you to leave me alone. No matter what."

"I won't," Clarke said.

"You promise?"

They lay in bed until their father woke and rose from the couch. They yawned and stretched and brushed their teeth. By late morning, they decided to head to the grocery store. In the driveway, the neighbor in the dark robe stopped them as they were about to get in the Ford. She came at them so that the sun angled behind her. A cigarette dangled from her lip. Her hands were in the robe's pockets. She said, "I'm Roseanne Small," and her mouth wrinkled around the filter and the cigarette burned orange. A paisley scarf covered her white hair.

Dominick said, "Nice to meet you." He turned away from her toward the truck.

She turned to the kids. "What're your names?"

"I'm King," said King. "My brother's Clarke."

"*Howland*," Dominick cut in. "I'm Jon Howland." The kids turned to look at him.

"You look familiar," Roseanne Small said. She coughed into a closed fist.

"This is our first trip to Maine," Dominick said.

"Will your wife be coming to stay?"

"No," he said. The kids inched toward their truck.

"Why not?" she said.

"You always ask questions like this?" The collar of Dominick's dark red vest was zipped tight to his neck.

"I guess so," she said. "The kids are missing school, aren't they?"

"Is your husband inside?" Dominick said.

"He passed away four years ago," she said.

"Sorry to hear it, Roseanne." He turned toward his children, gestured toward the Ford with his thumb and index finger.

"What are you doing up this way?" she said.

"The kids wanted to see the ocean." He did not turn back toward her. He pulled the handle of the door and began to usher the kids inside.

"You might have picked a warmer month," Roseanne said.

"Sure," he said. "You might have picked a friendlier mouth."

In the afternoon when they got back from the grocery store, Dominick had his children do exercises on the back lawn while

Clarisse Parish watched. She brought them a tray of sandwiches. "Anyone for salami and avocado?" She perched a pitcher of water on the patio and filled blue-lipped glasses.

His kids stood side by side. Syrupy light lit one-half of each of them. Dominick positioned their feet by pushing them with his own. He taught them to tighten their stomachs and roll in their hips. He pushed on their shoulders, quickly, knocking them over. "Again," he said, "again," until the kids' palms and knees were green, and their muscles shook, and they were two child-shaped pools of molasses sucking off the ground.

"Now it's your turn, Clarke," Dominick said. "Use my strength against me. Come at me and get me on the ground. On the ground, we're closer to equal. Learn to take me down." Dominick spread his legs to shoulder width and tightened his stomach and rolled his hips inward so that his spine straightened. "Go on," he said, "come after me."

Clarke felt the twinned impulses, the impossibility of hitting his father and the desire to shove him hard enough to hurt. Clarke thought about his sister in the room at night, asleep and shaking under the influence of some dream. He reached out hard. Hard enough that his father ought to have gone over, but he was like a rock beneath Clarke's hands. Then Clarke struck again, harder, but when his hands reached his father, Dominick folded backward, pulling Clarke with him. Clarke's toes ripped the grass out by the roots, but he had gotten strong, and he dug his shoes in and steeled his arms and held out, pulling back. He watched his father's brow wrinkle in surprise but before he could begin to feel any sense of pride or triumph he was lifted up and slammed back into the ground and his father had somehow swiveled around on top of him, his forearm pushed against the back of Clarke's neck. Then King launched herself at her father like a rag doll and draped herself over his chest and neck and wormed her thin white arms into her father's armpits and tickled. When Dominick smiled, King began to laugh.

Dominick took hold of his daughter and positioned her elbow around Clarke's neck in a blood hold. He prodded Clarke in the side. "Doesn't matter that you're big," he said. "If King squeezed you'd be unconscious in seconds." He took Clarke's elbow and wrapped it around his own neck. Clarke squeezed and Dominick's face reddened. "It doesn't matter how big I am, either," Dominick said.

He lined them up and had his kids strike out at him, their slow fists caught and twisted until a whole child lofted forward and over his outstretched leg and into the air. Dominick caught them and lowered them to the flat grass where they stood rubbing their arms. He did not stop until his children's bodies began to shake violently.

"Sit down," Dominick said.

Clarke said, "I'm gonna keep going."

"I don't want you to keep going."

"How else am I going to know what to do?" spat Clarke.

"Okay," his father said. "The next thing you need to learn to do is run." He pointed to the end of the line of houses along the shoreline and to the wooden staircase. He had Clarke sprint up and down the beach while he timed his son with a wristwatch.

AS HE DROVE the D.C. beltway, Charlie Basin called Dominick's sister Annie Sawyer in Rockford, Illinois. She had a sweet voice, calm and self-assured. Charlie liked talking to her and stayed on the line longer than he needed to. She said she hadn't heard from her brother. She asked what Dom might have done. She sounded concerned and protective. Charlie believed her and he liked that he believed her. He liked the person he was when he chose to believe people.

Traffic on the beltway moved haltingly. When Charlie got off the phone with Annie Sawyer, he dialed the number for Duke University Hospital. Why hadn't anyone told him that Charlene had been seeing a therapist? Would he have wanted to know? Why didn't she want to speak with him now? Charlie had never understood what a father ought to say to his daughter. She had always been so angry. Was it his fault? What of his life was he supposed to share? What was he supposed to live with alone?

The phone rang at his ear until someone picked up the line. Charlie asked to speak with Charlene Basin, a patient on the psychiatric unit.

"Hello, Dad," she said. She spoke too quietly. She dropped the ends of her words. "What's going on?"

"Just driving the beltway," he said. The gray-green station wagon in front of him had left its right turn signal on for the last twenty miles.

She didn't say anything. He could hear a slight mucusy catch in her breathing. "I can't do this," she said. He waited until she spoke again. "I don't want it, Dad."

"Don't want what?"

"Whatever you have to say."

"I'm not okay with that, Charlene," Charlie said. "I talked to Oswell the other day. He tell you I called?"

"He did."

Brake lights glowed red before him. Traffic began to slow. She wasn't going to tell him anything. "He said you're seeing somebody new. Dating. It might be serious."

"I don't know," Charlene said.

"What's his name? Tell me what he's like."

"He's okay. His name is Kurt."

"Charlene," said Charlie, "I might drive down this weekend. Would that be okay?"

"It's a long way from D.C. to Durham."

"I know it's a long way," Charlie said.

"I'm pretty busy. I'm trying to pull my life together in here."

"I'm pretty busy, too."

"Dad," Charlene said, "I'm trying to find a nice way to say that I don't want you to come."

A MIST FELL outside the windows of the garage apartment. The kids stood inside the glass. They could see nothing clearly. Behind them Dominick walked shirtless to the single closet. His skin was the tan of desert. The floor creaked beneath his weight. He was banded with muscle. He had the body of a man who'd run miles with a weighted rucksack and crawled under fences on his stomach and sweat and bled and carried heavy weaponry. He stopped in the middle of the floor and began to shake. He dropped to his knees as though someone had pushed him. The floor shook hard and the kids turned from the window and Dominick pushed back at whatever pushed at him until his body calmed and his knees unbent. He swept his hair back. He smiled at the kids until they turned back to the window.

Clarke and King watched two old women argue in the rain. Clarisse wore a patterned scarf knotted around her neck. The old neighbor wore her dark bathrobe. The neighbor gestured toward the garage with the burning point of her cigarette. The old women's mouths opened into small dark holes. King's hand crept over toward Clarke and latched on to his arm and Clarke felt his sister's need of him spider across his skin.

Their father pulled a shirt off a hanger and pulled it on.

"Dad," Clarke said, "you better look at this."

"I don't need to look at it." Dominick pulled his socks on hard enough that the kids could hear the heels tear.

"Yes, you do," Clarke said.

"We were never going to stay here forever."

The fog thickened until they could no longer see out the windows. Wet chilly air worked its way through the cracks around the door, along the windowsills, and, more slowly, through the walls. They played Chinese checkers. Dominick went out and came back with fried chicken and coleslaw. He put his kids to bed and lay on the sofa and listened to the gradual evening of their breath. When they were asleep, he went out. The cold wind on the beach chapped his face. He walked the beach and the water ran under the soles of his boots. He retreated. Lights winked out along the line of houses. The air blew and his pants and shirt began to whip around him. Short trees bent landward. The surf began to crash. He looked out over the ocean and couldn't see what pushed the wind. A great black mass stretched over the water. He pulled up the hood of his sweatshirt. His heart pounded. He counted the beats. He knelt in the sand and water welled in the shallow depressions.

Dominick couldn't see very much after the dark set upon him. Clouds rushed in and covered what was left of the sky. He wet a finger and held it up to test the direction of the wind but it came toward him from all sides. Everything before him was indistinct but loud. The gathering waves. The water rising up into some huge form, leaning over him like a great tower waiting to fall.

WHEN KING HAD swelled like a soft tick inside Sarah's belly, Dominick was on a two-month leave. He'd been sent to a twenty-week training course in military free-fall operations: survival, evasion, resistance and escape, marksmanship, and advanced navigation. Then he'd been promoted to sergeant in the Regimental Reconnaissance Detachment, Seventy-Fifth Ranger Regiment, and sent to Kosovo. By the time he got back, he'd forgotten what it was like to be stuck inside a cabin.

At home, Dominick and Sarah argued about his going back to the army, and they argued about King coming. He said he wanted to serve his country, that he loved what he did. He said the A-frame cabin felt too small for four. She said he'd barely been home enough to know Clarke. His hands were more comfortable holding a rifle than a child.

Dominick sat at the kitchen table while Sarah washed dishes. Her hands dipping into the water and out again, covered in soap bubbles. Her yellow apron wrapped around her. Her voice reasonable as he argued for abortion.

"No," she said. She stood in front of the sink. Water beaded on the silver lip of the faucet. Heat blew in the open window and the curtains lifted like long white arms. He lost himself then. The desert heat rose in his face. His heart pounded hard as gunfire. He reached out and picked her up by the neck and slung her across the room. A bar stool skittered away. Utensils scattered across the floor. She caught herself and held one hand over her belly and looked up at him with graceful cheekbones and fair skin. Her head cocked to one side as though she was listening. She wasn't afraid as he was afraid. Sometimes he felt like he was always afraid. This pissed him off. She reached up her hand to him. Her fingers were long and slender, the nail beds little perfect half-moons. He reached out for her, and picked her up, and spun his body clockwise, and threw her again, and she was spinning blindly through the air above the countertop in the way that their whole lives were spinning, and when it all stopped for a moment, he looked down at her and months had passed. She had landed in the hospital bed, holding the child he hadn't wanted, free of the bruises he'd left. A fat healthy child. So quietly regal. Kingsley. Her tiny eyes roved the room, moving across the great stretch of her father again and again, and Dominick wanted her so bad, wanted to lift her up, and hold her above his head, and take her out of the room, and show her to each nurse so that every one of them could marvel at her healthy rolls of fat, and her alertness, and her mess of wild dark hair, and the grip, my God!, that hurt when she latched her hand around your finger and squeezed. Dominick looked into those wet blue eyes and knew that certain mistakes were unpardonable, that certain errors would echo forever inside the four chambers of his life.

ON THE DRIVE to see his daughter in Durham, North Carolina, Charlie Basin listened to uninterpretable lyrics on college radio stations that faded in and out like better intentions. He whistled. When he arrived, he drove around campus, past Duke's gothic chapel and then over to the squat beige-and-glass medical center. He parked and walked the bright halls, following signs for the inpatient psychiatric unit. Finally, he spoke to a nurse, a man, who led him into the locked ward. A long pleasant hall with doors to each side. Pictures of beaches screwed onto the walls. Tan drywall and blue trim. Not a bad place, Charlie thought. The nurse, a thin sparse-haired guy, stopped at a set of large windows. He gestured with an elbow. "She's there," he said, "in the cafeteria."

Charlene sat at a stainless-steel table. She was reading a book. A small vase of fake flowers sat in the middle of the table. She wasn't wearing a gown, just jeans and a red sweater. She had a single dimple on her right cheek. She looked thin but muscular, a woman at the height of her youth and health. She wore slipper socks on her feet. Bandages wadded at her wrists.

When Charlie sat beside her, she said, "Hi, Dad," and looked down at her feet.

"Hey," he said. He pointed toward her slippers. "What're you wearing?"

"These?" she said. She raised a foot off the ground. "They gave them to me. No shoelaces allowed."

"Oh," Charlie said. He passed his thumb over his right eyebrow. "I want you to know that I listened when you said not to come. I thought about it. Then I came anyway."

"You want some lunch?" she asked. "I'm hungry."

Charlie could smell fried vegetables, oil, garlic. "I'll take whatever you're having," he said.

She stood and went over to speak with the male nurse in the hallway. She came back and they waited, neither knowing what to say, until the nurse brought plastic trays filled with food Charlie would rather not eat. Ginger carrot soup and something with tofu. "This is good," he said and pointed at his plate with his fork. She looked up at him through strands of long hair. Her eyebrows rose slowly. She didn't believe him. "I mean it," he said. "It isn't my style, but it's good." He pushed his plate toward the center of the table. "Can I get you out of here for a little while?"

"I don't think they'll let me out," Charlene said. "Maybe you can tell them you're a senior special agent with the FBI."

They took a walk around the campus. Charlene's lips kept moving as if she was about to speak. Charlie was quiet, trying to work out exactly what it was that he was there to say. It was easy to imagine that the white bandages around her wrists were some kind of fashion statement. Her legs were bunches of muscle. Her cheeks looked like they'd been pinched. She had a kind of impermeable beauty, like a statue, and Charlie understood that it could scare people away.

Finally, Charlene said, "You know this is the first time you've come down to visit, Dad?"

"Is it?" he said.

"Why do you think that is?"

"That's hard to answer," he said. "Work, I suppose."

"You don't have work now?"

"I don't want to talk about work, Charlene," he said. His voice was soft. "Is that okay?"

"What do you want to talk about?"

"How about depression?" he asked. "How about what you've done to yourself? How about you seeing a psychologist?"

"Jesus," she said. She stopped beside a stone building and leaned against a wall. "What is it that you want to know?"

"What do you talk about?" Charlie said. "With this therapist."

"Lots of things," Charlene said. "Sometimes my therapist wants to talk about you."

"He does?"

"*She* does," said Charlene.

"Me?" Charlie said. "What for?"

"I don't know," Charlene said. "I told her about the days that I couldn't get myself out of bed. It made me so angry."

"What's that have to do with me?"

"You're a cold person, Dad," Charlene said. "You're unemotional."

"I am?" he said. "I don't feel cold."

They began to walk again, between two buildings set close together and across a field where the ground was soft. They were conscious of the distance between them and of how, occasionally, their arms brushed together.

"Tell me about something else," Charlie said. "How about this guy you've met. Kurt, right? Tell me about pre-law. Tell me about what kind of law you're interested in. Criminal? Malpractice?"

"You don't usually ask me so many questions."

"I know," Charlie said. "I should have."

"What's going on with you?" Charlene said.

"I don't know." He stopped walking. They were surrounded by cherry trees in a terraced garden. He turned toward her. He reached out and touched the soft knitted material at the arm of her sweater. She pulled away and he let his hand drop. He bent an elbow so that his forearm crossed his torso and his hand rested on the biceps of his other arm. "You want to know what really surprises me about this?"

"What?"

"You're feeling pretty bad, I guess," he said, "but you look fine."

She looked straight at him. She held her own arms. "Get out," she said. "I want you to leave."

IN THE EARLY evening, Clarisse pounded on their door. Their father was out. The children were in their pajamas, side by side on the bed, watching cartoons in which violent actions were carried out but no one ever got hurt. The pillows lumped beneath them. Clarke got up to answer. Curtains obscured the windows. No matter what was there, Clarke decided, he'd stand between his sister and the spit of the future. He did not open the door. "Hello," Clarke said loudly.

"It's Clarisse. I came home from the library and my house smells like something's burning."

Clarke turned the deadbolt. Clarisse's brow was furrowed, but she didn't hurry as she stepped inside. She wore flat green shoes with bows on the top. King jumped off the bed. She had on a ripped T-shirt and blue pajama bottoms. She said, "Your house is on fire?"

"I don't think so," Clarisse Parish said.

"What does it smell like?"

"It smells like coal," she said. "You guys know anything about this?"

Both kids shook their heads. No, no. Clarisse squeezed her hands together. A light dangled from a wire that hung from the ceiling. Clarisse turned toward the door and opened the gingham curtains. The moon seemed to float in the sky like a curved fishhook.

"Where's your father?"

King shrugged. Her hands pushed down against her hips as though trying to retreat into pockets that her pajamas didn't have.

Clarke said, "Errands, I think. The hardware store. Groceries."

Clarisse said, "There's something else."

"What?" said Clarke.

"Come on. I want you to see it."

The children put coats on over their pajamas. Phlox grew along the edges of the stone walk. Every window in the house in front of them glowed with harsh light. Clarisse Parish walked briskly and the children hurried after. They felt a kind of cold terror that they would never in their lives come to put into words. Clarisse walked them through the house to the bathroom. The salt shaker lay on the floor. The stainless top, shoved a few feet away, looked like it had been smashed beneath a foot. Clarisse pointed at the tub. On the bottom, among the scratches and rust stains, salt curled into distinctive shapes.

Woodpile, scrolled the letters in salt, *Sylphine, Basin.*

Before they left, Clarisse served the kids apple cider, and King asked to borrow a dictionary. Clarisse wore a ribbon in her hair, a pale blue sweater. "A dictionary?" she said. "Sure." She touched King's shoulder. She pulled a small volume off the shelf in the dining room. "You can keep it," Clarisse said.

In the apartment above the garage, King sat cross-legged on the bed. She set the dictionary in her lap and took a deep breath. Clarke knelt on the floor and pulled a pistol from one of the bags beneath the bed.

"Let me see that," King said. "I want to hold it."

"Careful," Clarke said. "It's loaded." He handed the gun to his sister.

"It's heavy," she said.

"Better give it back to me."

"It says 'Beretta' on the side," King said. "What's that mean?"

"That's the kind of gun it is."

"What if Dad comes back?" King said.

"He won't."

"Where'd he get this gun?"

"The Army, I guess," Clarke said. "Why're you pointing it at me? Give it here."

"Why's he keep it under the bed?"

"Shhhh!" said Clarke.

"What?"

"You hear that?" said Clarke.

"Nuh-uh."

"Somebody's on the stairs," Clarke said. "Give it to me!"

"Here, here! Take it!"

"Oh, God," Clarke said.

"Put it back!" said King

"Which bag was it in?"

the people of the broken neck

"He's coming, Clarke, he's coming!"

Clarke slipped the gun inside a bag and they threw themselves onto the couch. The door opened hard. Dominick scowled. "Let's go," he said. "Ice cream," and he hustled them outside.

The Ford bumped hard over the ocean roads. A few dozen snowflakes fell and scattered around in the cement. The sun was a low slit between clouds, the sky a dark flat gray. Dominick whistled in the truck's cab, trying to unwind. His knees moved up and down casually. He said, "Let's try to imagine this is a real vacation."

"Okay," King said, but her leg shook back and forth. Clarke kept looking out the window at the way the snow seemed to dart around on the surface of the road. He reached over and steadied King's leg against the seat.

Dominick's eyes swept the houses alongside the street. "Look at that," he said. He was smiling. Two kids in red jackets walked a fence rail like a balance beam, their hands stuck out to their sides. "Reminds me of you two," he said. His arm lifted from the steering wheel and stretched along the back of the bench seat. "Funny that something far away can remind you of something that's right beside you." The weight of King's head pressed against his arm, between wrist and biceps. When Dominick's hand reached Clarke's shoulder, he cupped it hard enough that he could feel the sharp ridges of his son's bones.

Dominick pulled into a parking space in front of a white ice-cream parlor and sat quietly for a minute. Dry heated air blew from the vents in the truck's dash. Bits of ice flurried on the glass. They watched the parlor's door open and a family of five come out, wearing gloves and carrying ice-cream cones.

"Come on," Dominick said. "Let's go inside. I'll get you anything you want."

On the way back, they sat packed in the cab. Each held a cone in their hand. Chocolate peanut-butter cup. Peach sorbet. Pralines and cream. The nose of the truck dipped over the little hill of the driveway and bounced across a pothole. Roseanne Small stood in the middle of the pavement. She wore a fur coat and a long brown scarf. She flagged them down with both thin white hands. Dominick unrolled the window but stayed in his seat.

"I know who you are," Roseanne said. The ocean wind picked up and rushed over them and pushed her hair into a seabird's nest.

"Who am I?" said Dominick.

"I seen you on TV."

So easily was he transformed. One second he was a father in repose in a driver's seat, a rock beside a river, the next he was beside the truck with an arm pressed around Roseanne Small. With Dominick squeezed so close to her thin old body, King could see that he wasn't their father anymore. This new man was huge and strong and as foreign to her as another's tongue. Dominick's hand squashed Roseanne's mouth. His forearm was thick with muscle. He held her hard enough that she stayed still. He lifted her as though she was a briefcase or a hair dryer—something practical and meant to be carried.

Clarke glanced around. The road was clear in both directions. Snowflakes chased each other on the cement. The windows of the houses were almost all dark. Nobody jogged or walked a dog or stumbled drunk. Behind them, in the main house, the shape of Clarisse Parish darkened half a window.

Their father climbed the stairs to their room and set Roseanne on the bed. Her limbs sprawled and the fur pooled around her. The kids trailed after. Their father knelt beside the bed as though he was about to pray. "Don't talk now," he said. It remained unclear to each of them whom he was speaking to.

"You can't do this!" Roseanne said. Long yellowed fingers tightened around bed rails. Her feet scrabbled against the sheets.

Their father sat on the edge of the bed. He laid his hand gently on Roseanne's ankle. "It's okay," he said. "You're going to be okay." He looked at her and she looked back. Her cheeks blew in and out with her breath. "This isn't going to hurt," he said. He pulled the Beretta from under the bed and put it in the holster attached to his belt. He turned to the kids. They stood next to each other. He reached in his beaten satchel and tossed Clarke a roll of duct tape. "Tie her up," he said.

The children looked at one another. Clarke tightened up, a current of electricity causing his muscles to jump. He didn't like this old woman. "How?" he said.

"Not too tight. But tight enough to take her a long time to get out."

By the window, King fingered the gingham curtains. She felt faint. A single crystalline snowflake pressed against the glass. Clarke tore the duct tape and it sounded as though some great fabric was being ripped in two again and again. The corners of the window fogged. The rear light was on at the main house. King watched the back door open. A figure stood in the opening. It could have been King's mother. The silhouette moved forward until, beneath the porch light, Clarisse walked out in a gray housecoat. Her hair blew around her head in dark threads. Her hands held her sides. Halfway down the driveway, she stopped. She looked up. She mouthed King's name.

"Dad," King said, "she's out there."

"It's okay," Dominick said. "Go out and see what she wants."

When King opened the apartment door, a half-dozen gulls flew off the roof. She shuffled down the iced steps and up half the driveway to meet Clarisse. Dominick took King's place at the window. His daughter looked so small beside the old woman. King's head bowed. She took Clarisse's white wrinkled hand. They leaned toward one another as they spoke. King tipped her head upward and Clarisse leaned down. Whatever noises they made were for each other's ears alone, swept aside by wind. Then King came running back. Her shirt, an old red Henley of Clarke's, flapped around her. Her down-and-corduroy vest was unzipped. She moved outside the view afforded by the window. The old floor joists shivered as she ran up the steps, each leg a scrabbling piston. The impact of ball of foot on board like an infant's heartbeat. The palpitation of the brief wooden landing. The doorknob turning slowly to the left.

King looked bright-eyed and feverish. Her hair was damp. She stopped still and stared at the old woman in furs, limp, duct-taped and gagged on the bed. Roseanne Small's eyes pooled with spite.

King raised up on her tiptoes to whisper in her father's ear, "She says she didn't see a thing."

They left Roseanne Small tied on the bed and went to see Clarisse Parish. Every light burned in her kitchen. A fluorescent fixture was suspended overhead, two incandescent bulbs hung beneath a wrought-iron pot rack, and five halogens adhered to the underside of the old cabinetry. Dominick and his children squinted when they came in from the dark. They put their hands up to shield their eyes. Clarisse Parish had poured four glasses of milk.

"We owe you for the stay," Dominick said. His head was too close to the low ceiling. His hands tucked into the pockets of his jacket.

"Sit," Clarisse said. She wore a brown velvet skirt and a cable-knit sweater and a pastel scarf around her neck. Clarke and King took stools at the island. Dominick did not move. The muscles clenched in his squared jaw and his unwashed hair stuck to his head in a great block. "She's a royal bitch," Clarisse said. "What exactly did you do with her?"

"Duct tape," Clarke said.

Clarisse's head fell back, and her mouth opened enough to sip water, and she snorted. "I'll wait until morning before I find her," she said. She smiled and her teeth looked like they belonged to someone forty years younger.

"Thanks for this," Dominick said. "I don't know what to say. You've been kind to us."

Clarisse stood behind Clarke and King and put her hands on their shoulders. "Drink your milk," she said. Dominick still had not moved past the doorway. His shoulders nearly touched the edges of the door frame and his head was about even with the lintel.

"What do we owe?" Dominick asked.

Clarisse took a canvas bag from a shelf and filled it with canned peaches, beans, brown pears, a loaf of bread. "You'll need to eat," she said. She looked straight at him and held up the canvas sack. "And you can keep your money."

Dominick pulled out his leather satchel and dug for his wallet and began counting out bills. "I'm grateful," he said, "but we don't need charity."

Clarisse folded her hand over his. "Yes," she said, "you do."

When they drove out of Maine, the heat in the Ford was stifling. No one spoke. The three of them sank inward toward the kind of quiet antagonistic isolation that binds people unhappily together. Each of them felt conscious of how every movement of any one of their bodies on the single leather seat brought them into contact with another's skin. When one moved they all jostled. They passed through long tunnels of skeletal trees and past arched banks of snow and water frozen tight against the faces of cliffs. They drove without destination until King fell asleep. They drove unmapped miles and Dominick's eyes began to winnow closed until he pinched the thick of his leg and turned to his son, Clarke, to see him passed out, head back and mouth open. Dominick kept going. The Ford's metal frame hummed beneath them like something alive. The truck seemed to float upon the road and the night to fly against the windshield and minutes to uncount before them so that the country opened up in time. Dominick had to pull the wheel hard twice to keep the truck from spinning off into the grass and the thin patches of snow, so he pushed the brakes and turned onto a narrow dirt road and drove until the highway was far enough behind them. He killed the engine and slept.

There, King dreamed. She dreamed of her past, of things that had already occurred. She watched herself outside playing with her mother. Her mom wore a deep green skirt and stood behind King with her arms open. Even just two years ago, King had been much smaller, so low to the ground. A child, thought the new King. If she was no longer that kid, what was she now? What had changed? Just her size? The A-frame cabin sat behind them. She ran with her mother through a field being overtaken by purple loosestrife. They ran in rings beneath the trunk of the plum tree. King could see the shadows of her brother and father in the house windows. On the roof, a section of cedar shingles needed to be replaced. The window trim needed a new coat of paint. Her father must have been just home from the desert. She remembered that he would fix these things within weeks of getting home.

Her mother caught her up. Her shirt pressed against King's skin, her hair wreathed her face. King blew, trying to push the strands away with air from her mouth. The King who watched the two of them remembered that she had forgotten the smell of her mom, the wood smoke and syrup and salt and vanilla bean. Her mom smelled like something sweet baking and, though the King in her mother's arms struggled to escape, the King who watched wanted to burrow into her soft warm heart.

King dropped free and ran to the woodpile. Each hurried step sent up a small clump of earth. Her mother walked behind, breathing hard, smiling. Her cheeks had reddened. Her hair was held in a ponytail by a bit of blue ribbon. At the woodpile, King's mother sat on the ground with her back against the stacks. A double-sided ax stood buried in the chopping block. "Here," her mother said and patted the ground beside her. "I want to show you something."

"What is it?" King said.

"See that split log?"

"Which one?"

"The one at the bottom of the pile," her mother said. "There's a notch in the bark."

"That one?"

"Pull it out."

"It's at the bottom."

"Just pull it."

King pulled the log and it slid smoothly out. A half-cylinder with its flat surface placed against the ground.

"Turn it over," her mother said.

King flipped it. The heartwood had rotted out, leaving a darkened hollow. King said, "It's like a treasure chest!"

"What kind of things do you think we can hide in here?" her mother asked.

◄ˑ The morning light woke King to the cold. Deep internal shudders rumbled up from inside her. Her father's breath was visible inside the cab of the Ford. The insides of the windows were lined with thin sheets of ice. King's jaw chattered. "I'm really cold," she said.

"We all are," said Dominick. He rubbed his hands together, then slapped his thighs. "Let's get out."

"Outside?" said Clarke. "I don't know." He pulled his coat tighter around him and slumped into the seat. A cornfield stretched around them. The brown stumps of the stalks covered by white frost.

"Let's move," Dominick said.

He ran them through drills. Sprints through the shallow snow. Push-ups. Squats. There was a slight hill that he had them run up and then crawl down. Their legs fishtailed in the snow. They slid against one another and pushed off and laughed and scrambled to their feet and raced back to their father. "Jumping jacks," Dominick called. "Sit-ups." When they took off their coats, he nodded. "That's good," he said. When they took off their shirts, he smiled like they had traveled closer to a simple time in a simpler country.

CHARLIE BASIN WAS in bed when his phone rang on the nightstand. Rosamund leveraged herself up on one elbow and her dark hair cascaded. "It's awfully early," she said. "Something happened."

Charlie rolled to one side. He rubbed his eyes and turned on the lamp. Had something gone wrong? Was it his children? Was it Charlene? He answered the phone. "Charlie Basin."

"Hey, Charlie, I'm Jo-Ann Putnam, chief of the Wells Police Department. Up in Maine. You looking for Dominick Clarke Sawyer?"

"I am." The white sheet lay across his chest. Hair sprouted like thin seedlings. Charlie looked at his wife beside him and shook his head to say that everything was fine. Rosamund smiled. Her eyes were deep wild pools. Her hand tunneled under the covers.

"He's been here. Tied up a woman in her late sixties. Roseanne Small."

"Didn't hurt her?"

"Nope."

"Did he have two kids with him?" Rosamund's hand touched his side and her fingers spread and latched on to him and pulled.

"He sure did."

"When did he tie her up?" Charlie Basin said.

"Last night. Duct-taped her, actually. She chewed her way out, gave us a license-plate number. He's driving a white Ford F-150."

"You put out an APB?" Charlie asked. His wife's hand pulled at him and she slid across the sheets until her warmth added to his.

"We did."

"Good," Charlie said. "Try not to mess with anything. I'll be there soon."

"One more thing. He didn't tie her up."

"Come again?"

"It was the older child, the boy, that did."

Charlie hung up. He stopped Rosamund's hand on his thigh. Outside the window between clouds, the moon flashed like a falling coin. Charlie glanced at his wife, then dialed his boss. When Fry answered, Charlie said, "You up, Andy?"

"No," Andy said. "Why are you?"

"Just got a call from a local police department," Charlie said. "Dominick Sawyer's up in Maine."

"Maine? What's he doing in Maine? How many people do you need, Charlie?"

"He's out of there already," Charlie said. "He tied somebody up. A woman. I'll go this one alone."

THEY DIDN'T KNOW where they were going. They drove the small roads. The tires kicked up dirt and gravel and dust into a dark plume behind the truck. They didn't talk about where they were headed or what they might find. They made excuses to touch one another's faces. "Hey, look at that!" and a hand on a cheek and a finger pointed toward a heron slowly walking beside a creek that wound though etiolated grass. And "There, there!" and an elbow gently rested against the side of another while one of their heads nodded toward a herd of whitetails eating bark from the contorted trunks of dwarf apples. A whitetail's flag rose behind its rump and then, in concert, the deer stomped against the earth, leaping above the shrubbery in perfect arcs.

In the afternoon, they told jokes and at each joke they laughed outsized laughs.

When it got dark, they stopped driving and spent the night alongside a road. They slept piled against each other until dawn settled on them like a giant cataract. They stretched and yawned and, taking a risk, Dominick drove the highways into New York State, and the hills trammeled gently away from them. When the F-150 shot beneath the graffiti-covered mouth of an underpass, a police cruiser turned on its lights and inched to follow.

"Dad?" Clarke said. His head craned backward. His hand grabbed his father's forearm.

"I know," Dominick said. "We should have already dumped Howland's truck." His eyes were on the rearview mirror. He gunned the truck and it jumped forward, the engine rumpling like a congested lung. The Ford raced up the hill before it, the cruiser falling behind but gathering speed, its headlamps feeble in the light. The siren washed distantly around them. They crested the hill and sank toward the saddle point between two hills. The police cruiser passed from sight, the hill sweeping up between them like the rise of a dark volcanic mountain off the seafloor. Dominick pushed the truck faster, toward the highway exit. He watched the rearview mirror for headlights behind them but they did not appear. He pulled through the exit fast, the tires squealing, and onto an evergreen-lined street that ran toward the small town of Keeseville, New York. He came to a red light, turned right, traveled three blocks before turning into an alley, pulled behind a Dumpster, and killed the engine. They sat in the quiet, breathing. A long-dead leaf fell overhead. An orange cat walked along the top of a white fence. They sat and waited.

After half an hour, Dominick started the engine again. "I've got to be more careful," he said. His hands were still anchored to the steering wheel.

"With what?" King asked.

"With everything that happens from now on."

They stopped at a well-lit gas station and Dominick paid in cash. He came out past the glass walls and a bell rang on the door. He walked past the neon signs that hung in the windows. He hunched his shoulders. A rounded man pumping gas glanced at him, smiled. He wore oversized wire-rimmed glasses and a gray scarf. "Cold," the man said.

"Sure is," said Dominick. He opened the door to the Ford and tossed a paper sack onto King's lap. "We're dressing up in disguises," he said. Inside the paper bag was a pair of steel scissors and three boxes of hair dye. Off black, medium auburn, and light ash brown.

"I want black hair," King said.

"You got it."

"This is ridiculous," Clarke said.

"Come on," Dominick said. "Think of it like a game."

They drove farther south and found a padlocked restroom near Dix Mountain in the Adirondacks. A wooden sign read CLOSED in raised black letters. The narrow roads were deserted. The trails unkempt. "This is it," Dominick said. He took a pair of bolt cutters and a slim-jim, a small battery-powered drill, and a flathead screwdriver from his duffel bag in the bed of the Ford and cut the padlock with a single gesture. He found the water main in a supply closet and turned it on. He twisted the knob by the faucet until water sputtered into the sink. He pulled the pair of scissors from his pocket and held them up. "Clarke?"

"Go ahead," Clarke said. "Don't make it too choppy."

Dominick cut Clarke's dusty brown hair to a one-inch length. He handed him the medium auburn. "Wanna try this?" he said.

"Why not?" Clarke said. He almost smiled.

Dominick turned to King, who sat on a toilet tapping her feet against the cement floor. "Your hair's already growing out,"

Dominick said, "so we'll let yours get longer." He tossed her the black dye. "Follow the directions," he said.

The children spilled dye on the floor. They held their heads over the sink. Despite the plastic gloves, they colored their hands. When they were done, King looked at Clarke and laughed. "Dad can't cut hair," she said. "But the new color isn't much different."

"You look pretty different," Clarke said. King's newly black hair was slicked to her head. "You look pretty good."

Then they turned on their father. Clarke took the scissors to his head. "How short?" he asked.

"Close as you can get it."

Each lock of their father's dark hair fell as slowly as a feather. King pushed in. "Let me get a turn," she said. When they finished, Dominick stood in front of the mirror. He ran his hand over his short, rough hair. His jaw had darkened with stubble that he intended to let grow.

"You like it?" Clarke asked.

He ran his hand over his head. "Yeah, I like it," he said. "Reminds me of boot camp."

"Can I feel it?" King said.

"Sure."

Their feet made whisking sounds on the tile floor as they congregated by the scuffed mirror to feel one another's heads. Patches of dye had spilled on their clothes. Their fingers were darkened. It didn't feel like dress-up anymore. King's breath came too quickly and her face set hard as baked earth. In front of her, Clarke practiced styles of walking where he rolled his shoulders, or strutted, or dragged one foot. He affected a bad Boston accent until King almost smiled.

They went outside, where Dominick located the screwdriver in his satchel, knelt by the Ford, and pulled the plates while the kids waited beneath a giant fir.

"Look at this tree, it's huge," King said.

"What're you doing, Dad?" asked Clarke.

The ground beneath the tree was soft with moss. King lay down. "It smells good here," she said.

"Wait here," Dominick said. They looked up at him. His two children. Two parallel lines. Knotted roots unearthed beside them. "It won't take long," he said.

The entire time he was gone, they did not move. While they waited, Clarke imagined what might happen if his father didn't come back. His thoughts crept inward like the cold. Where would he and King go? What would they do? What had their father changed them into? What would happen if he took King's hand and tried to lead her away right now?

The forest smelled good. Shelves of mushrooms bloomed from reddish bark. Underfoot, a carpet of long pine needles. He walked toward the sounds of civilization, the deep-earth rumble of heavy trucks and the whoosh of air brakes. Electrical lines, draped between transformers, hummed with static. A distant horn. He walked out of the woods into a parking lot behind a glassworks, a long tan building with hundreds of mullioned glass windows. He walked among the rows of cars. He stopped beside the tail of a gray Dodge Ram, looked quickly around, then pulled the license plates from his satchel and switched them with those on the truck. Then he jogged out of the parking lot into an industrial neighborhood. Plumes of black smoke rose from great chimneys. Machines clanked behind loading-bay doors. Dominick jogged slowly up and down a few streets until he found another gray Dodge Ram. Again he switched the plates. Then he opened the driver's-side door with the slim-jim and pulled out the drill from his satchel. He drilled two small holes through the keyhole and into the lock pins. Then he turned the ignition with the flat-head screwdriver and the engine guttered to life. Dominick pulled smoothly onto the road and drove to collect his two kids from the bed of needles beneath the fir tree.

Driving west in the Dodge Ram, they crossed the Hudson River near its confluence with the Mohawk and followed green signs to Cohoes Falls. They opened the windows and the cold rushed in. They could hear the water before they could see it. The sound of a great spigot. They parked on the side of the road and walked toward the noise. Past the tree branches stood high rocky bluffs that looked down at the broad falls. The water had churned white as butter. The air was wet with mist, the noise loud enough that they couldn't really speak to one another. They were left to their own thoughts, their own impressions. King thought about how cold the air must feel in the thick mist that floated on top of the river. To Clarke, the water at the base of the falls looked like it boiled. For Dominick, the river basin was a great wound in the ground.

IN OCTOBER 2001: Dominick had jumped out of a Lockheed MC-130 and parachuted into Afghanistan to secure a desert landing strip south of Kandahar. Objective Rhino. Two hundred men plummeting earthward. Private Floyd landed hard and snapped his pinkie finger. This was for real. Everything was dun colored and dusty and the ground was covered with small rocks. The land was flat but they could see mountains in the distance. DeJesus wrapped Floyd's fingers together with medical tape. DeJesus and Floyd and Benny Ward looked like they belonged here. Did he? Did he look like that, too? AC-130 gunships circled overhead. They moved out with psychological operations loudspeaker teams and cleared an enemy compound. The Taliban surrendered or fled before them. They were U.S. Army Rangers. They scared the shit out of people.

They were out of Afghanistan within five and a half hours. Almost nobody but Floyd got hurt. Aside from the jittery fear, the whole thing felt like a celebration. They'd shown they could strike in the heart of the country. This was just the beginning. There was a lot more to come.

CHARLIE BASIN DROVE slowly on the road that shadowed the Maine coast. The tide was out pretty far. Seagulls swooped and strutted in the sand. Sharply angled rocks bulwarked the coastal edge of the road against erosion. He pushed on the brakes and the car slowed. The waves out there were white-tipped. A lobster boat bobbed. He came to a stop in the road. Far to the south, a lighthouse winked on and off, on and off. He called his wife and she answered, "Hello?"

"Maybe we ought to retire up here."

"Maine? You're already there?"

"I'm in the middle of this little coastal road." A white Volkswagen stopped behind him and honked. Its engine revved up. It pulled into the opposite lane and passed. "We could get a little house," he said. "A boat."

He could hear her breathe. She was getting a cold. Her lips clicked as they parted. "I talked to Charlene."

"She okay?"

"She's doing better." Rosamund sniffed harshly. "She thinks the therapist is helping."

"Helping with what?" Charlie asked.

"She's angry."

"She's always been angry. Ever since she was little."

"She's angry with you, Charlie."

"What for?" he said. Her breath rasped on the line. He said, "Christ, Ros. What was it? Did I yell at her too much? Was I gone too often? Did I like the house too quiet? Didn't I talk to her enough? Maybe I made her feel like she didn't do things well? I did, didn't I? Was it my fault that she was prone to breaking things?"

"You're a good dad, Charlie. I think kids just get mad at their parents."

"For no reason?"

"For not enough of a reason."

"Is she pissed at you?" Charlie asked.

"Maybe you should come home," Rosamund said. "You could pass this case on to somebody else. If you wanted."

"I don't know," Charlie said. "I'd just be put on something else. Maybe something worse."

"All right," his wife said, "you want to move up there to Maine, I'll go with you."

Charlie sat in the car for a few minutes before he started the engine. He drove to Clarisse Parish's house. She invited him in. She made chamomile tea. They sat at an oak table in Clarisse's dining room, which overlooked the ocean. A wall of mist rolled from above the water. Wind licked at the windows; the yellowed grass bent inland.

Charlie Basin had one leg folded beneath him. He cupped the teacup between his hands and held its warmth. He smiled. "Thanks for talking to me," he said. "I appreciate it."

"I'm afraid I won't be too much help," Clarisse said. Her hair was swept up in a bun and held together with two dark sticks. She wore a light green shirt with a broad collar beneath a zippered wool sweater. Her hands were finely veined. "I should tell you," she said, "that I liked them very much."

"Who?"

"All of them. The kids. Dominick, too." Her hands gripped the arms of the high-backed chair.

"It's very beautiful here, you know," Charlie said. He looked out the large windows. Indiscriminate shapes scrolled around in the mist.

"Most of the families aren't in yet. They don't come up until June or July."

"You like the quiet?" Charlie said.

"I do."

"Would you mind showing me the apartment where they stayed?"

"Of course not." Clarisse began to push upward with her arms.

"In a second," Charlie said. "Can I finish my tea?" She looked at him blankly. He touched his cheek with his fingers. He said, "Would you mind if we sat here for another minute?"

Her slippered foot tapped against the pine floor. She said, "You're not what I expected."

"What were you expecting?"

"I don't know," Clarisse said. "Someone younger? Somebody in a hurry, I suppose." She gestured at his navy-blue jacket with a pinkie. "The suit, I expected."

"I used to be younger," he said.

"Have you finished your tea?"

"Just about."

"I have something I think you'd like to see."

"I'm interested."

"Just follow me," said Clarisse. She stood, straightening her long pale skirt. They walked through the sea-blue hall toward the bathroom and she turned her head around to speak to Charlie. "I got to know them quite well," she said. She cleared her throat. "It's my opinion that they are very good people."

He leaned his hand against the bathroom doorjamb. The walls were a dark green. A great porcelain tub with brass handles sat in the middle of the room.

Clarisse stood next to the tub. She reached behind her and flicked on the vanity lights. She pointed into the tub. "Look," she said.

Charlie leaned forward and peered down over his nose. Smooth white porcelain. On the bottom salt spilled in thick words. He squinted.

Woodpile, he read, *Sylphine, Basin*.

"It's my name," he said. "That's odd. Who did it?"

THE RAIN BEGAN the longest night that Dominick could remember. It washed the dust from the new truck. It knocked on the steel roof of the cab. It came hard and, mixed with air and bits of ice, hammered against the hood of the truck and bounced off in unpredictable arcs. They drove down a road that none of them could name. Water flooded the windshield and the wipers, set on high, couldn't keep the glass clear. The brake lights on the station wagon ahead lit up. Its hazard lights began to flash and it pulled to the side of the road.

"Whoa," King said, "can you see?" Clarke sat tight-lipped.

Dominick said, "I can't see much." He pulled onto a side road in a town and parked. The rain fell all night and as they drifted in and out of sleep, scenes seemed to play themselves out before them in the downpour. At some point, Dominick threw a single blanket across all three of them. King took off her shoes and socks. They shared a can of pineapple rings and half a loaf of bread. When the electricity failed, every town light went out at once and total darkness settled down on them. The kind of dark in which they could not see one another. The kind of dark in which they couldn't see their own hands and the wind screamed with a young woman's voice and buffeted the truck hard enough to rock it back and forth on its shocks.

They looked out. Dominick saw things he shouldn't have seen. Dark shapes. A woman beside the window with hands clasped around her throat. Swollen-bellied beasts running out of flooded gutters. The inky triangular masts of great vessels.

They passed the night listening to the white noise of the rain and, when they'd heard enough, they finally slept soundly.

When King woke, she felt grit at her feet. The sun cracked the low clouds open. The lawns of the houses around them were flooded. Water rushed in the gutters. King looked down at her toes on the floor mat.

Splitlog, read the words in salt, *Rallentando, Doll*.

Clarke rubbed the words out with the sole of his boot. Dominick started the truck and they drove to Illinois in a single stretch. They traveled through Pennsylvania and Ohio and Indiana, staying mostly on the back roads, the old highways, so that a drive that might have taken ten hours took twenty-four. When they got out of the truck in the cement lot of a strip mall overlit with sodium lamps, they groped forward toward a pay phone like the undead. The three of them looked dirty and mean. When the children stood across the lot from their father, a woman walked out of a Dollar General and stopped in front of them. She was dyed blonde and smelled of more than one soap. "You look lost," she said. She tilted her head to one side and half smiled. A single dimple pocked her right cheek. "You okay?"

King took a step toward her and Clarke caught his sister by the shoulder. Clarke asked, "This is Illinois, right?"

"It is," the woman said.

"What town are we in?"

"Rockford." The half-smile widened. Her teeth were too white and too straight.

"We're not lost," Clarke said and he pointed across the lot to Dominick standing beside the booth with the phone to his ear. With his shoulders hunched, their father waved his hand broadly.

The woman said, "My name's Rachael." She lowered her voice. She pushed an overly blonde curl from her cheek. "Do you need any help?" she said.

"Why would we need help?" Clarke asked.

On the far side of the parking lot, Dominick used the phone book to find the number for Saint Anthony's Hospital. He dialed the front desk, and a woman answered, and he said, "Hello, I've got to get a message to Annie Sawyer."

"She's in Critical Care. I'll put you through."

"Wait, wait," Dominick said. "I don't have time. Can you take a message?"

"A message?"

"Please give her this phone number." He read the number from the pay phone. "815-967-0299."

"What's your name, sir?"

"Just tell her that she'll know who's calling." He hung up and waited. Across the lot, by the entrance to the Dollar General, a thin blonde woman in a thin white leather coat talked to his kids. He waved his arm again. What did she want? What business did she have with them? Didn't she understand that some people preferred to be left alone?

When the phone began to ring, Dominick lifted the handset. The receiver touched his ear as softly as a human finger. "Annie?" he said.

"Oh, Jesus!"

"I've got the kids with me," he said.

"Are you all right?"

"Fine," he said. "I'm fine."

"How are they?"

"Okay. They could use some help."

"People've been calling, Dom. The police have been stopping out front. You can't come here or to the house."

"Who's been there?"

"I've got to get back to work."

"Where do the kids and I go, Annie?" he said. "We need a place to stay for a while."

"Have you got something to write with? Take down this address."

"I'm ready."

"Twenty-six hundred Will James Road. In New Milford. It's a trailer home on the Kishwaukee River. It belongs to friends. Nobody's there. The key is under a flower pot. I've got to go."

They bought a map of Rockford at the gas station on the fringe of the strip mall. They found the trailer parked in the middle of a ring of willows beside the Kishwaukee River. No other homes were visible but they had driven past mailboxes planted at the edges of gravel driveways. A path of flat stones led from the road over a slight hill to the single-wide trailer. They walked around the building in a wide circle. The grass at their feet had begun to green. The outermost reaches of the willows' branches were limned with furry buds shaped like arrowheads. The willows at the rear of the home gave way to a stretch of pines and cottonwoods that led to an island near their side of the river. They walked to the mud banks and looked around. The sun shone off the surface. The water ran clean and clear. Dark roots rose out of the ground and arched into the silt at the bottom of the river. There was a small sandy area, a boat launch, and an overturned green canoe. The water deepened quickly as it fell away from the bank and the stones at the bottom were rounded and the size of a child's fist and colored white and red and brown and black. On the far side of the river, a great red-billed sandpiper pulled its beak from the sand and its head moved toward them with the jerky time-stop motion built into the musculature of birds.

The soft burble of the river was a nice sound. They stood on the bank and the sunlight caught the top half of them so that their skin warmed. They felt good. This was a nice place.

"Look at that," King said. "There!" She pointed.

A tiny bluish figure was swept down current, pulled under, and then pushed to the surface again. Dark curls on a doll-sized head. A pair of stiff legs rose up and then sank as though pulled from underneath. The doll swept into the channel between the bank and the island and then eddied before sticking against a fork-shaped root. Clarke and King trammeled through the poison ivy. They approached the bank of the river and bent down.

River snakes darted toward deeper water. They caught the figure up. It was plastic. Its blue dress had been ripped across the top, exposing hard smooth breasts.

Dominick went up to the trailer and found the key on the steps beneath a dead chrysanthemum. Inside, King put the doll on the kitchen table. They all sat. Clarke put his head on the table. Neither King nor Clarke moved. Nobody spoke. Dominick reached out and put the tips of his fingers on King's wrist.

When they heard wheels turn into the gravel drive, all three Sawyer bodies tensed. Dominick's sister, Annie, drove up in a hardtop Jeep. A lean-muscled rangy woman with short dark hair and a husky voice, she moved with the powerful grace of her brother, of someone riding on top of a bull. "Kids!" she yelled and the three of them swarmed outside and Annie caught Clarke around the waist. "Jesus," Annie said, "you've grown."

She turned to King and picked her up. King pressed her face against the skin of Annie's jacket and breathed in. She closed her eyes. In King's ear, Annie said, "You look so much like your mom." She touched her niece's dark head and said, "What've you done to your hair?" King opened her eyes and squeezed her aunt tight. Over King's shoulder, Annie stared at Dominick on the cement steps. His hair had been cropped close and his jaw was deeply stubbled.

"You see a way out of this mess you're in?" Annie said. The wind pushed a bit of her bangs into one of her eyes.

The kids hung their heads. Dominick looked at her, eyes level.

"Let's go inside," Annie said. "Let's talk about it."

"ROSAMUND?" CHARLIE BASIN spoke quietly into his phone. He sat in a red-cushioned seat inside Gate 9 at the Portland International Jetport. He could see his reflection in dozens of panels of dark glass.

"Where are you, Charlie?" Rosamund asked. Her voice was nasal and congested.

"At the airport in Portland, Maine."

"Where are you going?"

"To Rockford, Illinois," he said. "You've got a cold?"

"It's terrible. Maybe it's better you're out of the house," she said. "I talked to Charlene's doctor today. She mentioned her being released from the hospital. She talked about the need for a support network."

"She's got a support network."

Rosamund said, "Maybe you ought to come home."

"I don't know, Ros," Charlie said. "She doesn't want to see me."

"Yes, she does."

Over the line Charlie could hear Rosamund walking through their house. "I'm not sure I want to see her," he said.

"Of course you do," she said.

A European voice announced that Charlie's flight had begun boarding. He felt comfortable holding the phone to his ear without saying anything, imagining that she was listening.

"What's in Rockford, Illinois?" Rosamund asked.

"This guy's sister," said Charlie. "It's time for me to talk to her in person." He got up and stood in line to board the plane. "You should have seen this house where they were staying up here in Maine. Pretty nice place."

"Uh-huh," she said, sounding as though she was wiping her nose.

"Somebody wrote our last name in salt," Charlie said. "In the bathtub."

"What for? That sounds dangerous."

"I have no idea," Charlie said. "I don't even know how they know my name."

"Who do you think did it?"

"I'm not sure. One of the kids, maybe."

INSIDE THE TRAILER home, Dominick stood in front of a cracked windowpane. He looked down the long lane of grass, past the scattered trees, to the river where King stood with a filthy blanket wrapped around her shoulders. Her jeans were rolled to her knees and her feet were in the shallows. The setting sun hung in the pale fleshy sky. The pool between the bank and the island was shaped like an arrowhead. The light was so dim that what Dominick could see was leached of color and nearly two-dimensional so that King looked indivisible from the pool behind her. She looked thin and frail. His younger child. A dreamer. So much like her mother.

By her feet, water snakes slithered into the mouths of the dens between roots on the bank. King waded back to shore and shook as she flipped the old brown canoe. She stepped into the boat and, still standing, pushed at the muddy bank with the flat edge of a rotting wooden paddle. The boat wobbled out into the river, caught the current, and turned downstream.

Dominick leaned forward and the tip of his nose pushed against the cold window glass. From this distance, the lowering sun caught the skin of the water on fire. King's mouth moved and then stopped. She made a sweeping gesture with her hands. Her arms moved back and forth across one another, palm out, as though signaling *no, no, no.* Her mouth stretched open and then closed as though she was shouting at someone.

From the trailer window, the crack in the pane split the scene in two. Watching his daughter struggle, Dominick wanted to rush outside into the river. But he stopped and steadied himself against the wall. He sweat. What could he do to help his daughter when she faced a problem he couldn't see?

At dusk, Clarke wandered off the property by himself. He passed the border of the grass and into the greenery's bric-a-brac, where the monkey vines led into the branches of the trees. There was a lot of garbage. Tin cans. A rusted pie plate. Plastic gallon milk jugs. Constellations of burned cigarettes scattered along the edges of a thin path. He counted his steps and estimated that he'd walked a quarter mile before the trail flushed out into a dead lawn beneath a huge tree house. A staircase spiraled up the trunk of an old oak. Multiple roofs peaked up there. Asphalt shingles. The river ran behind the structure. The lawn was sloped and rectangular and on the far end sat a pink double-wide.

A cold wind caught at the cuffs of Clarke's pants and at the nape of his jacket and trickled inward along his chest toward his stomach. In the tree house, an orange point of light burned fiercely and then dulled. He stared until the point of light came again and he waited, unmoving, to let his eyes adjust to the shadows. Inside the tree house, he made out a figure, a woman, he thought, lifting the fire toward her mouth.

"You can come up here if you want." It was a woman's voice, or a girl's, and she spoke quietly.

He looked at the double-wide. A light shone in the northern window.

"Come on up," the girl said, "or fuck off."

"I'm coming," he said.

The ascent was like vertigo. He wound up the stairs, each plank of wood burrowed into the trunk, and the whole rickety affair gave off the sweet woodsy smell of sawdust. He stopped at the top landing, where a girl slumped in the doorjamb of the small house. She wore an unzipped sweatshirt that folded around her and a cigarette dangled from her right hand like something forgotten. Her nose was pierced with a small silver star. The tip of the nose was overly bulbous and reddened as though it'd been recently rubbed, and a spread of freckles on her cheeks called attention to her pale skin. She wore a thin flowered dress through which Clarke could see the splayed angularity of her pelvic bones and the sheeted mounds of her skinny knees. She looked at him and put the cigarette to her mouth.

"Who built this?" Clarke asked.

"What, this?" she said. Her leg rose and the yellow flowers straightened out of their folds and draped against the shape of her leg. It hovered there, her leg, and then she let it fall so that her heel knocked against the wood floor. "My uncle, he built it." She was quiet and he waited her out, unmoving. She said, "He was like a giant fat child."

"He lives in the pink house?"

"I live in that pink house."

"With your uncle?"

"No, he's dead." She brought the cigarette to her lips again. He watched her mouth open and her tongue flick out and her full lips purse together and wrinkle up. Everything she did was a little too slow.

The pink screen door on the pink house screamed open. A large woman in a beige housedress stuck her head out of the door. "Elsie!"

"Who's that?" Clarke said. Again too much time passed, and the woman yelled again, and Clarke said, "She sounds like a band saw."

The girl crossed her arms over her chest. "We haven't been properly introduced," she said,

"I'm Clarke," Clarke said.

"Get the hell down from there!" the heavy woman yelled from the door.

"Elsie." She held out her hand in front of her so that Clarke had to squat and fold his arm to take her hand.

The woman yelled, "Who the fuck is that boy up there with you?" Then she let the door bang shut.

Elsie's hand pulsed gently around his. She let her free arm fall out to her side so that her hand rested like a cup against the wood. Her chest arched forward until her breasts pushed against her flowered dress. Her eyes were an intense blue peppered with black filigree. "You want to kiss me?" she said.

"I guess so," Clarke said. "I do."

"You want to kiss me," she said, "you'd kiss anybody."

"No," he said. "I like that you move so slow."

"I don't always move this slow."

"I didn't always want to kiss you."

She put a finger to her lips. "Down here," she said. He bent forward at the waist and she stretched upward and their mouths met wetly in the middle. Her breath tasted charred and bitter. Their lips pressed together, and hers opened greedily and wide, and her mouth was hot and smoky and fouled.

When they broke apart, Clarke asked, "What's wrong with your aunt?"

"For starters," said Elsie, "she's a bitch."

"Does she always yell like that?"

"Since my uncle died," Elsie said, "sometimes she won't talk for a few days."

"Why doesn't she come up here?"

"She's too fat."

"I guess so," Clarke said.

"I don't really want to live here," Elsie said. "Do you?"

"I don't live here," he said. "We're just staying for a little while over there." He pointed. Their bodies were pressed against one another. He could feel her breathing quickly.

"Where're you from?" Elsie said.

"Pennsylvania."

"What's it like there?"

"I don't know. There are more hills. How old are you?"

"I'm seventeen." Her gaze was as flat as the Illinois countryside. "How old are you?"

"Fifteen."

"You're jailbait," she said. She touched his lips with her fingers. "My dad went to jail a few years ago."

"What for?"

"He hurt my mom. Bad. It wasn't an accident."

"Hurt her how?"

"Hit her."

"Oh. Is she okay?"

"She's fine. She met somebody else. That's why I'm with my aunt. It's just for a little while."

They were quiet. The moon looked like an empty plate. Clarke didn't know why she'd told him these things about her family but he could feel what the options were. He could clam up. Which meant leaving this girl who wanted to press close to him and kiss him with her undead breath. Or he could stay and talk. Tell her one or two things. Maybe ask a few questions.

He asked, "How do you tell if someone's a bad person?"

"Who?"

"Anybody. Your aunt or your dad. Or my dad. It doesn't matter."

"You've got to say who," Elsie said. "Or I won't fucking answer."

"Me, then."

"What've you done?" Elsie said.

"My dad doesn't want me to talk about this stuff."

"Do you care what he wants?"

"Sometimes," Clarke said. He paused. "No."

"I want to know things about you," Elsie said.

"You won't tell anybody?" said Clarke.

"No. I won't."

"Okay. We're on the run from the cops."

"What'd you do?"

"I tied up an old woman."

Just before sunset, a half-mile from the tree house, King paddled the canoe down the Kishwaukee River. Past stock-still herons fishing for bluegill. A bald eagle's nest pyred atop a pine tree. Near the bank, sharp rocks rose to the surface. A turtle slowly climbed atop another turtle, their hard shells clicking together. King held the paddle tightly with both palms. The sun felt like soft warm hands on her skin.

She drifted and paddled in turns. She pulled the dictionary from her pocket and rifled through the pages and looked at *renascence*. She came to the cement footing of a bridge that arched over her. A road hummed above. King splashed into the shallows and tied the canoe to a sapling. Her feet left wet prints in the gray dust on the cement. She scrambled up the embankment to a gas station. A Sunoco. On one side of the lot was an air pump. On the other a pay phone. A paunchy couple argued over a slip of paper as they pumped gas. She walked to the pay phone and dialed the operator and asked to place a collect call to Jon Howland. The phone rang with a faint echo.

"King?" Jon Howland said. "You guys okay?"

"I got a favor to ask you," King said.

"Where you at?"

"I'd better not say."

silas dent zobal

"All right."

"Can you go over to our woodpile?" King said. "Look for a big loose log with a notch at the bottom of the pile. It's hollow."

There was a pause. "Can I talk to your father?" Jon Howland asked.

"I don't want him to know about this."

"Okay, King, I'll get it done."

"Thanks. You can't call here. I'll call you."

"What's in this log?"

"Maybe nothing. I don't know."

DOMINICK REMEMBERED THE times that he and his wife had gotten along well. He remembered how, when he'd come home from Operation Enduring Freedom, his fat infant daughter had been replaced by a thinner toddler. She could walk. She could say, "Da da." Below Sarah's waist, Clarke peeked at him from under the V of her legs. His daughter's hair was the same brown as his wife's. She held King up before him by the armpits and King struggled as though she had no interest in rising for any will other than her own.

Dominick threw himself into the idea of home. He fashioned a child's bamboo fishing pole. He carried King in a pack on his back and Clarke in his arms. Down by the Susquehanna River, they watched their red-and-white bobbers float downstream. They waded in the shallows. Dominick held King as she slapped the flat of her small palm against the water. His wife walked down the hill with a basket of tomato sandwiches. She nursed King against a burled oak and Dominick ate sitting beside Clarke. When the kids fell asleep beneath a shade tree, Dominick and Sarah lay back in the grass. This was what Dominick wanted, what he dreamed of when he was gone. When he looked at his wife, he was assaulted by the ferocity of his own love. Paper wasps flitted among the leaves of the aspens.

The hills were patchworked with the shadows of clouds. He couldn't stop smiling even if his fatherhood was a pretense.

In the evenings, he built a long freestanding woodshed. He painted the bedroom. He pressure-washed the log cabin and resealed it with tung oil, and regrouted the kitchen floor, and rolled insulation into the attic. When he dropped into bed, covered in primer and bits of pink fiberglass, his wife flopped beside him. She flung one arm so that it lay across his chest. He rolled halfway toward her and watched as her eyes opened and closed more and more slowly. When had his own eyes begun to close? What terrible dreams had he dreamed?

In the morning, Clarke burst into their room to find his parents asleep in their clothes. The door slammed against the wall and woke Dominick and Sarah at the same time. Clarke wore long blue pajamas. He rubbed his eyes with his knuckles. Dominick waved Clarke in. His wife's arm was still across him and he picked it up and felt its weight. He did not feel rested at all. His son flopped onto the bed and crawled over Dominick into the hollow between his parents' bodies, and they waited together for the baby to cry.

THE AIRPLANE JOLTED against something and shuddered and threw Charlie Basin awake. His eyes were closed. Fear arched like electricity through his body as he bounced. The seatbelt cut his waist and he jostled into his seat. There was a lot of time contained within the millisecond it took his eyes to open. Enough time to wonder if time itself was a function of his mind, a kind of gatekeeping device to elide one moment with the next, the easy passage of the Boeing 747 into a mid-flight crash with a commuter plane, or a lightning strike, or a sudden halting mechanical failure, or the loss of a wing. All bad things come together at once.

Without time, the plane could not crash but would always be crashing. Without time, the present becomes an unfettered umbrella, expanding like some dark tulip of a universe. Without time, the future opens up before us as accessibly as the past. And there aboard the airplane, with all of our eyes still closed, we think of our two children with their slim faces that are timelines of our own. Do they look up? Do pieces of metal tear apart in midair and rain down upon our kids? Is that great roaring sound from the wind or the crash or is it somehow greater than either of those things? One thing is not nearly as distinct from the next as we must necessarily believe. We think of our children, and we are with them, both of them at once, as though what had separated us before had been as thin as thought. One stoops at a broad desk and the pencil in his hands loops against yellow paper. Oswell. His eyes are watery with fatigue. The other, Charlene, lies half underneath a pale-skinned boy on a hospital bed. A discarded law book on a brightly lit floor. Then nurses or orderlies sweep in and pull the boy out by his arms. We don't want to be here with our daughter in such a private moment but when we turn to the pale window, the orange behind our closed eyelids, we see another son, a huge boy with auburn hair and his arms wrapped around a girl, their lips mashed softly together like the mouths of two sea cucumbers.

Charlie's eyes opened and closed again. Beneath his eyelids, his pupils began to dilate. In the fraction of time before Charlie's eyes bounced open again, a thin girl wrapped in a blue blanket screams as she stands in a shallow river. A great communal heart pounds once in Charlie's chest. He is no longer his own, until time stutters forward and his eyes open into a separate dream.

Charlie Basin looked out the window at the needle-shaped control tower and the rushing lines and the smaller jolt of the front wheels pounding into the runway. The cabin of the plane held the passengers together the way that a rib cage holds heart and lungs and spleen. Sweat leapt to his skin. He reached inside his coat and steadied his hand on the handle of his gun. He leaned his head forward and pressed it against the small cold window. The sun slanted over the edge of the earth between two great bands of clouds in broad semicircles. One a sunny rose, the other a slate gray. Two clashing visions of the future. The beautiful collision of two colored smoke rings.

WHEN THE SAWYERS all collected in the house again, each of them carried a secret. They carried them carefully, like they'd carry a glass jar overfilled with water. Annie had gone home in fits and starts as if pulled by an invisible string. She walked away, turned, came back to Dominick.

"I might be gone for a few days," she said.

"I know."

"I've got to make sure I'm not watched before I come back."

"Go on," he said.

"I'll bring some food," she said. She walked down the driveway, turned back, rubbed her eyes, watched her brother waving her on.

When she was gone, Dominick wanted to do something to bring them all together. He wanted his kids to relax so they could be the family they ought to have been. So, on the next warmer afternoon, he gathered white bread, bologna, mustard, American cheese singles and made sandwiches and packed them in a basket for a picnic on the lawn. That night, he found a deck of cards beside the television set and they all knelt by the coffee table and played gin rummy. In the morning, he found two fishing rods in the basement and tied on weights and bobbers and they fished off the island right in the backyard, in the curve of the Kishwaukee River. The light shone pale and cool through the branches of the hackberry trees. He tried to get his kids to talk. He asked questions but they weren't interesting in answering. The fishing was good, though, surprising for a small muddy river. King's bobber dipped twice and she pulled up a smallmouth bass, then Dominick caught three walleyes in a row. He pulled out the hooks and tossed the fish into a bucket filled with water.

Clarke kept moving away on his own, casting his line far upriver toward a dark hollow beneath a fallen tree. Dominick sat beside King on the cold ground. He held his hands out in front of him, looking at the calluses, at how the deep lines intersected with smaller lines and the smaller lines intersected with lines even smaller still.

"What is it?" King asked.

"What's what?" said Dominick.

"What're you doing?"

"I don't know what I'm doing."

"It's cold out here," she said.

"I know."

"Maybe we should go in."

"Maybe," Dominick said. "But doesn't the sun feel good?"

They angled their faces toward the light. They watched Clarke set his pole in the grass and step onto a stone in the river. He moved quickly from rock to rock, sometimes leaning over to touch a stone with a bare hand. The moving water caught his reflection in bits and pieces. A piece of red sweatshirt, a coin of light skin, a brown shoe. He scrambled alongside the riverbank, jumped toward a small cliff, caught at roots and scrambled upward into the brush.

"There's poison ivy in there," Dominick said.

"Clarke doesn't get it," King said.

"What do you mean, he doesn't get it?"

"I've seen him pull it out with his hands," she said. "He doesn't get it."

"How didn't I know that?" Dominick said.

King shrugged. "Do you get it?" she asked.

"I do."

"Me, too."

Dominick lay back on the bank of the river and ignored the cold seeping upward from the ground. King leaned against him. They sat like that for a while. They were only able to stand the cold spring air as long as the sun shone directly on them. When a cloud blocked the light, they began to shiver. They got up, brushed at the backs of their pants. They felt damp. Dominick tried to holler, "Clarke," but it sounded like a dog's bark. A funny sound from a man. Beside him, King looked up. Her face cracked open and she laughed. Dominick cleared his throat and tried again. "Clarke," he called, "we're headed inside. I'm going to fix something to eat."

In the small kitchen, he dipped the fish in milk, then in cornmeal. He heated oil in a pan. He whistled. King snuggled into a blanket on the couch, watching her dad.

Clarke closed the door gently when he came in. "Smells good," he said.

Four days later, Annie brought a space heater, jars of peanut butter, raspberry jelly, chocolate donuts, hot dogs, canned vegetables, noodles, ground beef. The carpet in the trailer ran from wall to wall in a yellowed beige, matted with dark burns where the tips of the fibers had melted together into dark glossy ovals. Strange ovoid footprints. "This place is a pit," Annie said. The kids looked around and nodded. The vinyl flooring in the kitchen peeled upward from the particle board beneath. A large crack rose upward from the phone jack in the middle of the living room. The dark brown couch looked like a cigarette burn. They hadn't noticed.

Annie stood at the sink and washed the dishes. Glasses clinked against porcelain. Her eyes narrowed to slits. She turned her head toward Dominick. "I couldn't make it over here sooner," she said. "There's been people coming by the house."

"You being careful?"

"I waited," she said. "I drove here on back roads. Nobody followed."

The entire time Annie was there, the children stayed inside. She found a vacuum and ran it. She turned on the radio and listened to a Cubs game. She preheated the oven and made blueberry muffins and the house warmed up and smelled good. Her arms reached for the kids every time they walked by. She touched their shoulders and said, "I can't stay too long."

Dominick sat at the head of the table. He said, "Let me make us all hot dogs."

"I ought to tell you," Annie said, "this guy has been to my house three times."

"What's his name?" asked Dominick. He leaned against the kitchen counter. Light from the window scattered on the glass of water in his hand.

"Basin. He's with the FBI." King and Clarke looked at one another.

"What's he look like?"

"Dark hair. Thin but fit. Probably in his fifties."

"He give you a hard time?"

"He's nice. He brings me things. He keeps coming back."

"What's he bring you?"

"Tickets to see the Rockford Symphony Orchestra at the Coronado. A key-lime pie. A doily that his mother made."

"What's he want from you?

"He thinks I know where you are."

"Do you?"

"No. I have no idea where you are."

When King left the trailer again, she slipped away in the quiet afternoon, wrapped herself in a blue blanket, and floated the canoe. Yellow daffodils spotted the hills. The wind blew the water into little white-tipped peaks. Blue crocuses opened their mouths in the sun. She paddled downstream to the sign that rose beside the bridge. A bright yellow diamond split by a red arrow. The dark embankment led up to the Sunoco. She paddled the canoe to the bank.

A car idled at the top of the embankment, close to the guardrail. A dark rounded car with daytime running lights. In the window, a man opened his mouth and spoke soundlessly to someone invisible in the driver's seat. He was a thick jowled man in a dark suit. Heavy eyebrows. He gestured loosely with his fingers like he was telling a joke. King looked up with her head angled sideways like someone watching a bird in a tree. The jowled man glanced once or twice in the direction of the unseen pay phone. A thin pearlescent scar ran under his chin as though from cosmetic surgery. The jowled man looked cold and hard, the kind of man you could trust only in a few ways. In the way that you could trust a teacher to do, without listening, whatever he thought was best for you.

King couldn't go up there. Not now. Not ever.

ANNIE SAWYER'S HOUSE was a steepled two-story. Yellow brick. Old and small and charming. She pushed aside the green curtain of the living room window. A black Chevy Tahoe idled outside. She shaded her eyes and looked at the tall healthy man in the driver's seat. She looked down at her bright yellow shoes against the old chestnut floor. She smoothed the hair over her right ear. She looked back up at Charlie Basin and waved. This was pointless. What was he doing out there?

When he knocked at the door, she left him waiting. She had been baking bread. She took off her apron and hung it on a small iron hook. She stopped at a mirror in a gilded frame and wiped the sleep from her eyes. As she walked through the hallway her shoes clipped against the tile. She looked out at him through the small arched window in her front door. He was smiling broadly. His eyes were crinkled at the edges. He held a bottle of wine in the crook of his arm.

She opened the door and the air that flooded inside smelled of hyacinth. His shoes were black and recently shined. He still wore a suit.

"You're here again, Charlie," she said. "You keep coming back."

"It's my job," Charlie Basin said. "This is for you." He hitched the green bottle in his arm. "French," he said, "a Vouvray." He moved so deliberately that Annie supposed he was older than he looked. His dark eyebrows held small lines of gray.

"Are you married?" Annie asked.

"Thirty-five years," Charlie said. "Her name's Rosamund. She has a cold."

"What are you doing here?"

"I like spending time with you," he said. "Seriously."

"What's it like to spend all your time looking for somebody?"

"I don't know," he said. "Same as everybody else, I guess."

"Do you want to come in?"

"No, not really," he said. "Can I ask you one or two questions before I get back in the car?"

"Go ahead." She leaned against the door frame, her head cocked to one side.

"He's somewhere nearby, isn't he?" he said. "He's close?"

"I don't know," she said. "I don't think so."

"Okay," he said. "Here's one that's got me stumped. What do you think happened to your brother's wife?"

"I don't know."

"Have you asked him?"

"He doesn't know."

"You're sure?" Charlie said. "She called us, you know."

"Oh," Annie said, "she called you?" One foot tapped twice on the ground.

"She called the local Pennsylvania police. She said he was hurting his kids."

"You know where she is?"

"Not exactly," Charlie said. "She called from Beloit, Wisconsin. Not too far from here. We haven't been able to find her."

"They weren't getting along," she said, "Dom and Sarah."

"They weren't, huh? That's a familiar story."

"He's hard to get along with now," she said. "He wasn't always."

"I imagine that's true," he said.

"Dominick's not coming here, Charlie."

As Charlie walked back across the lawn toward his Suburban, he called the FBI headquarters. "Hey, Andy," Charlie said. "He's still here."

"You got him cornered?"

"Not yet. But I got a feeling it's going to happen here, in Illinois."

"When I hang up," Andy said, "I'll round up the Chicago division and the Rockford field office. Anything in particular you want me to tell them?"

"It's not going to go easy, Andy. Make sure they take a close look at this guy's file."

"What you need will be waiting for you," Andy Fry said. "I'll line it up."

WHEN HAD DOMINICK'S dreams soured? When had so many of his dreams turned into a search? At night, he searched the caves at Tora Bora, peering into dark entrances blown wide by bunker bombs, and going in to find what had been the bodies of al-Qaeda fighters, and kicking rotting hunks of flesh hung with tattered cotton into the hot clean outside, and looking up at the sawteeth of the White Mountains. This battle, the Battle of Tora Bora, occurred in the opening days in Afghanistan. Osama bin Laden was suspected to be hiding in the giant cave complex. Air strikes pounded the hillside. Soldiers combed the hills. Circling far around Tora Bora, Dominick's fire team—Ward and DeJesus and Floyd—passed through the hilltop village of Maduu. As they approached the town, they passed through an entire herd of dead sheep and goats. Dust hung in the air. Warplanes and smart bombs had flattened the adobe houses. A crowd shrieked and wept outside the fallen mosque. A silver-bearded man collected body parts, wrapping them in plastic bags. A leg. A hand. A hunk of meat. Dominick's job, his duty, was to show his men how to walk in the midst of this. How to pass through. Never should he fail his comrades. He would shoulder his share of the task and then some. For the most part, he kept his eyes fixed ahead. It was a small village, it wouldn't take long. But then his eyes wandered past the threshold of a crumbling adobe wall. Two small bodies, children, leaned against the wall, the larger with the smaller pressed behind. Was the larger one a boy? The hair was long and dark. Blood had turned the earth beneath them a darker shade of brown. His throat was missing, carved out. One of his hands was flung out, missing a finger. Dominick swung his eyes around, checked the positions of DeJesus and Floyd, looked ahead on the road. This was Afghanistan, and it was late November, and the weather was okay for a long hike wearing a combat uniform and body armor and a helmet. A bright day, hazy and mild, but on the road Dominick began to shiver. His jaw chattered and something shook around inside him. It was rage, sure, but that was just on the surface and he had felt that before. It was blind, and ugly, too, and violent and free, and other things, nearly all nameless and bad. His body clenched and released. He kept his eyes on the ground. There, two steps ahead of him, a small bleeding finger curled in dirt.

THAT NIGHT, **IN** the trailer, Dominick cleaned a parade of guns. Cold gray metal aligned on the scarred coffee table. Handle and barrel. This was the only task that had to be done. This mechanical fulfillment of duty. The arrangement of time like some pointless game. The tired kids asleep on the couch. Why had his life been a kind of waiting room? Night settled around them like a wool shawl. How many times had he lain flat and held his rifle still atop a roof in Fallujah or outside the caves at Tora Bora? What had he seen? A man wearing a green military-style jacket over a long robe dragging unexploded ordinance beside a dirt road, or a group of men laughing and holding AK-47s and standing near a black-veiled woman tied to an olive tree, or a boy, no older than Clarke, raising a rifle scope beneath stalactites of glass in a broken window. Had he fired at that kid in the window? The lost time had felt purposeful then, the air around him charged with the dust of meaning. When had the circumference of his life been ruptured? He picked up a greased gun from the coffee table. Oil dripped from his fingers. Wasn't there anything more than this? The kids' feet wrapped in white socks. The little house like an oven or an incubator. The dead metal in his hands so cold it hurt his chapped skin. The way his body could lift his children so easily and carry them to bed.

Later that night, Clarke swung his bare foot over the side of the top bunk and onto the first rung of the ladder. It creaked as sharply and loudly as a crow. Clarke froze, one leg suspended in the air. His eyes processed the room into patches of relative darkness. Shapes were semiobscured. The curtains were open and the night outside was like a black eye.

The wooden crow's caw woke King. She opened her eyes. The dark shape of her brother climbed down rung after rung. He was shirtless, his skin luminescent. His jeans were folded at the cuff. He bent to pull a wad of shirt off the carpet and his ribs rose to the sides of his spine.

King rolled to her side and the sheet pulled against the blanket with a hiss.

Clarke turned toward his sister. "You awake?" he whispered.

"Uh-huh," she said.

"Be quiet, okay?"

"Where are you going?"

"To meet somebody."

"Who?" said King.

"A girl."

When she fell back asleep, King dreamed pale and pleasant dreams. She walked through their A-frame cabin with the colors softened into weakly sketched pastels. Her hands were closed into fists. A full laundry basket—sheets and socks and shirts and underpants—waited to be folded. On the counter sat a handful of raisins in a blue handkerchief and a glass of milk that held, in the condensation, the fading impression of someone's hand. The whole place seemed timid with its own fragility. The front door stood open and air whistled through as though sucked between teeth. The ground outside was covered with sparkling snow and night hung over the snow like a hooded figure in a dark robe. A single pair of bloody tracks marked the snow. Above, the stars opened like tiny trapdoors. She opened her hand and found a thin white bone on her palm. King wished she was a stone.

She woke and sat upright in the bunkbed. The room was still dark. "Clarke?" she said. She wanted to explain what she could never explain. The sheets twisted in her hands. The lower bunk was empty. Clarke was still gone. She wanted to ask, How can a black robe absorb light? What lies beyond the trapdoors? Who left the shape of a hand on a glass? Why does it fade? Where does it go?

Clarke and Elsie walked together past an old frame house that leaned toward them. A doorless entryway. A gap-toothed chimney. Fire-blackened beams. Soot. The intimate smell of burned things. They walked an arm span apart. Long dead grass caught at their pant legs. Burrs gathered in their shoelaces. The river gargled and spat in the dark.

"Where we going?" Clarke asked.

"Come on," Elsie said. "This way." The high moon washed the color from her cheeks.

Clarke stopped walking. "Tell me," he said.

"I'm parked over here."

Elsie's rusted-out Dodge Charger was parked along a dirt road a quarter of a mile from her house. Elsie sat on the hood and the car sank on its shocks and squealed and did not fully rise again. She faced down the road toward a boat launch and the river. He sat beside her and wanted to hold her hand. Down the road near the water, something darker than the darkness that surrounded it slumped across the dirt. Clarke could feel the heat that rose off Elsie and filtered out into the cold air.

"What happened?" she said.

"With what?"

"What do you think went wrong?"

"How long ago do you mean?"

"I don't know."

The thin metal of the hood popped underneath them. He looked at her arms crossed over her breasts, her sad eyes. Neither one gave in to the impulse to tell the other that everything would be okay. In a minute they would get into the car and press themselves against one another. Now they sat apart, the space between them the width of a person. The dark horizon smelled of the burned house they'd walked past. One of them reached a hand toward the other and a spotlight split the sky into strange, radiant plumes.

King woke again. Her father and her aunt argued on the porch. For a few seconds a light rain fell at oblique angles. It pattered against the roof and against the window and stopped suddenly. With Clarke absent, King felt fragile and light, as though her bones were hollow. She held her own arms as though to restrain them. She looked at the dark window and the thin lines of water pushed along the glass by wind. Her beech-twig arms slid upward along the window frame and pushed against the wood until it cracked open.

Her aunt's voice was soft like a child's blanket. "Can they take this, Dom?"

"They're military kids," he said. "They're hard."

"Maybe Clarke," Annie said, "but not King."

"She's tough," he said. "I'll take care of both of them."

"Jesus Christ, you're so full of yourself."

"I don't mean to be, Annie." He put his huge hand on her shoulder and its weight seemed to lean her toward him. "I'm sorry," he said.

Annie's head bent forward so that her forehead leaned against his shoulder. "I'll get in trouble if you leave the kids with me, Dom. I'll probably get in trouble anyway."

"It's okay, Annie," he said. "I need them with me, and they need me."

He scraped at one of his cheeks with his palm. The rain had lightly wet the porch and the gray-blue paint shone for a moment before the water evaporated or absorbed into the wood. A few moths circled the light. The temperature was falling.

Dominick and Annie breathed in tandem. Dominick could see the shape of their breath like lost parts of themselves made visible.

"What happened to Sarah?" Annie said.

"You know this, Annie. She was just gone. Like that."

"What do you think happened to her?"

"The feds asking questions?"

"A lot of questions."

"Sometimes people just disappear," he said. "She'd said she was going to leave me. Maybe she doesn't want to be found."

"The FBI agent, Charlie Basin, said she called the police. About you hurting the kids."

"Oh, my God!" Dominick said.

"When she left, why didn't you try to find her?"

"I had two little kids."

"I know you did, Dom," Annie said. "I'm fully aware of it."

"That's why, then."

"But here you are," Annie said, "dragging them around with you now."

Clarke and Elsie pressed against one another with excited desperation. Each body an uncharted country. The other's name as awkward as a first attempt to whistle. Their cold hands groped beneath each other's clothes and found shockingly warm flesh. They fumbled with each other's buttons and touched each other without the hesitation reserved for sacred things. They gave off heat the way a fire gives off heat. They panted. They couldn't catch their breath. They felt hot and cold and alive. They were so human.

Her breasts hung over him. He stretched up to take them in his mouth and saw a great white furrow beside her left breast. A luminescent slash, puffy and thick-skinned. An awful scar. For a moment he stopped at the sight of it and she tensed, knowing why he'd become still. Then, tentatively, he licked it like an animal cleaning a wound, and she pushed her weight against him until he felt that he was holding her up.

In the middle, they paused. Their eyes had adjusted to the moon-blanched landscape. Each of them tasted of salt. Clarke's shirt and jeans had come off and Elsie straddled him. They could see one another well enough for comfort. They could taste the metallic tang of each other in their mouths. Elsie's hand had stopped just under the waistband of Clarke's underpants. There was still a lot that hadn't been explored and a momentary reluctance to go further, as though under the last layer of clothing they might find the end of the mystery.

She slipped him from his underpants, turned and plunged down on him all at once. The Dodge Charger pressed around them, so the elbow of the seat jammed against Clarke's thigh. The roof curled like a great tongue over their heads. The shocks bounced and shrieked. The dashboard held Elsie's hands.

In the trailer, King's eyes opened. Across the room, a great dark bruise in the night. A stifling human heat. Larger than the bunkbeds, her father overwhelming the bedroom. Darker than the dark. His breath like a sip through a straw.

"You awake?" her father said.

"Uh-huh."

"You want me to turn the light on?"

"No," she said.

"Where is Clarke, King?"

"I don't know."

The great bruise moved from one side of the room to the other.

"Are you okay?" her father said.

"I had bad dreams," she said.

"Me, too."

"Was it scary?" King asked.

"Yes."

"Are you still scared?"

"Uh-huh, I am," Dominick said. "Can I come in and sit with you?"

Elsie drove the rusted Charger past blinking neon signs. Bars and nightclubs. Red ropes around entranceways. A line of people waiting before a green door. Plate-glass storefronts that reflected their images back at them, their faces frozen in happy lines. They drove past fast-food restaurants. The flat-roofed and recumbent architecture of strip malls. A yellow neon cowboy hat. A giant fake windmill. The curlicued maze of driveways. Sometimes when Clarke leaned against Elsie, he could feel a pulse. His or hers, he didn't know. Colored lights glared on the windshield. The car smelled ripe as sex and fruit.

"What kind of things do you like to do?" Elsie asked.

"When?"

"Back at home?"

Clarke didn't know why it sounded like she was asking a question. "I don't know what I like. Sometimes I went bowling."

"I hate bowling."

"I don't feel that strongly about it."

"Who'd you go with?" Elsie asked. "A girl?"

"Sometimes. Mostly people I didn't really like from school."

"Why'd you go, then?"

"I don't know."

"You don't know?"

"I don't know why I do most of the things I do."

"That's your problem," Elsie said.

"What's my problem?"

"You've got to know what you want."

They pulled into the parking lot behind a Dairy Queen. Elsie lowered her head into Clarke's lap and tugged at the crotch of his pants with her teeth.

BECAUSE CHARLIE BASIN could not sleep, he drove the mostly deserted streets. He made a circuit between Annie Sawyer's small Victorian house and the Sunoco gas station. He sat beside them both, waiting, until he felt compelled to move. Not a single light shone in Annie's windows. He liked that woman, something about her reminded him of Charlene. How was he supposed to talk to Charlene? Could they, maybe, just leave each other alone? Did she need him in some way that he couldn't see? Pure-white moths swirled around the single streetlight. At the Sunoco, someone stumbled to the phone wearing a black sweatshirt with the hood up. The arm of the black sweatshirt reached out and lifted the black phone and the steel cord caught the light and hung like a cable on a suspension bridge. Charlie's hands grabbed the steering wheel. He felt hot. He leaned forward toward the windshield, then he relaxed. Too tall, too stooped, too drunk to be a little girl. The black sweatshirt spoke into the receiver and Charlie wondered about the pitch of the drunken voice and the shape of the ear that listened on the other end of the line. How much didn't he know about his daughter? Had she wandered around in the night? As he shifted out of park, he eyed his phone in the cup holder near the gearshift. He drove through mostly empty neighborhood streets. A pale dog snuffled at a storm drain. A hydrant poured water onto the road. What was Charlene doing right now? Where was Oswell? In the business district, he passed restaurants and bars with lines of people. Were both his kids awake? Were they, like him, circling? Did they think of him? Were they alone? Were they wondering what the use was?

◄·· The radio played songs about longing as Clarke and Elsie bulleted down roads. The sun began to rise. At the center of Clarke sat a deep sexual ache and his mind whirred with images that had been only magazine fantasies to him the day before. The furred arch between thin legs. The pliable lemniscate of breasts. Nipples rising like time-stop photography of a burl growing on a silver birch. The pornographic way that his body could merge with another's. Were there other ways of doing things? The headlights of the oncoming cars splintered into moving shards. All those people drove toward them and then passed. A round-face woman in pink with one hand against her cheek. A tiny blue car filled with shorn-headed boys. A black Chevy Tahoe driven by a thin man in a navy suit. The suit's eyes narrowed, his brow furrowed like an accordion. His head swung toward Clarke as the two cars passed one another, the distance between them bridgeable by an arm.

Clarke turned to stare at the rear of the Chevy Tahoe. The half-darkened windows. The brake lights that burned red. It turned sharply to the side of the road. "Shit," Clarke said. "Drive."

Elsie's fingers curled against his thigh like fishhooks. "You know that guy?"

"No," he said. "Drive fast." And Elsie pushed her foot down heavily against the gas pedal.

◆⁓ Charlie Basin recognized the hulk of the boy behind a cracked windshield. Two teenagers with their faces flushed red in a tattered Dodge Charger. He knew that look. He'd once caught his older son, Oswell, the unlikely one, naked in a car with a fleshy girl whom Charlie had never seen before. Years later, emptying the trash, he'd found two condoms in the bottom of Charlene's wastebasket. Charlie leaned forward over the steering wheel and wrinkled his brow and tried to get a better look at the two kids in the car. Clarke Sawyer. His hair had been shortened and died reddish brown. Clarke's hand ran down the arm of the girl in the driver's seat. She had thick dark hair. Swollen lips. The kind of skinny that makes you think of something dead.

The kid's eyes locked on his. He knows, Charlie thought. This was his moment. He could get inside this kid and work his way out. Through him he could reel in the father, go easy on him, talk about shell shock, argue PTSD. This poor goddamned kid. Out on some kind of joyride. Look at him.

The cars flashed past one another and the insect eyes of brake lights winked on the road ahead and Charlie swept the steering wheel with one hand. The wheels caught at the pavement. His whole body pushed forward against the seatbelt as he turned.

Elsie drove fast and poorly. She cut across a busy intersection and the driver of a blue minivan braked hard enough to slide and push his horn and peer at them over the dash with soft wet eyes. Elsie gunned into a side road too fast and the Charger spun. They came to a stop beside a street sign, the engine stalled.

"Start it," Clarke said.

Elsie turned the key and the ignition gave an electric hum and the engine turned once and died. The black Tahoe pulled behind them slowly as though there was no hurry at all. The driver's door cracked and the blue-suited man stepped out. Long, thin cheeks. Clarke watched him out the rear window of the Charger. The man had his hands up. His face looked calm. He said, "Clarke?" He spoke loud and slow. "I just need to talk to you."

Clarke looked down at himself. His jeans were unzipped. Elsie had shrunk into the seat. The bulk of her dark hair lay against one freckled cheek. She said, "What do we do?" Her hands still held the steering wheel.

"It's okay," Clarke said. He zipped up his pants. He reached over and peeled her right hand from the plastic wheel and placed it against her skirt. He looked at what lay around them. They were on the side of the road next to a short run of yellow grass that turned into a parking lot.

What did Clarke want? He couldn't see it clearly. He wanted to make decisions for himself and he didn't want to sit in the car, looking as afraid as he felt, while Elsie waited beside him. He opened the door. He stepped out.

The suited man stopped beside the Chevy Tahoe's fender. He didn't come any closer. He said, "My name is Charlie Basin. I'm with the FBI."

"Okay."

"I'm looking for your father."

"What's he done?" Clarke asked.

Charlie Basin looked overly relaxed. His face sleepy, his knees bent. He had kind tired eyes. He said, "You know Dallas Pope, right? The sheriff?"

"I know him."

"He's dead. I think your father killed him."

"No, he didn't," Clarke said. "He let him go."

"I pulled him out of a drainpipe. He's pretty dead."

"If he did it," Clarke said, "he's probably got a reason."

"Everybody's always got a reason," Charlie Basin said.

"What's that mean?"

"It means I need to find your father," said Charlie Basin, "and ask him."

Very distantly a siren began. Clarke looked around. No one was even looking in their direction. Fifty feet away cars passed on the main road.

"You're not in any trouble, kid," Charlie Basin said. "I just need to know where your dad is. Come over here and sit down."

"Fuck you," Clarke said. Clarke didn't know what he wanted to happen to his father but he wasn't going to turn him in because someone told him to. Clarke's father was his to reject when Clarke decided. Right now he wanted to be alone with Elsie, to work out his thoughts with her. He'd left the door open behind him. "Elsie," he said, "start the car."

Charlie Basin took a hesitant step forward and in his reluctance Clarke read fear. Clarke rolled his shoulders forward and felt the bands of muscle. He knew he was big for his age, bigger by far than Basin, and he felt an electric current crackle upward into him from his gut. Why should he care what his father had done? Clarke reached out for Basin in the way he might once have reached out to smash one of his sister's toys. He was going to hurt the man badly enough to make him reconsider saying that Dallas Pope was dead, but those smaller hands met his and Clarke's fingers bent backward and his body went with. He could only see the ground over his shoulder, and then he felt pressure along his arm and he stumbled forward over something, Charlie Basin's foot, and sprawled out against the cold hard ground. Basin's knee pressed into his back. Clarke's arm was still twisted behind him.

"Calm down, kid," Charlie Basin said. "Everything's going to be—"

Flesh pressed against Clarke, but his back and arm were freed, and he put his hands against the slurry of dirt and rock that ran along the side of the road. Clarke pressed upward with thick arms and felt the weight slide off him.

Charlie Basin lay facedown on the side of the road, bleeding from behind his right ear. Elsie held a tire iron. She knelt beside Basin and put her cheek next to his. "Good," she said, "he's breathing."

"Okay," Clarke said, "okay, okay."

In the trailer beside the Kishwaukee, Dominick sat on the couch. His younger kid slept. His older was missing but Clarke would come home again. Dominick knew how to wait. He looked around the squalid trailer, then pushed the walls of his hands into the wells of his eyes. He rubbed and felt hard grit turning against his skin. Pinpricks. Tiny wheels. Tracer rounds. Behind his eyelids, red waves burst into sad uninterpretable forms.

NEAR TAKUR GHAR mountain along the eastern edge of the Shah-i-kot Valley, Dominick had sat beside all the other Rangers in the belly of a twenty-seven-ton Chinook helicopter. Operation Anaconda. The rotors chopping above obscured all other sounds. They flew at night. Nineteen rangers sent to rescue a special operations SEAL team. How had it begun? With a long flight, a wait long enough that hearts calmed and legs ached and fear did not go away but calcified. At the tip of Takur Ghar, Dominick's face pressed against one of the Chinook's round windows. Pure darkness broken by the flashing line of light that marked the path of an RPG. The Chinook tumbled in the air and the noise of the explosion overwhelmed his thoughts. Bodies tumbled around him and people shouted and pushed their hands against him. When the Chinook crumpled against the ground bullets began to ring from its steel skin. Dominick picked himself up. He ran his hands over his body, then over his M4 carbine. He looked up. One of the pilots stumbled from the cabin, an arc of blood from his hand rising six feet into the air. Other Rangers gathered around him. Hard good men whom Dominick knew and loved and trusted. Benny Ward and DeJesus and Floyd. He waved them forward and they pressed out of the Chinook into heavy fire. They fell in the snow and the cold bit them like a child's teeth. How many had been shot? There wasn't time to count. He was okay, his men okay. They'd crashed on a mountaintop near an al-Qaeda camp. They were pinned down. Bullets whistled overhead. He felt the fear that would later make him feel ashamed. He pushed his gloved hands against his face. DeJesus's voice, loud and high and vast, called in air support, AC-130 Spectres, then F-15s with 20-mm multibarreled guns and heavy bombs. They hunkered down and waited. The medics with the injured in the Chinook waited for the bleeding to stop. The dead waited to be picked up and carried out of the snow. Bullets waited for flesh. Dominick's team fired hundreds of rounds of suppressive fire and they waited, waited for the moment when they'd be called to push forward toward the nearby rocks or toward the al-Qaeda encampment or toward the lost Navy SEALs, and, when the wait was finally over, their mouths would run dry, and their guns would spit fire into foreign bodies, and that rare dazed moment of fearlessness would set upon them.

When it came, when they pushed forward into the snow, Dominick laughed. This was being alive. He could feel it coiled inside him. Bullets whined near his helmet. The enemy's hardened positions exploded with a heat that felt like it came from inside his stomach. He pushed forward with DeJesus and Ward and Floyd and, when he glanced to his sides, their faces flickered in and out. Shadow and light. He fired and they gained the position between rocks. Burned al-Qaeda bodies, still smoking, melting snow. They shot those who were still living. They occupied the new position but it ended up feeling no different _the people of the broken neck_

from the position they'd occupied before. They found things that weren't theirs. AK-47s. A bayonet. A porno magazine. A backpack filled with dates and rice. By an outcropping of rock, they found a puddle of blood but no body, reddened footprints loping toward another hill. Under a shrub, they found a dead insurgent curled around his stomach wound. In a pool of melted snow, they found a woman, long-haired and stripped to the waist, drowned in bloody water no deeper than a sink. They stared and stared. Somebody, maybe Floyd, made a joke about her tits but nobody laughed. Finally, they had to stop looking. They took deep breaths. They felt the cold air whistle into their lungs. They felt themselves expand.

SOFT LIGHTS INTERRUPTED the dark behind Charlie's eyelids and a rough voice called his name. Why couldn't he wake up? Was he home? Charles Basin? The bed beneath him had calcified. A hand washed across his face like something he'd forgotten. Someone fumbled with his limbs, cradled his head. What had happened to him? He had two children. One boy and one girl, right? Was that it? Was that what he had? Someone was speaking to him again in a slow calm voice. Rosamund? His wife needed him but his tongue wouldn't answer. He made a fist with one hand. The voice spoke again. It was way too deep to be Rosamund's. He felt himself being lifted and set down again. A soft fabric beneath him. He heard the static crackling of a two-way radio. Someone said his name again—"Agent Basin?"—and he raised one shaking hand. He felt someone hold the cold round metal of a stethoscope against his chest. A band of fabric tightened on his upper arm. A finger burrowed beneath one of his eyebrows and pulled his eyelid open and the darkness cracked apart like dry earth.

CLARKE DROVE THE Dodge Charger though he didn't really know how. The car jerked forward and braked too hard. Elsie braced one hand on the dash and threw her head back and laughed. Spit stretched in a shimmering line from an upper dogtooth to her lips' lower vermilion border.

The darkness had lifted suddenly like a window shade. They drove past a dun-colored suburb, every house pockmarked with the dual rectangles of sliding doors, and they took a left into turned-earth fields where a huge red tractor pulled a red twelve-row corn planter. Elsie ran her hand up Clarke's leg and left it sitting on top of his crotch.

"You hit him with a goddamn tire iron," Clarke said. His voice was louder than a whisper.

"You wanna see something?" Elsie said. She unbuttoned three buttons on her shirt and pulled it underneath her bra. She pushed her chest forward.

"Oh," Clarke said. He kept his eyes half on the road. Three silos rose on the horizon as the nose of the Dodge pushed forward. Her hands moved toward him. He said, "They're going to find out you own this car."

"It was my mom's," she said. Her mouth curled as though she was going to spit. "Let's see them track her down."

A tiny hill rose and then fell as they passed it. Their stomachs heaved inside them. A lane led toward a tired ranch home. A dog barked. Clarke didn't want to think about what lay ahead.

"You know what?" Elsie said. "It felt kind of good."

"What did?"

"Hitting him with the tire iron."

"It did? Good how?"

"I don't know. Scratching poison ivy until it bleeds. That kind of good."

The vinyl whispered as she slid across the seat. She took one of his hands off the wheel and put it to her chest. Her lips against his neck were wet. Alongside the road, two children dressed in dark coats stared and waved as they passed. In the rearview mirror, the two kids fell behind, losing facial details, and then the distinction between cloth and skin, and then any sense of shape or size beyond two black gnats in a dust cloud.

Elsie's hands burrowed into him. He felt soft and earthen. "I don't care if your father kills people," she said.

"You don't?" Clarke said.

She opened the fly of his pants. The road ahead curved to the right and then ran straight as far as he could see. Not another road in sight. Not a building. Nothing but tilled earth. Her mouth pressed close to his ear. He grunted and said, "I don't know where we are."

"I do," Elsie said.

In the trailer, King dreamed that the back field was filled with bees. Hundreds upon hundreds of them. King was in the

174

field, too. The bees skittered in the air and she held still. Some dangled long dark legs, some were covered in soft fur, and some had wet shining midsections. Dozens alighted on clovers in the same moments that others took flight. They made as much noise as an airfield. Near the plum tree, her mother waved at King with both arms. Her mouth moved but King couldn't hear beyond the buzzing. Her mom wore a red scarf and hat but her eyes looked like they were all pupil. She gestured at King with both palms spread. Don't move! Don't move! Even across the spread of grass, King could see her long hair twitching with insects. A hornet crawled across an eyebrow. Both of her hands remained outstretched and the small dark shapes began to lace between her fingers. King froze in the field. The air held an autumn chill. Her mother's mouth opened and the tip of her pink tongue touched her bottom lip. She gestured with her hands. She pointed at herself, then at the ground. She tried again to speak. She tried to say something to King and some sound must have come out and trailed across a few feet of withered grass. King cupped a hand behind an ear so that the soft cartilage hooked forward. She couldn't hear anything beyond the bees' communal hum.

Outside the door to King's room, Dominick sat on the stinking couch and loaded a clip for his Beretta handgun. Each bullet clicked into place with the satisfying sound of a routine. The metal held the bullets in a straight line. Dominick's eyes were half closed and unfocused. His hands moved with the rote swiftness with which an adult ties a shoe.

Clarke drove back to find a dark cloud atop the trailer home. The gravel driveway crunched beneath the Charger's tires. Elsie's eyes were wide. When the car stopped, Clarke said, "Wait here." As he got out of the car, the trailer door opened and a huge man stood on the threshold. Hair cut close to his scalp. Squared jaw. The skin by his eyes was wound tight. Clarke walked up the stairs. The father leaned forward and put his arms around the son. They stumbled backward into the house.

Inside, a shotgun leaned beside the door. A pile of thick red shells. On the coffee table sat three handguns and boxes of bullets. His father's Wharncliffe knife. A scoped rifle. The house was filled with some dark vapor. Clarke had trouble seeing clearly. The ground seemed to shift beneath his feet. Something rumbled intestinally. His father said, "Jesus, Clarke!" His voice sounded faint. He said, "Don't do this to me."

"Do what?" Clarke's body stiffened. He felt the stiffness of a tactical vest beneath his father's shirt.

"You scared me," his father said.

"Scared you?"

"I didn't know what happened." His father seemed to collapse against him. His arms feebly held his shoulders. His neck leaned forward. "God," he said, "*God*, I'm glad you're okay."

Clarke exhaled hard, as though his lungs had collapsed. He pushed his father back. "Fuck you," he said. His voice was low and tight. He stepped toward his dad. He raised his voice loud enough that others could hear. "What the fuck's wrong with you?"

The trailer seemed to shake. The guns vibrated against the coffee table and the single bookshelf seemed to waver as though it was about to fall. King appeared in the doorway to the hall that led to the bedrooms. She held a blue blanket. She braced herself against a wall with one arm. Outside, the darkness gathered at the windows in loose bodily shapes and pressed inward and the house timbers groaned as they shifted. "Stop!" King yelled.

Dominick pushed Clarke onto the couch. He swelled upward, his strength returning. The floor felt uneven. Dominick was not surprised, he had spent so many dark hours fumbling with the flint and steel of his narrow mind. The dark outside pressed inward so that the indoor shadows crept across the floor toward them. Something outside pressed its great dark face against the windows and looked in. "What's it want?" Dominick shouted. He thrust himself over the trembling floor out into the hands of the darkness, and stumbled, and came up looking at a young woman with long dark hair and a tiny star in her pierced nose.

"Are you okay?" Elsie said. She pulled her shirt tightly around her. "What's going on in there?"

The kids gathered in the door frame and looked at their father on the gravel. He pushed himself up and swept inside and through the house, searching, until he stopped by the bathroom sink. He saw the lines of salt on the vinyl floor.

Elsie stood on her tiptoes behind Dominick's kids. Her mouth hung open.

Map, read the words in salt, *Finger, Bone.*

CHARLIE BASIN SWUNG his feet out of a hospital bunk. He wore a greenish gown. He flexed his thigh muscles, then rolled his head on his shoulders. His navy blazer hung on the back of a chair near the door. His shoes sat on the seat of the chair, their fine black laces were untied and the tongues had slipped into the cavities. With his right hand Charlie felt the bandage on his head. He took careful inventory of his body. Feet hanging over the edge of the high bunk. Mild ache in his calves. Legs like sandstone plinths waiting to bear weight. An intestinal barrenness. How long had it been since he'd eaten? He needed to piss. Throat a little dry. A mild wooziness. He held a palm out in front of him. It did not shake. He could get up. He could stand.

He knew what would happen now. It was what always happened. Dominick Sawyer would run and run hard. Charlie needed roadblocks. He needed police cooperation, search parties, a SWAT team. He needed a helicopter. His phone began to ring. Where was it? He put his hands against the white sheet and pushed himself up. He pulled his phone from his jacket pocket. He lifted it slowly.

"Charlie?" Andrew Fry said.

"I'm here." Charlie Basin's voice cracked like a stone snapped in two.

"You sound like shit," Andy said. "The hospital called us. You okay? What the hell happened?"

"Fine," Charlie said. "My head hurts. Got taken by surprise. Can I tell you the particulars later? They're right here, Andy. We need roadblocks. We've got to move."

"You're up for this?"

"I told you I'm fine."

"You want me to call Rosamund?" Fry said. "Let her know what's going on?"

"I'll get in touch with her after I take care of things here."

"Okay, then," Fry said, "get over to the Rockford field office. I'll let them know you're coming. You're in charge."

KING WADED OUT into the cold river. She shivered. She was waist deep and she pressed in further. A muskrat worked its way upstream. On the far bank, hundreds of small dark birds blanketed the cottonwoods. The spaces between trunks were filled with knotted brambles. Her wet jeans and shoes held her down like ankle weights. Her jaw chattered. She pushed deeper.

Beneath her the water ran clear and she watched her shoes curl around colored stones. Deep blue stones the size of her fist. Chips as red as blood. Orange-and-white striations. Black orbs. Smooth white eggs. When the water deepened, she treaded water. Slow circles with her arms and legs. She floated downstream. Way down the river she thought she could see someone else in the water. The dark figure of a woman. After a while King stopped shivering. Rectangles of light shone from the trailer home. The air around her face felt superheated and the water on the surface felt good. The river seemed to be separated into layers or bands of temperatures. Eighteen inches of warmth sat atop the surface. A colder layer ran underneath and washed around her chest and thighs. She stopped moving her arms and let her legs hang, and the water rose up and covered her mouth. Like that, her dangling feet sank just deep enough to touch the icy undercurrent that ran like a secret life beneath the surface.

King waded back out of the river and hurried to the trailer. She put on dry clothes and sat at the table with Clarke and Elsie. A few moments later, Aunt Annie pushed through the front door and stood in the middle of the living room. She wore a dark blue fleece. She carried two brown bags of groceries. "What?" she said. "Why the long faces?" For the moment, she ignored Elsie.

No one had anything to say. At the table, Clarke's brown hair curled across his forehead. King, hair still wet, squeezed both hands between her knees. Elsie held a glass of milk. Dominick rustled about in the bedroom, packing. He appeared in the hallway with his arms full of backpacks and duffels. The handle of the Beretta jutted from the holster beneath his belt.

"Where you going?" Annie asked him. "What's happened? And what's that for?" She pointed to the pistol at his waistline.

"That guy you spoke to," Dominick said. "The fed."

"Basin?" Annie said. "He's been here?"

"No," Dominick said. "Clarke ran into him."

"Where?"

"Out joyriding," he said.

"Shit, does he know you're here?"

"Not yet," Dominick said. "Anybody follow you?"

Annie set the bags on the table. "I snuck out the back door," she said, "and borrowed a friend's car." She pulled Clarke's chin up toward her with one hand. "You okay?" she said. Clarke nodded. "Who's this?" Annie asked him. With her other hand, she pointed at the thin round-nosed girl in the chair a little too close to Clarke's.

Loose-wristed, Elsie held out her hand. "My name is Elsie,"

she said. She flicked her long hair back over her shoulder with a toss of her head. The silver star glittered in her nose.

Everyone was quiet for half a minute. A cold draft rose from the floorboards. Through the windows, light winked behind broken clouds. King's chair scooted back from the table with a low judder and she stood. She said, "If we have to leave, I want to go home."

Dominick walked out the door and corralled the bags in the bed of the truck. Annie followed his broad dark back. King stood near the front door. Clarke and Elsie walked out of the trailer and onto the lawn. Putting her hands on Clarke's shoulders, Elsie whispered in his ear. "You can stay," she said. Her lips touched his ear.

"I want to," he said, "but I can't. I've got to take care of my sister."

On the porch, King looked back into the house, first at the phone in the living room and then at the kitchen counter, where she had left her belt behind.

The bags knocked heavily against the metal truck bed. "Jesus, Dominick," Annie said, "I hope you didn't do these things." He noticed that her hands had begun to wrinkle. Her hair was drawn up in a braid that looked like a vestigial tail.

"What things?" he said. He tossed the last bag into the bed.

"The things they say you've done," she said.

Dominick turned and looked at his sister. "Sometimes everything falls apart," he said.

"What does that mean?"

"Most of it I can't remember." He put a hand against the side of his face and took it away again. Dried blood sprayed against dun-colored walls and a wet breath loosed against his face. He felt his finger curled around a metal trigger, heard voices like curses in a language he didn't understand. His hands were around a thin throat. The crack of bone. Blood running past yellow marrow. Bruises welling like black ink beneath paper skin. The edge of a knife pressed against the slender joint of a slender finger.

"I'm going to miss you so badly, Dom," Annie said.

"Me, too, Annie." He turned away from his sister and gritted his teeth to suppress the pressure in his throat.

"When we were little," she said, "you were the kindest boy."

Behind the truck, Clarke and Elsie had latched their arms around one another. Her eyes were huge and wet. One of her hands made circles against his back. The other fished in a coat pocket for a pen. She pushed him a half-step back and, in blocky black letters, wrote 815 966 4774 on the pale underside of his forearm. They leaned into one another like falling fence posts. She moved so close that her lips touched his ear as she whispered, "You call me. Then I'll come get you."

The sun sat low and orange in the sky. From the driver's seat, Dominick murmured to his sister as she leaned against the side of the Ram. She felt the truck's thin metal cladding give a little beneath her weight.

King walked out onto the creaking porch, turned around,

and ran back inside the trailer. She hollered back, "I forgot something." She dropped to the floor beside the phone so that she was completely out of view of the windows. She dialed Jon Howland's phone number. The phone rang, and she whispered, "Hurry, hurry," until Howland answered. King asked, "Did you find anything?"

"Are you kids okay?" Howland's voice graveled and static jumped across the line.

"I only got a second," King said. "We're fine. Please, you've got to tell me what you found."

"Okay, okay. A picture of you and your mom. She's got you on her shoulders. Looks like you're carrying a turtle. There's a crucifix. A glass vial filled with something."

"What's in it?"

"Looks like water. Hold on." King hears a muted pop and a snort. "Smells like perfume."

"That it?"

"There's a handkerchief. White. Maybe looks like it used to have something written on it. That's it," Jon Howland said.

The truck's horn blared. King let the receiver fall into the cradle. She walked slowly back toward her father, her feet knocking against the wood floor and echoing into the crawl space beneath. She left the front door gaping open and leapt down the steps onto the dark springy earth with one arm raised above her head, holding the belt that swung like a black adder in her hand.

CHARLIE MADE A phone call from the satellite FBI agency on West State Street in Rockford, Illinois. It was a nondescript brick building with black awnings. Charlie had taken over a corner office. He swore into the phone. The bandage on his head had a small stain the color of rust. Dark-suited men came into the office when he beckoned through the great windows and left again when he motioned with his head. The office phone had a long spiraled cord that stretched across the office and knocked over the pencil holder and the stapler and a stack of paper. Charlie went round and round the desk like a tetherball. He called for roadblocks and traffic stops and an aerial search.

Charlie paused and wiped the edges of his lips with his thumb and forefinger. Then he called Rosamund.

"What's wrong, Charlie?" she said.

"I'm fine. Don't worry. I just wanted to hear your voice."

"I can hear it," she said. "Something's wrong."

"What does it sound like?"

"Tinny. Higher-pitched than usual."

Charlie lowered his voice to a strained, breaking baritone. "How's this?"

"Sexy."

Outside the office, a burly man beckoned to him with one hand. Charlie held up his index finger. "I had the older kid," Charlie said to Rosamund. "His name's Clarke."

"You had him? Past tense? You don't have him anymore?"

"This girl he was with hit me in the head with a tire iron."

"My God, Charlie! Are you okay?"

"I got a few stitches."

"Have you thought about calling the kids?"

"Not really."

"Maybe you ought to call them. Especially Charlene. She needs to hear from you. She's struggling."

"She's having a hard enough time, isn't she?" Charlie said. "Without adding on my problems."

"Call her, Charlie. Tell her what's happened."

"I got a lot to coordinate right now, Ros," Charlie said. "The Rockford police. The satellite bureau."

"Then hurry up, Charlie, catch these people and then come home."

THE RAM TRUCK scuttled out of the narrow driveway and the tires spat gravel as Dominick turned onto a cement lane not wide enough for two cars. A woman with her hair tied in a handkerchief planted bulbs and craned her head to follow the Sawyers' retreat, a cigarette dangling from her lips. They turned onto a two-lane drive with a twenty-five-miles-per-hour speed limit. A yellow hatchback seemed to follow them. It drove too close but then slowed and pulled into a driveway and idled while an automatic garage door yawned. They came to the busy four-lane artery that would flush them out of New Milford. Dozens of cars dopplered by in flashes. It seemed to Dominick that every head turned to look at them. Bright faces flashed questioning looks. There were raised eyebrows. Down-turned lips. Deep disapproving scowls.

Night fell over them like a tossed sheet. A giant orb of moon rose as though attached to a pulley. The Sawyers limped away from New Milford, the distance between sets of headlights widening until everything behind them sat dark. A helicopter droned overhead. The streets narrowed at each turn and the tilled fields expanded like a creeping mold. Dominick turned the truck onto a small road lined by thin trees that curved to the east. Far ahead, through the trees and across a field, they saw two pairs of brake lights slowing to a halt. Briefly, red and blue lights flashed. The beam of a flashlight cut the night into halves.

"What's that?" King asked. She was slumped against her brother on the seat.

"A checkpoint," Dominick said. He had taken his foot from the accelerator and the truck's weight began to work against its speed.

Panic pulled Clarke's voice into a higher pitch. He held one arm in front of his sister to hold her in her seat. "What do we do?"

"We walk," Dominick said.

They bumped off on a dirt road. Thin pale beech trunks loomed toward them in the night. Dust and insects glinted in the headlight beams. The truck rumbled to a halt. Dominick cut the headlights. He stepped out and walked around through the soft wilted grass and opened the passenger door. Clarke and King slipped out of the cab, leaving the door open behind them. The dome light shone as bright as a lighthouse. Dominick tossed each of them a bag from the truck bed and he shouldered what remained. He pushed the passenger door shut and the dome light faded.

They walked for three nights. The weather held out with sun-warmed afternoons and deep-starred evenings. When it was dark, they walked through fields and forests, the land before them great and flat and tame. When they saw the lights of cars, they hunkered down and waited for them to pass. They avoided roads. Sometimes smoke rose from distant chimneys and lights burned at farm windows and the kids looked longingly back over their shoulders as their legs carried them beyond the range of their desires.

"I'm really tired."

"It's not even that late, King."

"It feels really late. We've been walking forever."

"You're fine. Just stay behind your brother."

"I can't keep going, Dad. I can't."

"Come here, I'll carry you."

"All right."

"Hold on to my neck."

"Okay."

"How's that feel?"

"It's pretty good. Why's it so dark out here?"

"I'm *carrying* you and it's just pretty good?"

"It's nice."

"Do you think you can sleep?"

"I don't know. When do we get to stop again?"

"Not until it gets light."

"Can you carry me until morning?"

"I can carry you a long time."

At daybreak, they camped in stands of elms or amid firs or in patches of deer-flattened prairie. Daffodils wilted in small clearings. Red and yellow tulips poked from yellowed grass. At one camp, the ground was littered with cow bones. Skulls and vertebrae and scapulae. Dominick and King had a sword fight with thin ribs. At daybreak they ate bagels and salami and cans of beans and beets and corn. They stretched their mummy bags out on the ground in a triangle. They yawned and slipped inside. They rolled onto their sides. They curled into tight S's. The ground beneath them was hard but their minds had softened with weariness. Their breathing slowed and evened. They slept. Their sleeping bags were dotted by shadows shaped like the leaves of elms.

When King dreamed, she sometimes believed she was awake. At other times, she mistook the long night walk for a dream. They walked in a dark line, the taller figures that King could barely see in front of her in the dark. The earth felt as soft and smooth as skin beneath her feet. Sometimes she walked in the middle. Sometimes in the rear. Never in the front, not once. She counted each of them again and again, afraid she would get lost. One, two, three. One, two, three. She couldn't tell the shadow of her father from the shadow of her brother. "Clarke?" she whispered. Fir branches arched down and traced the curve of her chin with cold needles. Small four-legged animals scattered at their approach and pale gleaming eyes leered at them from the undergrowth. "Shhh," one of them said. Her father or her brother? One, two, three. Her legs felt leaden and her eyes closed and she stumbled and a hand caught her by the shoulder. The tails of the coat on the shadow in front of her flapped like small wings. The air smelled of fertilizer. The ground hardened beneath her feet, then softened again and then filled with ankle-sized stones. One, two, three. She reached her hands up to squeeze her own cheeks. Something wet squelched beneath her feet. One, two, three, four. One figure ahead of her and two be-hind. One, two, three, *four*. Her mouth went dry. Her lips stuck to her gums. She whispered, "Who's there?"

On the third night of the walk, a squad car's headlights flashed across the figures hurrying over the road. A moment before there had been darkness. Ahead of them sat a copse of trees where they meant to camp. Their boots felt heavy. They were tired. Dominick wasn't paying enough attention. The headlights burned toward them, the whine of the engine rising and the small pair of lights growing larger like some hostile eventuality. Clarke felt his bladder tighten. Something icy and hot prickled across his skin. Dominick pulled the Beretta from beneath his belt. He stood at the side of the road. He looked straight at the oncoming lights. He did not turn to his kids. "Run," he said, and they stumbled forward with the light hot on their backs. They passed a brown road sign that read MALTA, ILLINOIS 5 MILES. The squad car's brakes squealed. Clarke and King threw themselves onto their hands and knees in a drain-age ditch. They crabbed in the mud until they looked back toward their father.

The state police car was white with a long yellow stripe down its side. Dust billowed in the beams of the headlamps. A single officer in a brown shirt fumbled with his gun and opened his door and leaned out and barked, "Don't move!" The fear was a shadow on his face. His eyes were open very wide. They could see him shake.

Their father called, "Let's talk about it." He had his gun trained loosely at the officer. He stood with one shoulder toward the car as though to offer a smaller target.

"Put down the gun," the officer said. His voice quavered. He had a bristly mustache and close-cropped black hair that showed his white scalp. Clarke looked at his father's face. There was nothing. No fear. No satisfaction. *Nothing*. A slight tightening of his father's eyes as though he squinted at something in the distance. Curled calmly inside himself, he looked carved from stone.

"There's no way I'm going to put my gun down," Dominick said. He took two steps forward. His voice carried quietly. "Listen," he said, "*listen*. ..."

"Put the weapon down!"

"I don't want to kill you in front of my children."

CHARLIE BASIN FELT his stomach drop as his Suburban rose and fell over a small hill. There wasn't much else for him to do, so he'd joined the manhunt. Useless hours spent covering useless ground. All these farm roads looked the same. The fields running flat out in front of him. Miles of combed earth. Concrete silos at random intervals. A few old farmhouses with bowed roofs. How could anyone tell where they were going? Maybe the Sawyers were lost.

Charlie held his phone in his hand. What was this that he felt? A familiar sense of distance from everyone he knew. Was this a kind of strength or just loneliness? He let his hand dial his older child's number. The assistant district attorney. Oswell. His son shaped like a crane.

"Hey," Charlie said, "can you make a trip out to see your sister?"

"What for?"

"What do you mean 'what for'?" Charlie said. "She's in the hospital."

"I meant that maybe you should go down there yourself."

"I already tried that. She doesn't want to see me," Charlie said. "She's pissed at me. Are you mad at me?"

"Not really, Dad. What's she mad about?"

"I don't know. Have I been distant?"

"Where are you, Dad?" Oswell asked.

"This road doesn't seem to have a name," Charlie said. "I'm in Illinois."

"You're still looking for the two kids and their father?"

"Oz, when I'm done with this, you think you could take a week off work?"

"What for?"

"Come up to Maine with me and Charlene," Charlie said. "Sit by the ocean. I'm thinking about buying a place."

"Seriously?"

"Yeah," Charlie said. He paused. "These people. I think they've taken to the ground."

"Who?"

"This family that I'm chasing down."

"Are you getting any closer?"

"Not five miles from where I am right now, we found a stolen Dodge Ram out of New York State. It was probably theirs. They're on foot. They can't get far."

DOMINICK HANDCUFFED THE officer to a thin tree trunk in the copse of saplings. When he pulled the wrists together, he thought of a line of insurgents he'd pushed ahead by their arms, their wrists bound by flex cuffs, past rolls of razor wire into the yard of a detention facility, where lines of detainees prayed, folded over their knees with their heads pressed against the dry dirt. Where had that been? Somewhere outside Mosul? Dominick pushed the officer until he sat on the ground. He put his mouth close to his ear. "You look like a nice guy," Dominick said. "Everything's going to be fine." His kids looted the police car for a bag of apple crullers and a pack of peppermint chewing gum and a cell phone. Clarke picked up the officer's cell phone and dialed the number on his arm. The phone rang ten times. Eleven. Twelve. King held out the pack of gum and put her head back against the seat rest and looked at Clarke with her mouth slightly open.

"Hello?" Elsie said. Her voice sounded like linen run through the wash. Her voice was thick with sleep. Clarke imagined her hair twisted into its thick untidy strands.

"Elsie, it's me," Clarke said.

"Clarke?"

"Uh-huh. Can you come pick me up?"

"Where are you?"

"I'm not sure. Do you know a town called Malta?"

"Sort of. There's not much there."

"Meet us on the western edge."

"Now?"

"Right now. Really fast. We tied up a cop."

"I'm coming," she said. "Wherever you're headed, I want to go with."

They left the officer handcuffed to the tree. Clarke put a bottle of water in one of his hands. Dominick drove the police car. He drove fast, with the lights off, toward the town of Malta while, in the passenger seat, Clarke sputtered about Elsie. His fists were clenched. "I want you to drop us off in Malta," he said. Spit flew off his lips in little arcs. He expected his father to argue, to stop him, to say there was no way. "Elsie will pick me and King up," he said.

"You won't have long," Dominick said. "If she's not fast enough, I'll get you another car."

Clarke sat quiet. Why didn't his father argue? Clarke's arm muscles clenched tight. He tried to let them relax before speaking again. The eastern edge of the horizon had begun to lighten. King sat in the back of the car with their bags piled around her. Her fingers laced through the grillwork between the front and rear seats. She said, "I've never been in a police car before."

Clarke slapped the dash with one hand. "I'm taking King, and I'm leaving," he said. His voice shook.

"Of course you are," Dominick said. "That's just what you need to do."

Dominick's face looked slack, almost stunned. No one spoke. The squad car's wheels ground against the concrete.

"Did I mess up, Clarke?" Dominick said. "Should I turn myself in?"

"Don't do it," King said.

"No?" Dominick said.

Inside the shell of the police car, their ears played tricks on them. They shushed one another, cocked their heads to one side and listened for sirens. Then one nodded his head and said, "I don't hear anything," and another, "Me, neither," and another, "I think we're okay."

In Malta, Dominick turned south on the westernmost road, North 2nd Street, passed over a railroad crossing, and pulled the squad car into a red-and-white four-bay shed not far from a granary. He parked the car beside a huge yellow plow. Clarke pulled the bags from the backseat and piled them on the ground. The branches of the trees just across the street were tipped with budding leaves. Who among them first cocked their head to the side when the sirens began to swirl to the north? The father? The daughter? The son? Which of them led and which followed? Who listened the hardest? Who first felt their chest tighten with the sense that someone had come to pull them inexorably apart? Who first reached out to touch whom?

"Get out of here now, Dad," Clarke said. He pointed toward the stolen cruiser. "You have to go!"

"Go?" Dominick said. "Go where?"

They huddled together for a minute before Clarke walked past the shed and looked up the street. He waved his hands above his head. "She's here," Clarke yelled. "Elsie's here!" He sounded like he could hardly believe it himself. He was up standing on his toes and leaning in her direction.

CHARLIE BASIN'S PHONE rang. He was north of Rockford, Illinois, among soy fields and silos. Maybe it was Charlene. Was she trying to get hold of him, to draw a line between their lives? Maybe his wife had told her about the tire iron. When he answered, a voice he didn't know said, "Lieutenant Crosser here. We got an officer found your family."

"Where?" Charlie said.

"Off Route 38."

"He's got them?" Charlie said. He slowed the car, did a U-turn, and turned south.

"Afraid not," said the lieutenant. "They tied him up, took his car. He's a good man."

"You send people after?"

"Everything we've got."

"I'm on the wrong side of town," Charlie said. "I'll need a chopper to meet me."

"Done."

"What's the name of the officer who saw them?"

"That'd be Bill Hackenberg."

"Patch me through to him, Lieutenant."

Charlie gunned the car forward, racing toward the police helicopter that rose to meet him. The phone was pressed between his cheek and shoulder. He waited.

A quiet voice, almost a whisper. "This is Bill Hackenberg, sir."

"Hey, Bill, I'm not going to chew you out for this. But I'd like to know what happened."

"It's pretty simple, sir. They tied me up, then stole my squad car."

"Tied you up with what?" Charlie said.

"It's embarrassing to say, but the handcuffs off my belt. The thing is ..."

"What's the thing, Bill?"

"I had him, sir. I couldn't bring myself to shoot."

"It's not a small thing to shoot someone, Officer."

"Not for me, sir."

Farmland began to give way to suburb and, in the dark sky ahead, the flight lights of the helicopter swept toward him. Charlie said, "I got to go soon, Bill. A few quick questions. Where did you run across them?"

"Route 38, five miles west of a town called Malta."

"Small town?" Charlie said.

"Really small."

"What were they doing?" said Charlie.

"I caught them in my headlights, walking in a soybean field."

"You stopped them?" Charlie said. "By yourself?"

"First I called it in to dispatch."

"You did the right thing, Bill."

"There's one last thing."

"Go ahead," Charlie said.

"I'm not sure about it, sir."

"About what?" asked Charlie.

"Out there, in the fields, I saw four of them."

IN THE EARLY years, when Dominick came home on furlough, they couldn't get enough of each other. He and his wife. Sarah. He loved the feel of her name in his mouth as much as he loved to fill his mouth with her fingers or earlobes or thighs. He thought about her all the time. Sarah reading to the kids in bed at night, all of them lying side by side, touching. Sarah walking out into the sun of the front porch, squinting out into the brightness, sweeping her dark hair behind her ears, unconsciously, each time it fell. Sarah kneeling in the garden, the muscles in her forearms bunching as she dropped bulbs into holes in the ground.

The kids went to sleep earlier then, King just a baby or toddler or small child, and Sarah looked tired, so tired, but she'd stay up with him and get naked and drink cold beer by the fire. They fell asleep interlocked like jigsaw pieces. The fire in the hearth roared up as hot as the desert he'd come home from and, pressed against his wife, he twitched in his sleep and whimpered like a child and dreamed.

KING'S ARMS HELD her father's waist. The four-bay shed smelled good. Oil and sawdust. The eastern sky was a blade of light. Clarke motioned for Elsie's car to pull behind the shed. She stepped from the car. Her long dark hair was pinned against her head with pink barrettes shaped like insects. Her nose was running and she wiped at it twice with the back of her hand. Clarke lifted his bag and King's from the ground and tossed them into the Charger. No one else could move. The police sirens multiplied. Distantly they heard the *chop chop* of a helicopter rotor. Dominick pulled the armored vest from a duffel bag and put it on. He reached into a backpack for a second handgun, which he pushed into his belt. Then he slung the backpack over his shoulders. He opened a long duffel and pulled out a scoped M1A Springfield Armory hunting rifle.

Elsie sat back in the driver's seat of the Charger. Clarke guided King by the arm and led her to the car. Next to the door, Dominick picked King up in his arms. He put his mouth next to her ear. He whispered, "This is scary, isn't it?" and King's head nodded.

Dominick said, "You're going to be fine, you know that?"

He felt King nod again, the weight of her head so slight against his arm. "I love you so much," Dominick said. He slid his daughter into the backseat of the car and turned to Clarke beside the passenger door. Clarke's head looked first to one side and then to the other as though listening to competing voices. Dominick pulled his wallet from his leather satchel and fumbled with bills and pressed them into Clarke's hand. He was a few inches taller than his son. He stood there absolutely still.

The light wind died and the air suddenly felt warmer. Their breath came out in thin clouds.

"You head south, away from the sirens," Dominick said. "I'll stop them here. For a little while." He paused to wipe his lips. "When I get out of this, I'll head west on Route 88, cross the Mississippi River, and be in Iowa. Then I'll follow the river north to the town of Bellevue."

Clarke climbed into the passenger seat. "We're not coming," he said.

"Maybe you'll change your mind," Dominick said. He put his hands on Clarke's shoulders and pressed down and, though Clarke tried to stiffen his spine, his father's great weight pressed against him until he collapsed against the seat. His father's hand locked on his shoulder, holding him in place. He drew the seatbelt across his son's lap. Clarke's face was so close to his father's that he felt the scrape of the hair on his father's jaw.

"It's okay," Dominick said and he let go of his son and slammed the door.

He didn't watch them drive away but walked into the middle of the old tar-and-chip road. He wanted all of those coming for him to think he was all there was. He wanted them to focus, to see him as the threat that eclipsed all others. The sirens were close, the helicopter but a dot on the horizon. He closed his eyes. He heard the stuttering approach of the helicopter and saw the gray earth and mountains of the Shah-i-kot Valley and a line of Apaches and CH-47 Chinooks coming in low, nap of the earth, with the ground swirling into dust. He looked up. He dropped to one knee on the road's yellow dividing line. He swung the Springfield rifle onto his shoulder, rested the elbow of the arm supporting the rifle against his forward knee, and sighted north, up the road, to where they would have to turn from the highway. He felt the air bellow in and out of him as he breathed. The rising sun struck his face. He squinted against the low-slanting light. What about light was warm? He waited for the first car to make the turn. He felt steady. He felt weightless. He felt good.

When the first police car turned onto North 2nd, its lights washed the few houses that sat on the east side of the street. Dominick tucked his chin and followed the scope down the street, through the windshield. The tires of the second car squealed as they made the turn. The sirens waffled back and forth. He centered the crosshairs on a burly officer in the lead car, on his harelip and on the cleft chin and on the tense bob of his Adam's apple as he swallowed. Dominick took a deep breath and held it until he tightened into a single thought, until something in him swelled and filled the moment and extended out upon the line between him and the harelip that he could not miss. The weight of the gun rose off him like a dark angel, and his head buzzed with the held breath, and he waited, waited until the moment that the gun's trigger pulled him.

The windshield shattered and the squad car gunned forward and veered right. It bucked over the curb and shot across a blighted lawn and crashed into the corner of a dirty white house. Dominick held still against the wall of sound. He did not see the scatter of mildewed vinyl siding, or the hole in the house, or the rear of the car and its dark spinning tires. He did not think about the distance between his stance on the road and the officer behind the glass, or about the speed of the vehicle, or about the wind that blew from the east. He didn't think about what would come next, about the growing orb of the helicopter, about which direction he might run or which shabby house he might take cover behind. He did not think of the way that, when he'd been home from the war, his wife had cut unopened daffodils from the yard and left them on his dresser. He did not think of the great unnameable fear that often sat on him when he'd come home, a fear untethered from any cause, that made him snap at Sarah and shove her against a wall so that he found himself disgusted with his longing to be away from them—his wife and children—and back where everything was bloody and godawful enough to give him cause to be the person he was. He did not think about those he had killed at war, about the film that overwhelms one's eyes, about the arterial pump of blood, about the knife that cut flesh with the ease with which a kitchen knife splits ribs. He did not think about how he had once imagined people to be more solid, more sustained than they are, about what he'd learned of fragility, especially his own. He did not think about the way the honey his wife had left on the kitchen table solidified in the jar from a translucent amber to something almost opaque.

He did not think about what his children must have thought of him, or of what all children must think of all of the rest of us. What he thought about—what he imagined in slow sad steps—was all the times he had left his kids behind. The good-byes whispered to an infant in a crib. Lifting the puppy weight of a toddler from his neck. Waving back through the window as he walked away from the house. Clarke and King at the airport, Clarke with his hands in his pockets and King tugging her mother's hand out toward him as he walked away from them through security in his gray-and-green uniform. First it was Kosovo, then Afghanistan, then Iraq, then Afghanistan again, and all the times in between. Could he even remember where he'd been? When had leaving begun to grow easier? When had it started to feel harder to return to his family than it felt to leave them? When had his wife's hair been cut short? When had she begun to look like someone he'd never known? When had the cabin that he'd built with his own hands turned into something foreign?

In the middle of the road, Dominick Sawyer pivoted slightly on the ball of his left foot. The rifle moved half an inch. The sole of his shoe against the chip-and-tar roadway sounded like a cleared throat. The second police car bounced over a pothole. He put his eye to the gun and the town of Malta winnowed like a parfocal lens. The police car's windshield held a wavy reflection of the sunrise. The officer's face was a round of cured meat. Dominick took a deep breath. He possessed a sight not his own. The gun had a purpose. He would not stand in its way.

FROM THE COCKPIT of the OH-58 helicopter, Charlie Basin watched the line of flashing lights. The noise of the rotors pushed at him like a great rhythmic wind. The line of police cars jockeyed for position in the middle of a road that led in both directions as far as he could see. The pilot's eyes were fixed on the town. The nose of the machine pointed downward.

The first cruiser turned into Malta and Charlie saw the tiny figure of a man kneeling in the middle of the road. He pointed: "There!" The figure cradled a long rifle and the first cruiser cut sharply to the left and crashed halfway through a house. The sound must have been gut-wrenching and horrendous but Charlie could hear nothing at this distance over the chopping of the helicopter blades. A split second later that growing figure, Dominick Clarke Sawyer, turned his gun and a tiny fire appeared at the barrel. The second cruiser twisted too sharply, rolled across the cement and came down hard on its roof. The windows broke and the side panels crumbled and pieces of red taillight scattered, still scattered, across the road. Then the squad car started to burn.

The helicopter was just outside the town. A small clutter of mostly white houses. The line of cruisers began to brake behind the burning car. Dominick stood in the center of the road as though he intended to sacrifice himself. For what moment did he wait? Then his great shorn head tilted upward. His eyes were grim slits. Light from somewhere glinted off the barrel of the gun. It rose and fired and the helicopter jerked hard to the left, sheering so low that the yellow-green of the grass rushed toward Charlie. The chopper lifted and turned as if it wanted to spin. The pilot jammed the cyclic stick forward and the helicopter straightened and flew outside the boundaries of the town and into the great dark fields.

ELSIE DROVE OUT of Malta, and King pressed her face to the Charger's rear window. "What's going to happen to Dad?" she asked. "I can't see anything."

From the driver's seat, Elsie's hand slipped over to hold Clarke's bouncing thigh. She was driving too fast. "Oh, Jesus," she said. "Oh, Jesus!" Then her jaw clenched tight. The road was deeply pitted. The rising light flushed against the windows and the interior of the car felt warm and soft and artificial. A bug cracked against the front windshield.

"Don't speed," Clarke said. "Get on a busier street."

"What's going to happen?" King said.

"I don't know."

Elsie pointed ahead toward Route 88 with its stream of cars. King's face flattened against the glass. Not a single car traveled the road behind them. The Dodge nosed onto the access ramp and distantly the gunshots began.

Elsie's hands tapped against the steering wheel and she kept reaching up with one hand to wipe at her eyes.

In the backseat, King's head pressed against Clarke's headrest. She spoke quietly. "Is she okay?" King asked.

"You know," Elsie said, "I can fucking hear you."

"Are you okay?" Clarke said.

Elsie said, "That's a stupid goddamn question."

"I'm glad you're here," Clarke said. "I want you to be all right."

The Charger kept drifting toward the side of the road and running over the castellated rumble strip at the shoulder so that the wheels juddered up and down. "I want to ask something," Elsie said. "Back there in the trailer. What was that salt in the bathtub?"

"A ghost," King said, "maybe."

Elsie said, "A ghost?"

"No kidding," King said.

"No such thing," Clarke said.

"Whose ghost is it?"

"It's bullshit," Clarke said. "I haven't thought about it."

"Ghosts don't belong to people," King said. "They belong to themselves."

They were quiet for a while. Weakness poured between them as among parts of an hourglass. Elsie pulled herself together as King began to fall apart. "We left Dad behind," King said. "What's going to happen to us?" She held to the back of Clarke's seat. Between the front seats she could see Clarke's hand on top of Elsie's, their fingers woven together. Elsie had small bitten nails. Clarke rubbed his thumb over the knuckle of her pinkie. "Did you hear me?" King said. "What's going to happen to us now?"

"I heard you," Clarke said.

"What's going to happen? What do we do?"

"He said he was going to go to Bellevue," Elsie said. She

drove slowly enough that faster cars hummed past. Her free foot tapped hollowly against the floor mat.

"I want to go," King said. "I want to meet Dad there." Her hands pinched the back of the headrest.

"Did you see all the police?" Elsie asked.

"There were so many of them," Clarke said.

"You don't think he's coming?" King said. "I do. I do think he's coming. Don't you?" Her voice was smaller than her body. "I don't know what to do."

"You don't have to do anything," said Clarke.

"That's right," Elsie said. "We'll take care of you."

"I don't think so," said King

"If you'll let us," Elsie said, "we'll be like your mom and dad."

They drove, and clouds massed until the sky was almost as dark as night. The car was warm. King stretched out prone on the backseat, one arm dangling over the edge. She let her eyes close. Clarke and Elsie glanced back at her as lights winked on and marked the houses among the fields. The road hummed beneath them and the car hiccupped over the seams in the concrete. Headlights washed through the windshield, over the three of them, and on down the road in the direction of what they had left behind. Sleep closed around King like a great soft mouth and her dreams licked at her with long tongues. Soft reddish flesh squeezed white. The zebra-striped shadows of trees stretching out over a yellow field. Her hand engulfed by her mother's. The hand's dense warmth. A cup inside a cup and something stirring within. Something flitting and crawling like an itch inside her closed palm. She turned and looked at her mother's arms and saw that she wore a blue sweatshirt and a red scarf and inside the cuffs of the sweatshirt wasps hung on the threads with thin black legs. She shuddered but did not let go of her mother's hand. She looked at her mother's soft face, at the widening of her mouth, the thick lip skin stretching taut until her jaw seemed to unhinge and widen further as if, if King was to watch her long enough, she would turn inside out.

King woke to a parked car. Her eyes were closed beneath an unsettling stillness. A wet sound. A quiet slapping. A lip unsticking from skin. A heavy breath. She opened her eyes. In the passenger seat, Elsie's breasts were smooth and her hands were pressed against the ceiling. Her dark hair waved around her face in tangles so that King caught glimpses through brief opening and closing apertures, glimpses of shoulder bone, and navel, and the heaving void of her brother beneath Elsie. Elsie's eyes were closed, and her mouth open, and her tongue pressed against her teeth. King could hear her breathing, or them breathing, like something being consumed, and she fell back against the cushion and kicked out at the seats and screamed and screamed.

"Oh, my God, King," Clarke said. "I'm sorry."

"I don't want to go with you," King said. "I want to go with Dad."

"What for?"

"Take me to Bellevue."

"He's not coming," said Clarke.

"He is, too."

"He's dangerous," Clarke said. "I think he's going to get you hurt."

"I don't care," King said. "I want to find him."

"I'm sorry, King," Clarke said.

"What's wrong with you?"

"Nothing's wrong with me."

"Something," King said. "I could see it."

"It's normal, King."

"I could see it."

"See what?" said Clarke.

"Something buzzing inside you. I've never seen you like that before."

"It's just sex, King."

"No, it isn't. I saw something inside you."

"What is it you think you saw?"

"There's something gone wrong."

On North 2nd Street in Malta, Illinois, Dominick let the gun continue firing until the magazine emptied, then he ran. The duffel on his back thumped against his spine. He was off the road in two steps, across a front lawn in three more. He hopped a low white fence and sprinted across backyards, past a yellow plastic children's pool, a toy car, a trampoline. He hurtled some chain-link and ducked beneath a pear tree and raced through a brick-lined bed of ivy circling a white-painted Madonna. Something far behind him exploded and a great thrust of air pushed at his back. An empty doghouse sat in the most direct path, and he jumped it. He lost count of the number of yards, each one increasing the distance between them and him. He didn't think they had fired a single shot. Had they? A few fence lines ahead, a bone-dry irrigation ditch ran between two fields studded with dried cornstalks. The light struck harshly against the sharp lines of his face. He'd be too easy to see out there. Two blocks over lay a road that continued south. The road ran past an occasional house or farm. He looked behind him at the run of yards. No one in sight. When he turned back toward the field, he caught some dark movement in the irrigation ditch. A trickle of water? A snake? Then a dark cloud pushed in front of the low sun, and darkness gathered along the bottom of the ditch, and a pale fog began to gather against the ground and catch at the edges of things. He ran from the shelter of Malta, Illinois. The clouds descended and pooled in the irrigation ditch and spread across the fields and the darkness inside the split earth reached out toward him. He stumbled inside, and his hand scrabbled among the white bottom rocks, and the wet air licked his face. He pitched himself forward into dark heedless arms.

THE GROUND RUSHED toward the glass that curved in front of Charlie Basin's face. There was a high-pitched whine. The helicopter pilot did not spare him a glance. Charlie clutched the edges of his seat and the seatbelt burrowed into his shoulder. Ahead of them a thin line of trees marked the transition from one field to the next. The ground was a dark blur. This wasn't how he wanted his life to end. He wanted to work things out with Charlene, to talk to his wife, to Oswell. He wanted to ask his daughter if she could see forgiveness anywhere ahead. The helicopter shot forward and lowered toward the ground as if it was going to land like a small plane. A run-on landing. When the skids touched ground they threw up dark plumes of earth. They skittered and came to a teetering halt. Charlie and the pilot threw open the doors, and they stumbled out into the sweet air, and Charlie bent forward on his knees and emptied his stomach.

DOMINICK EMERGED FROM the irrigation ditch beside a farm that sat tight against the road heading south. A red grain truck idled beside a nest of silos. The fog lapped at its wheels. He swung himself up by the wing mirror, lifted the cold handle of the door, and swung into the passenger seat. The man behind the wheel wore blue jeans and a short-sleeved button-down with the name *Elvis* embroidered over the left breast pocket. His lower lip bulged. He turned toward Dominick. "Goddamn," he said, "you surprised me some bit." He eyed the rifle over Dominick's shoulder and the green duffel that he dropped at his feet.

"Drive," Dominick said.

"All right," the driver said. He shifted the truck into gear and pulled onto the road. "Where you want me to go?"

"What's south of here?" Dominick asked.

"Shabbona ain't much over five miles."

"Pick up the pace some."

"That an M1A?" The driver tilted his head toward the rifle.

"That's right," Dominick said.

"Where you headed?"

"You have children, Elvis?"

"One fully grown. My name ain't Elvis. This one is my brother's shirt. He don't need it. He's locked up in Statesville."

"What'll I call you, then?" Dominick said.

"My name's Allen Straub. You aren't gonna hurt me, are you?"

"What's in Shabbona, Allen?"

"What's there? Shit, we're a pretty small town. Got a bank. A florist. A gun shop. A supermarket. There's the country club. Shabbona State Park."

"This park pretty big?" Dominick asked.

"Damned big, I'd say."

The clouds cleared and the moon slowly rose as Elsie and Clarke and King drove the three hours to Bellevue, Iowa. Clarke drummed his fingers against the dashboard. Out here, on their own, he felt scared and no longer angry. Goose bumps kept rising on his arms. He didn't know where to take these two, he didn't even know how to pretend he did. His father probably wouldn't make it to Bellevue, anyway. How could he? But if he did, his father wouldn't hesitate. He'd know what to do. Clarke wanted that kind of certainty. He wanted to be able to see his next step as though it was drawn in a thin red line on an old map.

They crossed the Mississippi River on a steel-and-concrete bridge. The river snaked beneath them, its turgid brown-green water curving by pylons. They turned north and drove along the west bank for mile after mile. Blackbirds sat among tufted cattails. Red-tipped branches leaned over the water.

"You ever seen a river this big, Clarke?" King asked.

"Not even close."

"You've seen it before, right, Elsie?" King asked.

"Nope," she said. "I've never been out this way. I've never been anywhere."

Just outside Bellevue, they turned onto a dirt road and drove to the far side of a slight hill and parked the Charger among cast-off burn bins and old car tires. They got out of the car and walked into town. Clarke held tightly to King's hand and King did not pull away.

Before dark settled over Shabbona State Park, two men in green waders caught a glimpse of a giant man hurrying through ascetic trees. They looked up from their fishing poles for a moment. "Nice rifle," one muttered.

From one of the lake's artificially sanded beaches, a boy of eight caught a dark glimpse of Dominick on a fir-covered hill. In the middle of a raspberry bramble, a pair of spotted hounds snuffled past him, their noses against the ground. A group of pastel-sweatered women on a pontoon boat stared when he passed out of one patch of wood and moved through a field. At a concession stand, Dominick stood in line for hot dogs and French fries wrapped in greased paper and half-a-dozen hunters and fishermen took no note of him. In a virgin wood, he pressed through scrub brush and passed a lone turkey hunter in an orange vest traveling in the opposite direction who raised his hand and mouthed, "Good luck." The orange sun fell, and Dominick lay on the ground beneath a willow tree. He was tired. The earth was soft with decay.

In Bellevue, Iowa, the moon sat low against the horizon. On foot, Clarke led Elsie and King past a sign for a saloon, a line of shined-chrome motorcycles, Eagle's Rest Antiques, a True Value hardware store. At the riverfront park, they sat on wooden benches and stared at the moving river and watched the muskies jump. Dark backs and white bellies, hard landings splashing the water into hundreds of separate drops, each with its own narrow parabolic trajectory.

They waited for their father. Their heads lifted at every approaching footstep. King sniffed. She looked around. "Why does it smell like chocolate?" she asked.

Clarke and Elsie looked at each other. They sniffed. They held hands. It did smell like chocolate. "There," Elsie pointed down. "The flower beds are mulched with cocoa shells. Reminds me of my grandma."

"Why doesn't everybody do that?" King asked.

Elsie pulled her coat around her. "It's getting cold."

"Dad isn't here tonight," Clarke said. "We'll have to sleep somewhere."

"Where?" King asked.

The moon shone bright over the Mississippi. Its light came in low and white and caught at the edges of things and the barren riverside trees cast thin leggy shadows that blurred with the shadows of benches or rounded bushes or boulders and formed a new shape behind them that looked to King like a great dark centipede.

With the money his father had given him, Clarke bought corn chips and small chocolate-covered donuts and a half-gallon of milk. They walked back to the car in the dark. Elsie hung her head and pushed her hands into her pockets and shivered.

"There're sleeping bags in the car," Clarke said and Elsie

looked up at him from under her eyebrows.

They walked without speaking, their feet hitting the pavement with the noise of biding time. The rusted Charger looked appropriate among the long brown grass and the rusting metal cans and the cracked rubber of old tires. They wrapped themselves in the mummy bags and ate donuts and chips until their stomachs protested. The dark settled heavily on them, cold and close, as stifling as the growing sense that each one of them must have done something wrong. No one said anything. None of them had slept for a very long time.

When King's eyes closed, Clarke reached out for Elsie's shoulder. He said, "I'm sorry."

He said, "What did you think it'd be like?"

He said, "I had to leave him."

She reached out and touched him back. "I'm sorry, too," she said.

Then they all slept.

In the middle of the night, Clarke woke to their soft even breathing. His heart pounded. Stars pinched the black sky. Though the air was cold, his body was covered in sweat. He opened the car door and the cold wet air slipped over his skin like an iced tongue. He stepped out and closed the door softly. The town of Bellevue was invisible but surrounded by a soft hill of light. He set about gathering wood and kindling and threw what he gathered into a pile. He squatted down and cupped his hand and held a lit match to some cotton batting. Light welled as if out of the wood itself. A little fire. He held his hands out before it.

◄— A plastic grocery sack had caught on the knuckled branch of a fallen elm. All night, while Dominick slept, it fluttered hollowly, catching a breath of wind and bellowing full, then collapsing again like a thin pale lung. He had slept on the ground before, on sand and dirt and field, beside Benny Ward and DeJesus and Floyd, while the air cooled fast and they pressed together, any self-consciousness having long abandoned them so that their sense of themselves as individuals with sharp edges grew confused and they stayed as warm as they could. He woke before first light, shivering cold, and jumped up into the dark. He threw his bag over his shoulders and walked to stay warm. On a dirt trail, he passed a long-haired couple hiking with trekking poles and tall brightly colored packs. They stopped as he approached and offered him an avocado. He cut the avocado in half with his knife and scooped out its flesh with his teeth. His legs pinioned the hills beneath him and he rose and fell over grassy knobs of earth. In one moment he felt the immensity of himself, the way he rushed outward along his edges like burning light. But in the next moment the thorned brush rose up from the ground and obscured any possible view, the triangular trees leaned over the dark trail, and low branches pushed against him like the great pressing weight of his anonymity. He moved out of the brush on the south end of Shabbona State Park. A gray-green pickup sat on the side of a road. The plates were out of Iowa. Two men tossed a pair of turkeys into the truck bed. He approached them with a broad smile.

CHARLIE BASIN WALKED through the trailer home. He looked through the torn screen on the rear door. He pushed the coffee table aside with his foot. The beds wore the impressions of the bodies they'd held. Windows were open. The whole place smelled of unwashed skin. In the bathroom sink, he found a used bar of soap, a muddy thumbprint on the wall. On the vinyl floor beneath the sink, salt spilled into words.

Map, he read, *Finger, Bone.*

Charlie shook his head. He sat on the couch. When his kids were still in high school, he'd taken them to a place like this, a dumpy top half of a duplex a block off Rehoboth Beach. Oswell's tall white frame looked out of place in the sun. They got sand in their shoes. He had to drag Charlene out for French fries, banana splits, lemonade. She wanted to stay in the duplex listening to music on her headphones or turning on the TV and lounging on the dirt-colored couch. Mostly he let her. What did it matter? Maybe what people needed most was headroom, a place left open that they could expand into. At night, when Charlie lay in bed, half asleep, there was a slight electrical hum he couldn't source. Drunks gently cursed each other in the streets. The gurgle of Oswell's breath in the bedroom next to his. A creak inside the wall. A mantel clock that stuttered. Then the couch squeaked as Charlene rose off it. Her feet sounded softly. Her shoes were off. The slight sucking knock of the front door sticking in its frame. A pressure shift, a moist breath in the dry conditioned air. He listened to her leave. Where was she going? Did anyone care? Did a secret ever hide anything that mattered? Weren't important things always hidden in plain sight? Charlie reached over and turned the bedside lamp off. Wasn't it a mark of childhood to believe that something exciting, something undreamed of, could be found by sneaking outside?

In the morning, Oswell cooked sausage in a cheap aluminum pan on the electric range. The fluorescent overhead hummed. "She snuck out last night, Dad," Oswell said.

"Charlene?"

"She was gone a long time." Oswell pushed the sausages in the pan with a wooden spoon.

"How did you know?" Charlie asked.

"She woke me when she came in. She said she'd gone to meet somebody. A boy, I think."

"That right?" Charlie said.

"She was drinking, too. She smelled."

The bed creaked as Charlene rose. She came out of her bedroom in bare feet. She wore the jeans and brown sweater that she'd worn the day before. One of her hands was smudged with dirt.

Was Charlie supposed to come down hard? Was he meant to say something weighty? Was he meant to cut to the center of things? When she sat at the table, Charlie said, "You snuck out last night?"

"No, I didn't." Her face looked as innocent as a mirror.

Charlie put his hands against the edge of the table. "I'm not good at this," he said. "Am I supposed to say, 'Yes, you did'?"

"What?" Charlene said. "You're not good at what?"

"I don't know." Charlie shook his head. "Jesus, Charlene, I don't want to talk about this any more than you do."

"Are you okay, Dad?"

"Of course I'm okay," he said. "I'm pretty sure I'm okay."

"You don't seem okay."

"I don't?"

"Not really," Charlene said.

In the trailer in Malta, Illinois, Charlie stood. The floor shifted slightly beneath him. He rubbed his chin, ran one hand over his face and through his hair. He picked up the phone. He twirled the cord around one finger. He hit redial. The phone chirped and peeped and then someone picked up on the other end of the line. Charlie heard the scratch of rough skin across the receiver, a cleared throat, an indrawn breath, a voice.

"This is Jon Howland."

WHEN DOMINICK HAD finally come back to Pennsylvania for good, he felt like a distant observer. Which side of the line was he on, friendly or enemy? It didn't really feel like either. Driving home, in his uniform, he took his time. What was the rush, anyway? When he neared the A-frame on Flint Valley Road, he stopped the car in the middle of the street. Nobody was coming in either direction. The sun felt good on his hands on the steering wheel. He could smell heat and asphalt. He sat like that for five minutes. Nobody came by. When he'd made up his mind, he pushed the gas hard and drove fast to within a half-mile of the cabin. There he pulled to the side of the road, parked beside the black raspberry brambles, got out of the car, slipped into the woods. He knew he wanted to see them, his family. He wasn't sure he wanted them to see him. He took his time in the woods, listening to the knocking of woodpeckers. The trees were mostly oaks and white pines and hemlocks. He felt their barks with his palms. It felt strange being alone. He stopped among beds of drying pine needles and sunlight filtered through the lacework of leaves. He breathed in. He'd hunted this land all his life, and he knew exactly where he was going. He could feel the cabin up in front of him beating like the heart of the wilderness. He moved in.

Before he could see his family, he could hear them. The high pitch of his children. How much had he changed? Would they recognize him? The ground ahead lightened where the trees broke and the land turned to field. Then he heard Sarah's voice. Calm. Instructive. Sweet. He couldn't quite make out the words. He wanted to see them, just to watch. What did his family do when he wasn't there? He slunk toward the tree line and looked out. He let his eyes adjust. The corn was knee-high in the fields. On the lawn near the cabin was a table piled with cabbage. There was Clarke beside the table. How old was he now? Seven? He looked so strong, holding a cabbage in each hand. There was Sarah. His wife's thin arms moved back and forth, shredding cabbage on a wooden mandoline. At the far end of the table, his daughter, King. She had grown so much, her hair dark and unruly and curled around her neck. She poured cabbage and salt into a large bowl and put her hands in and kneaded. She handed Clarke the bowl, and he dumped the mixture into an earthen crock.

They sang children's songs, off key but beautiful. "My Bonnie Lies over the Ocean." "Little Po Beep." "Little Boy Blue." They worked so well together. The sun shone straight down on them so that their skin was bright. Dominick shaded his eyes.

EARLY THAT MORNING, on the path back to his kids—through state parkland and then hunkered in the extended cab of a pickup—it had seemed to Dominick that he was following a darkness that receded before him. His body felt smooth-skinned and calm and strong and he didn't worry once about his ability to find them. They would be found for him. Squeezed in the backseat, he woke from cramped tempestuous dreams and felt relief that the war no longer owned him. The pickup bumped along and the darkness passed away. The sun balanced like a ball on the flat horizon. Dominick watched and waited until they hit Bellevue, then he called out, "You mind pulling over here?"

"Sure thing," the driver said. A short man in hunter's camo with a pomaded curl over his forehead, he pulled the wheel and braked and the pickup came to a stop with one wheel on top of the curb.

"Good place to eat just there," the other man said and pointed across the street toward Richman's Café, "if you're interested." A broad scar split one of his eyebrows.

When King woke, she heard the crackle and spit of wood smoke. The car windows were fogged on the inside. She reached into the front seat and shook Elsie awake. Together they wiped the fog off the windows to look out. Elsie pointed with a bitten fingernail at Clarke, who squatted on his haunches before a small fire. The growing flames reached out and covered half of him with flickering light.

In the morning, the three of them walked into town, looking for breakfast. The river frothed at the mouth. Shivering, they walked fast along the road; their hearts quickened and the sun began to warm the outside of their coats. The water caught the light and held it close. The air smelled good, like frying fat, and Clarke's fear was overcome by a deep satisfaction for no better reason than that they were all walking together, all in the same direction, hungry and sharp-eyed and young. They all started to feel better, sure that after eggs sunny side up and maple syrup and pancakes and bacon, they would be delivered. One of them would know what to do.

A bell rang as they entered a bland-looking diner. Clarke stood next to King. Behind them, Elsie reached out and pinched the back of Clarke's arm. A meaty bearded man in a short white apron squeezed around them. "Pretty full up," he said. He spoke out of the side of his mouth as if he had something clenched between his teeth. Clarke surveyed the small full space.

In Richman's Café, Dominick ordered what his daughter would have ordered: blueberry pancakes and bacon. The waitress brought a glass of water, and he felt the cold move down his esophagus and spread like oil through his stomach. Before his breakfast arrived, his kids stood blinking just inside the entrance as their eyes adjusted.

"Dad?" King said.

Dominick rose and swept them up in his great arms and felt how solid they were, how real and how good. He buried his face against his son's shoulder and his son did not push away.

"You're okay?" Clarke said. "You're okay."

"I'm okay," Dominick said.

When they left the diner, the huge blue sky spread over Bellevue like an umbrella. Elsie and King walked back to wait in the gully with Elsie's Charger. That left Dominick and Clarke beside a low-slung medical building faced with brick.

Dominick pointed at a blue Honda in a half-full parking lot. Maybe his father was bad. Clarke didn't know. Right now, he didn't care. What he knew was that there was bad and then there was worse.

"That blue one?" Clarke asked.

"I'll teach you how," Dominick said. One of his huge hands caught his son's shoulder. "You've got to commit to this, Clarke. I'm going to need your help." He slung his bag against Clarke's chest. "Get out the drill and the screwdriver and the slim-jim, okay? You want to do this?"

"Yeah."

Dominick slipped the slim-jim between the window and the door, popped the lock, and opened the door. "You see how I did that?" he said.

"Not really," Clarke said. "What'd you do?"

Dominick glanced around once, not furtively but like a man surveying his property's imperfections. Then he locked the Honda door and pushed it shut. He handed Clarke the slim-jim. "Here you go," he said. "You try."

In the blue Honda, they stopped to pick up Elsie and King. Dominick asked Elsie to drive and they traveled west out of Bellevue. In the passenger seat, Dominick split a green apple with his Wharncliffe knife. Clarke and King sat close to one another on the rear seat. Elsie's dark hair curled behind her ear. Dominick passed out pieces of apple, then reached out and touched Elsie's shoulder. He watched the slow movement of his hand. The thickened knuckles and yellow calluses. Elsie's shoulder felt soft, her clavicle belonged to a bird. When he spoke, he was quiet. He said, "I can't say how much I appreciate you helping my kids."

She looked at him quickly and returned her eyes to the road. Her eyes were large and wet. Her teeth clenched and her round-ed lips bunched together. Dominick nodded. He understood what his son saw in her.

"You're all right with me coming with you?" Elsie asked.

"I am."

"That's good," she said.

"Maybe it's good, maybe not," Dominick said. He point-ed at his children. "They're the only things that make my life decent."

"HAVE YOU TALKED to her?" Charlie Basin asked. He sat on the side of a small road near a telephone pole, fields lying out in all directions. Buzzards circled around a barren patch of ground. Through the phone, he could hear the clip of Rosamund's shoes on the kitchen tile, a dish clinking into the sink.

"It's Oswell's birthday next week. We're having a party. She's coming. Charlene's coming."

"What do you mean she's coming?"

"She got out of the hospital yesterday."

"That's it? It's over? Just like that?"

"I don't think it means she's entirely okay, Charlie," Rosamund said. "It means she's better. She's still seeing a therapist as an outpatient."

"But she won't pull something like this again?"

She took a deep breath. "We'll miss you at the party. Are you all right?"

"It's a mess here, Ros," Charlie said. "I've got the bureau and the cops canvassing everywhere." He thought of the smell of home-baked bread, and the depth of the leather chair that was his to read in, and the small arts-and-crafts table where he'd left *Netherland* opened and half finished, and the flagstone patio he'd built with the help of his children, and the wet bar with its shining glass decanters of scotch. "I have no idea where they are."

"He got away?" Rosamund asked. "On foot?"

"Uh-huh. Let's not talk about it."

"Okay," Rosamund said. "What should we talk about?"

"I don't know. Maine. A summer house. Did I tell you I saw a fox while I was up there?"

"I miss you, Charlie. The house feels hollow without you here."

IN THE NIGHT, while Elsie drove, King sat in the passenger seat. Dominick and Clarke felt cramped in the back.

"Clarke," Dominick said, "we have to talk to each other."

"No, we don't."

"How else are we going to get through this?"

"We're not going to get through this," Clarke said. "Don't you know that?"

"Sure, we will."

"You don't know what will happen," Clarke said. "You always pretend like you do."

"That's true, I guess," Dominick said. "I want us all to stay together."

The road ahead played with conflicting lights and the night moved around them like a river. The dash glowed a spectral blue. The car smelled like athletic socks.

"So you're worried about where we're going to go next?" Dominick asked.

"There's nowhere," said Clarke.

"Sure there is. There's a whole world."

the people of the broken neck

For days they drove. The roads were like tarred veins. They stopped at picnic areas and rest stops and ate green apples, cucumbers, canned pork and beans. They drove across the young drift plains in Iowa, whose constancy suggested that the world might be a willful reiteration of a few small ideas. In the badlands of Nebraska, the car disappeared among striped rocks etched into great pinnacles and buttes and spires. They got out of the car and sat on ancient stones. They marveled and picked up pamphlets that told them about thirty-seven-million-year-old Oligocene fossil beds that held the evolutionary stories of horses and rhinoceroses. They looked out at a land that was vast and seemed dead. They drove on through South Dakota and Wyoming and Montana and detoured through Yellowstone and walked among the remains of stone trees. Broken stubs of immense trunks exposed hardened growth rings. Concentrically fractured rings of rock had eroded into pieces that could be carried away inside coat pockets. White-topped mountains rose around them in a semicircle. Mountains of so grand a scale that each could have held dozens of their Pennsylvanian mountains inside. They drove and they stopped and a rhythm established itself and, in this, they felt a kind of safety, a sense of their human concord. They stood looking out at the contorted lodgepole pines. They put their hands to the rear of their hips and stretched their backs. They brushed their teeth and spat milk on the ground. They traded places in the car with polite words. They pushed the accelerator through the slow climbs up mountain passes and then raced down steep inclines so fast that the landscape around them blurred into something as loose and unfixed as failing wallpaper.

King sometimes got excited. She asked a lot of questions. She said, "Where do we go from here?"

Her father answered her: "As far as we can."

They slept in the car beside mammoth brick buildings. Smoke rose from industrial chimneys whose tips burned with fire. An alleyway beside them was filled with stacked pallets and broken cement. The air was ripe with saltpeter.

They slept in a field beside a lake. The flat water rainbowed with petroleum. Fish afloat with pale open eyes.

They slept on cold stone. They wrapped themselves in their mummy bags. They padded blankets beneath them but still felt the hard mouth of the world siphoning heat.

In the Rockies they turned south. Though it was near noon, darkness beset the car in a gust of wind. Fingernail-sized hail bounced off the windshield. Air swept from the south and rocked them back and forth and pilloried the clouds into a great dark human shape whose head hung loosely on a thin insubstantial rope. Something struck the roof and left an indentation of great teeth. The car stumbled and moved again. They stared forward, loath to relinquish control. The road switchbacked upward among ponderosa pines and a latticework of branches and pine needles shook around them. The brakes bit hard and the car began to slow and the night glowed red. An uprooted tree had fallen across the road. Great strips of bark hung like razored skin. Mammoth limbs had snapped beneath the tree's own weight. To one side of the road, the roots wove together into a filthy nest.

"That's it," Dominick said. "We've got to turn around." The car shuddered to a halt.

They turned back north. In the rearview mirror, the figure in the dark clouds opened its arms. The hail became a light rain and the light rain turned to a warm breeze and the puddles at the sides of the road shrank and dried up and turned to a run of wildflowers. Ahead, the clouds opened up and the sun struck the wet road until it shone bright and white and obliterating.

"This can't go on," Clarke said.

"Why not?" asked Dominick.

"There has to be a destination."

"What for?"

"We'll run out of money," Clarke said. "Out of gas."

"So what?" Dominick said.

"What'll we do then?"

"Walk."

"Walk where?" Clarke said.

"You're not going to let go of this, are you?" said Dominick.

"How can I let go?"

"You're going to have to learn," Dominick said. "But right now I'll tell you where we're going."

"Okay."

"I've got an old friend."

"What kind of old friend?"

"Ex-Army friend," Dominick said.

"Where's he at?" said Clarke.

"Outside a town called Bellingham. In Washington state."

"That's where we're going?"

"That's where we're going," Dominick said. "He'll set us straight. He'll help us."

The four travelers took what time they were offered. They got out of the car to stare at rock formations that looked like human faces. They picked butterfly weed and angel's trumpet and wild petunia and vased them in soda bottles. They stopped at convenience stores and bought one another donuts or jellied fruits. Clarke and Elsie held hands and interlaced their fingers. They stopped at night, when all human luster had been extinguished, and they lay on the hood of the car and looked up at all the stars combining into great swathes of light. They touched one another. They drove until their muscles cramped and one of them groaned, and they got out with the sun burning overhead, and they ran, tight-limbed and awkward, until their bodies unclenched and their breathing came hard and raw. They leaned forward and braced their hands on their knees, their skins loose and slick with sweat. They stood amid crescents of thorned brambles and pointed things out to one another. Look there, a lazy creek bottomed with translucent pebbles. Or over there, a mounting scuttle of blue hills. Clarke and Elsie stood close enough to feel each other's heat. Dominick dropped to his knees. King turned her face toward the cloudless sky. They gathered round. They smiled at one another and it was not in consolation.

In Idaho, they peed off the sides of unnamed roads. Four

dark silhouettes. The sky behind them covered in a pale rosacea. When Elsie squatted, she said, "Turn your heads." Birds twittered unseen among the thorny scrub brush. The heads of the four shadows turned, and some bird of prey whirled and screamed against the sun, and urine ran in rivulets across dry earth. The bird's high raw bark was the sound of something split open for good.

It was night when they passed from Idaho's panhandle into eastern Washington state. The earth was a light dusty brown. Dominick stopped at a roadside recycling bin and pulled a black bag filled with glass out of the bin and pushed it into the car's trunk. They slept in the car until morning and then drove out along a small road, past sweet-clover pastures and white fences in great rectangles around quarter horses. He pulled over when they hadn't seen a farm in miles and bumped the Honda slowly through a brown field. The dead seeded grass pressed into ruts. The car stopped amid fluttering aspens. Dominick pulled duffel bags from the trunk. He spread a blanket on the ground and laid four handguns out in a line. Beretta M9. Glock G22. Ruger SP101. Smith & Wesson .357. He hefted the black trash bag, walked thirty paces, and began setting bottles against the ground and atop a stump. Light prismed though brown and green and clear glass.

Clarke bounced on his toes. Elsie clapped her hands. "This is going to be fun," she said.

Dominick picked the Beretta off the blanket. "The purpose of the handgun is to kill people. Pick one up." Each of them did. "You ever fire a gun before?"

"Not really," said Elsie.

"King can teach you."

The children squared their shoulders and shot at bottles. After each cracking shot, there was a dead eerie silence in which
they understood that they hadn't known they had been hear-
ing cricket chirps and goldfinch whistles until the sounds were
absent. Standing beside Elsie, King plugged her ears with
her index fingers. Elsie shrugged her shoulders and took aim.
Dominick stood just behind Clarke, watching. Making small
corrections. His boy's eyes ovaled into the shape of eggs. Bottles
exploded in a line as though connected by a fuse. Glass arced
into the sunlit air. Hot. Burning like a thousand tiny suns.

WHEN CHARLIE BASIN got home, the party was in full swing. He could feel the music from the street. Something with bass that he didn't like at all. Through the front bay window, he could see his son. In his right hand, Oswell held an orange martini. His Adam's apple was prominent. He wore a blue-and-red cone-shaped birthday hat, which had likely been Rosamund's idea. Oswell was a good sport. He was talking to old friends, boys from the neighborhood whom Charlie remembered as thin and covered in dirt but who, look here, had grown paunches and wide faces. Between them, they had lost an awful lot of hair, but they looked to Charlie, as they would always look, like children. In front of this crowd, Oswell moved his hands a lot, as though he was drawing pictures. Where was Oz's sister? Where was Charlene?

Charlie stood on the lawn holding a birthday present under his arm. It was dusk. A line of orange hovered over the horizon. Bats flitted against the dark blue sky. The present was wrapped in yellow paper and tied with a blue ribbon. He set it on the ground. He toed off his shoes, sat down in the grass, and pulled off his socks. Though he felt a little self-conscious, he didn't get up for a minute. He could hear all the sound from inside. The tinkle of glasses coming together. The high-pitched moments of recognition, of old friendships momentarily rekindled. The giddy peculiar laughter.

He felt comfortable outside, watching through the window. He didn't belong in there, did he? If they knew he was out on the lawn, they would want him to come in. At least Rosamund and Oswell would. Maybe Charlene was the honest one. Wasn't it all just a matter of form? Charlie understood that they couldn't let him sit outside. What would they want in their heart of hearts? To speak with him or to be left alone?

He went in and they were all over him. A neighbor whose name he didn't remember (Marilyn? Meredith? Mary?) put an orange martini in his hand. A few old FBI men slapped their hands down hard on his shoulders as though even the briefest of male touch had to hold the possibility of violence. Rosamund put her lips to his cheek and pulled him by the hand to see Oswell. Beside Oswell stood Charlene. Had she been there all along? Had he failed to notice her? Her face looked sharply defined by cheekbones and jawbones. She had lost weight. Her wrists were wrapped with flesh-colored medical tape. When she saw her father, she looked down, letting her hair mask her face.

"Oz," Charlie said. Oswell's friends nodded and smiled and faded back. Charlene turned and pushed past a purple blazer, past a yellow-and-orange dress, past the cabriole legs of the highboy, into the candlelight of the kitchen.

Oswell pointed at Charlie's feet. "You're not wearing any shoes," he said. His cheeks were flushed with too much to drink. He lurched forward. He'd always been such a good kid, a lightweight when it came to alcohol or any other kind of trouble. Oswell lifted the present from Charlie's arms and dropped it on the blue velvet couch, then he turned back toward his father with his long arms outstretched. Charlie stepped up into them. How long had it been? How long had he been shorter than his tall stooped son? Oswell held Charlie's shoulders fiercely. "I didn't know if you were going to make it, Dad," Oswell said, his mouth an inch from Charlie's ear. "Charlene needs you. I do, too. I'm really glad you could come."

"Wouldn't miss it," Charlie said.

Oswell put his mouth even closer to Charlie's ear. "I'm a little drunk," he said.

Charlie refilled his martini glass, then walked toward the kitchen on tiptoes. The fibers of the rug spread around his feet. He stepped on dropped bits of prosciutto, goat cheese, melon balls. Something wet and yellow had spilled on the kitchen tile. Charlene stood by the sink with her back to him, washing her hands. The soap smelled of his wife, of lavender and of thyme. Charlene's hair, dark at the sides of her neck, curled like a shepherd's crook. In the candlelight, she faded in and out of focus. "Charlene?" Charlie said.

"What?" she answered. Someone walked into the kitchen and out again. The flames on the candles bent over and then righted themselves.

For a moment, Charlie could see the pulse of a muscle in Charlene's jaw. "You want to talk to me about the hospital?" he said.

"No. I don't feel like talking at all."

"This isn't the way I wanted us to be." He leaned back and rested on his hands against the cold tiled countertop. "I don't want to talk, either, Charlene."

"What?" she said. "What isn't the way you wanted us to be?"

"Angry. I don't want us to be angry."

"Mom didn't tell me you were coming home," Charlene said.

"Are you doing okay?"

"No," she said, "I'm not okay. Nothing is okay."

"You still seeing the same therapist?"

"I'm still seeing her."

"That's good," Charlie said. "You still talking about me?"

"She thinks maybe I learned to be distant from you."

He took a deep breath, held it, then released. "You're not distant," he said.

"Last visit," Charlene said, "she told me I was acting like a child."

"Yeah? So how'd you like that?"

"I'm thinking about seeing a new therapist." She turned around from the sink and faced him. The edges of her mouth had been slightly downturned since she'd been an infant. Near her hairline was a slight indent from the obstetrician's forceps. Her thin eyebrows lifted and her eyes widened and her brow curled just as it always had, asking some question that a father ought to have been able to answer.

"Hey," Charlie said, "I've been meaning to tell you that somebody hit me in the head with a tire iron."

"Mom told me," Charlene said. "Who was it? Who hit you?"

"Just a girl. I woke up in the hospital, in a blue gown. Twenty stitches."

"Why'd she hit you?"

"She was with a fifteen-year-old boy whose father is the man I'm looking for. I guess she was scared."

"You got knocked out by a *teenage* girl?"

"That's right."

"You told people at the office?" Charlene said. "You're going to take a lot of shit for that."

"Haven't told them," Charlie said. "You know what I felt in the hospital, when I woke?"

"No."

"I felt pissed."

DOMINICK WAS BEGINNING to think that they might live a life like this. Raw and ranging. Sleeping in the open. Not minding. Seeing such great sights as this country had to offer. So when they neared the Columbia River and the Grand Coulee Dam and the chorus from the seats was that opportunity should be seized, Dominick saw no harm in stopping. Didn't such sights serve as a key to the landmarks inside them? Some dark hand guided them, didn't it? Was this not a wild country?

They joined a tour that got them inside the gates and they stood at the bottom of the dam. The breadth of the river made them hold their breath. Whitewater at the base. Hundreds of feet of concrete rising above them. A cold gray wall they couldn't see beyond. King leaned against it with both hands. "You feel that?" she said. A low vibratory noise moved things around inside them. A sense of weight waiting behind the cold wall.

"I feel it," Dominick said. His hands were pressed to his trunk but he pushed his cheek against the concrete. Elsie and Clarke slipped off their shoes and toed the sand. King sank her shod feet in the cold water.

Clarke looked up. "It's so huge," he said.

"It's bigger," Dominick said, "than I imagined,"

"I never heard of it," Elsie said. "What's it for?" Steelhead rolled across the water's surface. "What's that?" Elsie said. "Did you see that?"

"What?"

"There's something in there."

"No, there's not," Clarke said.

"Yes, there is."

"I don't like it down here," King said. "Let's go up."

They walked to the top and arrived out of breath at a great lake. The Grand Coulee Dam was a mile long. A two-lane road ran along the crest. Members of their loose tour group moved about in small bunches. Dominick looked up at the closed-circuit cameras affixed to each light pole. The others followed his line of vision to the camera lenses above them. The wind blew hard in such open spaces. They huddled together. Their clothes flapped around them.

King said, "Nobody is watching us, right?"

"Somebody's watching," Clarke said.

"Who?"

"Somebody in a uniform," Clarke said.

"Are they going to come get us?" King asked.

"I don't think so," said Clarke. "Not yet."

"They can see us," Dominick said, "but they don't know who we are."

The kids moved to one side and looked down over the edge of the dam. A placid lake. Millions upon millions of gallons trying to flow in one direction. Hairline cracks. The pressure of the water bulked behind the concrete.

"Dad," King called. "Dad! Come see how calm it looks over the side."

After lunch, the Sawyers left the Grand Coulee Dam behind them. Inside the blue Honda, time did not seem to move; outside, scenery rolled past as though projected by a magic lantern. They passed a few earth-colored buildings in some nameless place. A half-dozen trailer homes scattered loosely around a crossroads. A gas station with a single blinking light and a pay phone where Dominick called Benny Ward.

They abandoned the Honda and turned onto the roads in a Volvo station wagon. The miles metered the hours of their lives. Sometimes they talked and at other times they were quiet. Sometimes they passed around dried apricots or peanuts or a bag of small plums and sometimes they wished they had something to occupy their hands. If they gazed out the window, the glass became nearly opaque with condensation or it became a beacon of reflected light too bright to gaze at without pain. Sometimes they pressed against the hard interior paneling and held their own limbs close. Sometimes they liked each other and sometimes they did not.

They gazed out on vast hollow landscapes and felt broad and uncontained. But then canyon walls rose around them or they tunneled through banks of earth toward harsh and distant lights. They spoke to each other gently. They touched each other's skin as though it was something holy. Sometimes the soft silence gave way to gentle sleep.

The moments that tip the balance in our favor, or against, are always small enough to go unnoticed. The Sawyers spent the night on the roadside and in the morning drove the remaining miles to Leavenworth, Washington. They found a quiet chrome-edged table in a nameless diner. Elsie slumped against Clarke. King pushed the salt shaker in loops. A waitress wearing a faded purple apron and a nametag that read GLENDA served them French toast and eggs and orange juice. The plates rattled in circles on the tabletop. Glenda had a light fuzz of hair on her upper lip and her face hung too loosely from its underlayment. She had dark beautiful hazel eyes. She brought King a donut. She said, "You remind me of my son's little girl."

"I do?" King asked. The waitress's eyes were the shape of her mother's.

"You sure do."

Dominick swallowed the rest of his glass of juice and looked at the waitress as though she was a knuckled rock or a driftwood root. He tipped his empty glass. He said, "Can I get a refill on this?"

"Sure, honey," Glenda said. She retreated to the kitchen.

They all listened to the mindless sound of chewing and the low hubbub of older men. When they finished eating, Clarke and Elsie went to wait in the Volvo. Dominick rose and walked toward the bathroom. Outside the large windows, the sky looked like an old dishrag. By the window to the kitchen, Dominick passed the dark-eyed waitress, now laden with plates of pancakes and omelets. Her head pointed down so that the skin of her neck folded up against her chin. When the bathroom door squealed shut, she dropped the plates on a table filled with farmers and headed toward King. She set her hands against her hips. She asked, "You headed over the mountains?"

"I think so," King said.

"There's a lot of snow up there this time of year."

"There is?" said King. The waitress put her hand on King's arm. Her fingers felt cool and soft.

"Sure is," the waitress said. "My son's little girl, we call her Brit, she loves the snow. You like the snow, too?"

"I do. I love the snow."

"What's your name?"

"My name is King."

"Isn't that an unusual one," the waitress said. Gently, she turned King's arm so that the palm of her hand faced up and the veins rose like a blueprint beneath pale skin.

The Sawyers left Leavenworth behind. Driving westward, they began the ascent into the Cascade Mountains and the brown landscape gave way to green. Deciduous to evergreen. The engine revved to a great cry. Enormous rocks rose to either side. As they drove, they studied a map and saw how shortly they'd hit the ocean. A westward stopping point. No more space to run.

The pines in the mountains were as gnarled as ancient men. They drove into snow that seemed to multiply upon itself until great heaps ran alongside the road. The cement had dried white with salt. Snowy peaks reared to their sides and they took comfort in their own diminishment, the sense that they could disappear all at once into the great obliterating whiteness.

the people of the broken neck

After the mountain pass, they descended into deep fog. The car poked forward until guardrails loomed just in front of them and a great broken pine seemed to point left with one trailing limb. The nose of the station wagon tilted down and their bodies felt as though they were falling against their safety belts. When they began to drop out of the clouds that sat atop the mountains, the landscape stretched out fearfully before them. Steep hills slowly descended in hundreds of shades of green. Rock faces were still fogged over and murky at the edges as though the border between one thing and the next had begun to decay.

THE PHONE CALL from the waitress, Glenda, was routed slowly. She made the call from a pay phone in front of the diner. The air was still. Blue-painted letters swirled on the windows. The clouds clotted into stiff shapes and broke open and the light fractured into beams. The waitress spoke impatiently into the phone. No, she couldn't be put on hold again. She was tired of repeating herself.

"This is agent Charlie Basin," someone finally said into the line.

"Who're you?" the waitress asked.

"I'm the agent in charge of this investigation."

She watched two pigeons scuttle from the roof. "I'm tired of saying all this," she said. "My break was over twenty minutes ago."

"I promise you won't have to tell it again."

"Well, I seen them," she said. "That family. They got a teenage girl with them."

"You're referring to the Sawyers?"

"That's them," she said. "The father, he's grown a beard. The older boy's hair is short and reddish brown. That King's is long and black and pretty."

"They say where they were headed?"

"The little girl said they were going over the mountains. But she wasn't none too sure."

The cement beneath the waitress's feet was littered with bent cigarette butts. She answered Charlie's questions in short sentences. This man on the phone, she thought, had a soft voice, like a memory from her childhood. The light through the clouds cast its spectral architecture on a church steeple, a blue water tower, a peaked slate roof. She watched the light fall and her mouth hung open.

"Glenda, I've got one more question."

"Shoot," she said.

"How do they look?"

"I told you already."

"I mean, do they look tired? Worn? Do they look like people on the run? Do they look like they've been hurt?"

"None of that at all," she said. "They look good."

AT NIGHT, WHEN they all slept in the car, Dominick sometimes dreamed of his kids and woke and reached out to touch them. Their skins felt warm and damp and fragile, like exhalations of breath. He tried not to move too much, not to wake them. He looked at the way his son leaned against the girl who leaned against the car door. Her hand lay almost protectively across his chest.

Dominick blinked his eyes. His throat felt as though someone was squeezing it. The night swam, watery and alive. Out the windows he could see only a few feet before his vision faded away and he could sense, more than see, the great indecipherable forms heaving their way through the dark. He turned his eyes back on his children, then he opened the door to get out of the car. "Sometimes," he said so quietly that his lips barely moved, "I wished the three of us was all there was."

In the dark, King sat up. Her breathing came hard and her eyelids were clotted with sleep. They had pulled off on the side of the road. The air was dark and cold and, as her hand rose to her eyes, she had a feeling that she'd lived through all this before. She was half inside her sleeping bag in the far back of the station wagon. Someone was whimpering.

King remembered being woken by a soft whimpering in the time before her mother had left. That, too, had started quietly. A mewl. King had thought of a beaten dog. She'd gotten up and felt the cotton pajamas fall flat and warm against her and she'd followed the whimpering through the house. She stood at the front door, listening before she opened it. Over the crested pines, the moon looked like it had been pared with a knife. The night sky was brackish. Her mother sat on the front steps. She had her arms around her knees. Her hair was black, her skin white. Muscles ran in lines up her back.

In the car, King rose up to her knees. Moonlight filtered in. Clarke was stretched out alongside Elsie, both asleep in the backseat. Through the windows, she could see the hulk of her father among craggy pines. She cracked the door and cold flooded inside. The frozen ground crunched beneath her feet. Her dad was sitting on the ground. His face was knotted up. His eyes were pinched and unfocused and moving. His mouth opened and closed, making soft noises. King stood behind him a moment, hesitant. Then she reached out and touched her father's shoulder in just the way that she had once put her hand on her mother.

"What is it, Dad?" King asked. "What is it?"

When had the past and present begun to overlap? Was it her mother's voice or her father's that asked, "What happened to us?" The words sounded limpid and run together, as though both of their tongues were partially frozen. "One of us was always going to hurt the other."

"No, no," King said. For a second she pulled at both of their hands. "Come on inside." She pulled harder. "Out here it's too chilly."

⬖ In the morning, not far from their destination, they drove through tulip fields. Miles of flowers tended in squared lots. Red barns lumped beneath great firs. Geese in dark V's were backlit by the sunset. They passed through a yellow field into a valley of dark red blossoms. Cresting a long ridge, they turned into a violet tulip bed bordered by a white fence. The neighboring hill was covered in orange. The moon sat above it as white as bone.

"Oh, my!" Elsie said. All that beauty felt alien. Clarke and King pressed their faces to the windows.

"Look at it!" Clarke said. "It's like it's here just for us."

"Jesus," Dominick said, "I'm glad that we get to see this."

⬖ To get to Benjamin Ward's house, Dominick turned off a road onto a long graveled drive that led down to the Pacific Ocean. Apple and cherry and pear trees flowered in long lines that rose and fell across hills. Huge ferns swept up from beneath jagged pines. Behind them Mount Baker and the Twin Sisters rose from the Cascades. To the south hunched Mount Rainier, snow-covered and alone and massive.

They drove over a last hill and slowly descended a long slope, past a knee-high rock wall, through a field of clover toward a brown house. Beside the main building, a scattering of cabins nestled among trees. Just beyond the property, the earth gave way sharply, a bluff falling to sand. The ocean stretched out, jagged with light and dotted with triangular sails. The green mounds of the San Juan Islands rose up in the distance.

Though the air was chilly, all the windows were down in the station wagon. Elsie pointed her face into the outside air. "It's the first time I've seen the ocean," she said.

"You like it?" Dominick asked.

"I didn't think it would be like this."

As they pulled in, a man as large as their father came out of the brown house. The doorway behind him was filled with artificial light. He wore a white shirt and a jungle hat. He stood in gravel and waved them forward until they stood in front of him. "Goddamn!" he called, his voice overly loud. His features were oversized, his nose a thick mound, his lips ruddy and wide, his chin a landmass.

Dominick got out of the car and they put their arms around each other and waved back and forth like two wrestling giants. "What happened to you?" Dominick said. "You got old."

The man lifted their father off his feet, set him down again, released him, and came to stand by Elsie and the kids. "Who're you?" he said to Elsie.

"Elsie," she said. "Who're you?"

"I'm Benjamin Ward," he said. His thighs were round like Easter hams. He looked at the other two kids. "You're Clarke and King," he said. "Your dad used to tell stories about you.

You know that? I know some about you already. You're welcome here. Call me Benny."

The air smelled of pine needles, of salt and decay, and of the
blue hyacinth that bloomed around the window wells. Elsie
stepped closer to Clarke. Benny pointed at the two of them. "I
see how it is," Benny said. "This place used to be a resort. You
two want your own cabin?"

CHARLIE ROSE AT 5:00 A.M. in a hotel room that looked nearly identical to the room he had last been in. He had an early-morning flight to Spokane, Washington. His body groaned at being awake. What were the Sawyers doing in Leavenworth, Washington? Were they still there? What was the point in running?

His phone rang. Annie Sawyer. He didn't feel especially surprised. A paper cup of coffee in one hand, he answered his phone. "Hello, Annie," he said.

"Charlie, I've got something to get off my chest."

"Go ahead, then. But listen, I already know that Dominick was staying in your friend's trailer."

There was a pause on the line, not as if she was quiet but as if the line had gone momentarily dead. "It's not that," she said.

Her voice was deep and husky. Charlie could hear a catch in her breath. He remembered the coffee in his hand and took a drink. "You okay?" he asked.

"I don't know. All this is happening to my family."

"Have I told you that I've got a daughter named Charlene?" Charlie said. "She's been having some trouble. Neither of us is sure that we want to talk to each other."

"Charlene?" Annie said. "You named your daughter after yourself?"

"It was my wife's idea."

Annie Sawyer drew in a breath and held it. Charlie waited until she let it go. "It was me, Charlie," she said.

"What was you?" he said.

"I pretended to be her," Annie said. "I pretended to be Sarah."

"What do you mean?" Charlie said.

"I felt so worried about the kids," she said. "I didn't know what to do, so I called the police. I said I was his wife. I said I thought he was hurting his kids."

When he got off the phone, Charlie let his frame drop to the floor. A short cream carpet. The smell of antiseptic. The day curled ahead of him like a question mark. He lost himself in the physical rhythm of his push-up routine. He listened to his breathing. Someone began to run water in an adjacent room. He felt at home in hotel rooms, he'd lived half his life in them. His face brushed the carpet. His muscles began to tighten. His stomach began to churn. His body to live.

What makes a man hunt other men? What but a desire to look anywhere, no matter how brutal and low, other than at himself?

BENJAMIN WARD'S HOUSE was a fortress. He led them through the hallways. The wide pine boards creaked beneath their feet. Every wall was white and clean. Benny had little furniture beyond a leather couch, a table and chairs. He pointed out what mattered. Reinforced concrete walls. Steel shutters at each window. A gun rack. A bomb-shelter basement lined with a hundred gallons of water and canned foods stacked on steel shelves. Beside the fuse box, dozens of car batteries had been wired together and connected to the main power line.

"What are you scared of?" King asked. She stood beside him.

"I'm not that scared anymore," Benny said.

"You've been scared before?" King said.

"Sure."

"What'd you do all this for?"

"I don't know," Benny said. "It's home. I feel comfortable in here." He picked up a can of beets and set it atop another can of beets. "Don't you feel safe?"

"Is something bad going to happen?"

"Sure, something bad will happen." He waved his hand around him. "And none of this will do us any good."

Upstairs, Dominick sat on the couch. His body hurt. He heard his children's lighter footsteps on the basement stairs, then Benny Ward's clodding weight. Benny showed Dominick and King to separate rooms in the main house. For dinner they had pasta and sausages and sweet pickles. They said good-night.

Clarke and Elsie shared a cabin. The bed was old and bowed in the middle so they rolled inward and each encysted to the other. In the morning they woke with their limbs twined together. Their tongues adhered to the insides of their mouths. The green flowered sheets stuck to their skins. They lay in the bed and the room lightened in visible increments, as though someone outside held great sheaves of papers against the windows and cast them aside piece by piece.

It took some time to peel themselves apart. Elsie sat on the edge of the bed. "I'm homesick," she said.

"You are?"

They got up, reassembling themselves. Combed their hair. Gargled. Brushed their teeth. Slipped their legs into cold jeans. Clarke parted the yellow window curtains suddenly with both hands.

To the east, the clouds were pasted to the hills. A large brown puddle stretched across the ground outside the window. Rain puckered the water into tiny closing mouths. Rivulets etched jagged paths down the glass. Elsie's hand fell gently on his shoulder and turned him toward her. Dark wet hair curled across her forehead. Her eyelashes were clotted with mascara. Her eyes were tactile and wet. "What're we going to do?" she asked.

"Isn't this enough?"

"For a little while," she said. "Sometimes I feel bad again. Like I did before."

"I think we all feel bad part of the time."

Outside, on the main house deck, in the near dark of the morning, Dominick stood beside Benny Ward. They were three feet apart—two huge men. Neither of them said anything. The eastern sky was the color of rust. Each of them stewed in the memories that rose in the company of the other.

A crown of gold light rose on the eastern horizon. Swallows dipped beneath branches and turned. Dominick reached out and put his hand on Benny's shoulder. He said, "I remember that roadside IED going off under our lead Stryker like the world gone up in smoke, and all that dust."

"Yeah," Benny said. "The small-arms fire. Must have been a grenade knocked me out cold. I woke to see you lying ten feet over, against the side of a building, your face covered in blood." Benny Ward shook his head. "When you opened your eyes, you said, 'We're still here.'"

"Not a scratch on you," Dominick said.

"Two luckiest guys in Iraq." Benny clicked an odd noise, as if encouraging an animal to move.

"Then we fucked some shit up," Dominick said.

"It was a long walk back."

In the early afternoon, Clarke and Elsie walked out into the woods, far from the house and even farther from the road. Clarke dragged stones into a rough circle. Elsie gathered dead wood. The sun stroked them with a soft warm hand.

"Are you glad we're alone together?" Elsie said.

"Uh-huh, I am."

She held him off with one hand against his clavicle.

"We barely know each other," she said.

Their elbows scraped moss from the trunks of trees. They rolled on the ground crushing the ferns' fronds. They breathed into each other's mouths until they grew light-headed. They pulled off each other's clothes. Each felt something desperate and hungry in the other's touch. They left prints of the things they did in the dirt. They had no sense of how alien they might have looked from another angle or from a greater distance. Two soft figures and their thin limbs. Their pale skins like scars among the browns and greens of the dewed leaves and the variegated earth and the tessellated bark. They scrabbled atop and inside one another as though trying to disassociate from age-old wounds.

Afterward they lay on the warm ground with their hearts beating in their ears. Their limbs twined into a fragile human scaffolding. The dirt beneath them was wet. Clarke rolled on his side to face her. The corners of her eyes were screwed tight. "What is it?" he said.

She said, "It's a funny thing that I said."

"What is?"

"Alone together."

On the beach, King walked next to Benny Ward. Waves crashed against the shore and pulled back. The siphons of clams pushed through holes in the sand and squirted as King walked. Seaweed disintegrated in great piles. The shells of dead creatures lay half buried in sand.

"You ever see whales out there?" King asked.

"Sometimes."

"You do? What kind? Are they big?"

"Gray whales," Benny said. "They're really big, but they look small in the ocean. Over there, by the islands, I've seen orcas. Killer whales."

The brown house slipped invisibly behind the bluff. The beach turned to a churn of driftwood that they picked their way through with bandy legs. Then the driftwood gave way to a tumble of rounded stones and crabs skittered beneath their feet.

"You live here all alone?" King asked. She swung her arms at her sides.

"I used to be married," Benny said. "But she left. I'm hard to live with."

"You don't seem hard to live with."

"Thank you."

The rocky beach ended in a sandstone cliff. Sea stacks rose from the ocean and mussels clung to stones in wide tide pools.

White-tentacled anemones withdrew into themselves when King's finger approached. Orange and red starfish climbed atop one another with their arms moving in slow even arcs. Reddish crabs tucked beneath rocks. King put her fingers in her mouth, tasting the salt. Benny Ward squatted on his haunches.

"It's like another world in there," King said.

"It's weird," said Benny.

"How far are we from home?" King asked.

"Not far."

"It feels really far."

In time they gathered around the picnic table beneath the shade of the apple tree near the house. They drank tea from tin cups. Benny Ward cut great slices of melon. Then they took guns from the cabinets and shot at human-shaped targets pinned to hay bales. They walked down to the oceanside and pushed their toes into the water and felt the deep chill. They watched the tide come in and go out again. They let their bare feet feel the sun-warmed stones. They buried shells in sand. They dug for clams and baked them in an open fire. At twilight, Dominick and Benny drank cheap beer and Dominick passed cans to Clarke and Elsie and then shrugged and raised his eyebrows and let King have a few sips.

They passed a few days this way. They played checkers and

gin rummy. They took turns washing the dishes. They felt peaceful and temporary, as if the things they did were a pale mimicry of simpler lives. They spoke to each other softly. They tiptoed. They felt it could not last, felt it inside them, a kind of fragile shell around each of their hearts.

CHARLIE SAT UP in bed to answer his cell phone. The sheet rumpled down by his waist. How tired he was. His arms wanted rest. "Agent Basin?" a voice asked. Deep as a well. Saddened, too. A voice that had lost any sense of itself.

"Go ahead," Charlie said. The deep voice didn't respond. Charlie rose from the bed and cracked the motel drapes. He looked out at the sidewalk in Leavenworth, Washington. A dark car passed beneath a streetlight. Charlie watched the dust corkscrew behind the wheels and listened to the breathing at the other end of the phone. "Who is this?" he asked.

The deep voice started to speak and broke, then started again. "The reward," it said. "I'm calling about the money."

"What's your name?" Charlie said.

"I was with the Seventy-Fifth Ranger regiment."

"You're calling about Dominick Sawyer?" Charlie said.

"That's right," said the voice. "He's here in my house. He's my friend."

"DAD," KING SAID, "how long will this last?"

"Not long," her father said.

"Why not?"

"Nothing lasts very long."

"Why not?"

"I don't know why not."

"Where do we go next?"

"I don't know that, either, King."

Sitting beside one another on the porch steps, Dominick and King and Clarke were quiet for a little while. It was dark. All of them had their hands folded in their laps.

"What was the war like?" Clarke asked.

"The war?" said Dominick.

"Uh-huh."

"I don't know."

"Did you kill people?"

"Jesus, kid."

"Did it feel bad?" King said.

"I don't know. I guess it did. Like being a piece of a machine. I was afraid so often that I got numb."

"Did you want to leave?" Clarke asked.

"I tried not to think about it. Sometimes it felt really bad."

"Did you want to come home?" Clarke pushed.

"At first I wanted to. Sometimes it didn't feel like anything, like nothing happened at all, like people were just smoke."

The three Sawyers rose from the porch and walked down the trail to the beach. They sat in a line on the sand. Father beside daughter beside son. Bits of light tippled against the waves. Night birds cried in forlorn voices. King kicked her heels. Clarke smelled of oil and wood smoke. Dominick told Clarke and King that their mother had been eaten by bees.

"Eaten," he said. His voice was faint and whispery. "By bees."

"Bullshit," Clarke said. He laughed once.

"That's how she disappeared?" King asked.

Their father nodded sorrowfully. He glanced first at King and then at Clarke.

"You expect us to believe this?" Clarke asked.

"I don't expect you to believe anything." His hand reached past King and grasped Clarke's thigh hard. Triangular sails floated in the middle distance.

"What kind of bees?" King asked.

"All kinds," his father said. "Paper wasps and Africanized honeybees."

"Killer bees, you mean?" King said.

"Sure. There were mud daubers. Sweat bees. Hornets."

"You just don't want to say that Mom left you," said Clarke.

"Fine," Dominick said. "I don't want to hear it, either."

DOMINICK HAD AN urge to tell his kids about his relationship with their mother. That they had tried so hard. That they had pushed each other too far. That finally neither could look at the other without the urge to spit. That they had fought but not like lovers.

Day and night, they'd argued. Once, to avoid waking the kids, they walked by the Susquehanna River. Where the riverbank had eroded from beneath the great trees, a huge tangle of roots rose out of the water. In a willow tree, wasps swarmed around a papery hive. Neither of them was saying anything. The way she looked at him, he'd seen it before in the faces of men who wanted to pull a gun from their belt, or slip a knife between his ribs, or pull a thin wire around the soft skin of his neck. "God," he said to her, "what's happened to us?"

"We used to be okay," he said.

She turned her back to him.

"Sarah?"

She wore a white woolen sweater and a thin red scarf. The flat surface of the river was blanched with moonlight. A few brown leaves showed the current. Up the hill toward the house sat the woodpile and the chopping block and the ax handle with its head buried and its handle pointed up. The night was a many-headed beast. An ink-black sky filled with colonies of stars. A siphonophore spiraling slowly in the night.

She stood by the edge of the river with her back to him. "One of us," she said, "is going to have to leave." Her shoulders lifted and fell, then lifted and fell again.

They were supposed to raise their kids together, be a family. They were supposed to get along. They were supposed to put things behind them. But they put the kids to bed and fought like hungry animals, like they could smell each other's blood. In the morning, they woke with baleful eyes in the same bed. Their faces felt fixed in their positions. Their kids made noises in the kitchen. Spoons in bowls. Poured milk. His wife had a fist-sized bruise on the side of her chest. Claw marks ran across Dominick's face. Their bodies moved stiffly. Each had said so many things from which the other believed they would never recover. He laughed when she bit him, and her mouth filled with blood, and her face contorted into something hard and unfamiliar and wrinkled like a prune. He yanked his arm out of her mouth and shook it there in front of her as if to show her what she had become. Her face fell. She crumpled against the scab-colored carpet. She tucked her chin under and her hair lay flat against the dome of her skull. When she spoke, she spoke quietly. She said, "Why didn't you die in the war?" He had to strain to hear her.

CHARLIE BASIN DROVE west on U.S. Route 2.
Dark evergreens rose on either side of the road. An oncoming car dappled over small hills, its brights cutting across the windshield and leaving him with blotchy reddish afterimages. Twin suns hovering in a night sky.

The drive between Leavenworth and Bellingham would take three hours. He had wanted to be on the road before he picked up the phone to call Andrew Fry.

"Andy," he said, "I know where they are."

"Good," Andy said. "Where? How'd you find him?"

"He's staying with an old Army buddy. A Ranger. The guy turned him in."

"He deserves it," Andy said. "You want to have SWAT and the locals move in?"

"I'm driving now," Charlie said. Bits of dust or ash or ice rushed against the headlights. "I'll be there in less than three hours. I want to go in first thing in the A.M. Yes to the SWAT Team and get the Bellingham police up to speed so they're ready when I get there."

"Sure, I'll get everybody ready," Andy said. "We need to put an end to this. You up for it?"

"What do you mean am I up for it?" The thin trees blurred

273

at the side windows. A spatter of town lights hung in the rear-view mirror.

"I talked to Rosamund," Andy said.

"What for?"

"We bumped into each other at the gas station. She told me about Charlene."

"What'd she tell you?"

"The suicide attempt," Andy said, "the hospital." He paused and Charlie heard the noise of stubble grinding against the mouthpiece of the phone. "Jesus, Charlie, that poor kid. What can I do to help?"

"Shit," Charlie said. The line crackled. "You see your kids often?"

"Well, they went to boarding school," Andy said. "Then to Yale. All three of them moved out to the West Coast when they graduated. Two to LA. One to grad school at Stanford. We do our best to get together on holidays."

"How's that suit you?"

"It suits me fine."

"You talk to them on the phone?"

"Sure," Andy said, "when I've got something to say."

Bats flitted in the headlights. The road canyoned through a steep rise of coniferous trees.

"Listen, Charlie," Andy said, "there's nobody I'd rather have on this case. But if you need to you can turn around right now. You can go home. Let the locals take over."

"No," Charlie said, "I'm going to be the one to take this guy down."

THE WINDOWS WERE dark. Elsie rolled up onto her side and rested her head on one hand. She asked, "Why did your mother leave?"

"I don't know, Elsie."

"Do you miss her?"

"Yeah, I miss her," Clarke said. "She was great."

"How long has she been gone?"

"Just under a year, I guess."

"Did you know she was going to leave you?" Elsie said.

"No," Clarke said, "I didn't."

"Did you see signs?"

"What's with all the questions?"

"I want to know what it's like to be you."

"You can't," Clarke said.

"Maybe I can if you tell me about the signs."

"I found her packing a suitcase once," Clarke said. "I asked where she was going. She wouldn't tell me. It was a few weeks before she left for good."

"Anything else?"

"When my dad got out of the Army, she asked him if he would go back."

"Why?"

"He was gone so much she got used to it being the three of us."

"Were you mad when he came home?"

"I don't know. Sometimes."

"Did they get along?"

"They got along okay."

"Did they fight?"

"They fought," Clarke said. "They fought a lot."

"Like every night? Did they leave bruises?"

"Jesus, I don't want to be like them."

"That's not something you have to worry about."

"Why not?" Clarke asked her.

"Because you aren't."

Inside the house, Dominick paced. His feet knocked hollowly against the floorboards. He stopped in front of a photograph of a group of men, he and Benny among them. He scanned the faces. Half of them had died in the Middle East. One had killed himself stateside. The sky in the photo was just a shade lighter than the sand. Behind them were buildings and walls made of dirt. Nearly every one of them had a can of beer. Their M4 carbines piled on the ground. A few of them wrestled. Only one or two of them wore shirts. All of them were muscled and ruddy with health. Their skin swam with sweat. All of them wore Friday-night smiles.

Dominick opened the refrigerator and closed it again. He filled a glass with water. He held it up and looked into it in the light. The slow drift of particulates. Tiny bubbles adhered to the sides of the glass. When he swallowed, he listened to the epiglottal flap. He reached behind him, put his wrists against the small of his back, and thrust upward until his spine cracked.

At the kitchen table, he flipped through a stack of gun magazines. Inside one, he found a white paper folded in half. He unfolded it and found his own name.

UNLAWFUL FLIGHT TO AVOID PROSECUTION —
FIRST-DEGREE MURDER

DOMINICK CLARKE SAWYER

Aliases: Dominick C. Sawyer, Dominick Sawyer, Dom Sawyer

DESCRIPTION

Date of Birth: July I, 1977
Place of Birth: Pennsylvania
Hair: Brown
Eyes: Blue
Height: 6'4"
Complexion: Light
Weight: 230 to 240 pounds
Sex: Male
Build: Large
Race: White

silas dent zobal

Occupation: Former Army Ranger
Nationality: American
Scars and Marks: "sua sponte" tattoo on
back of neck

Remarks: Sawyer has ties to Pennsylvania
and Illinois. He is an expert marksman. He
may be in possession of a Springfield Armory
MIA rifle and a Beretta M9 handgun.

CAUTION

DOMINICK CLARKE SAWYER IS WANTED FOR MUR-
DER IN SNYDER COUNTY, PENNSYLVANIA, AND
DEKALB COUNTY, ILLINOIS. SAWYER ALLEGEDLY
SHOT AND KILLED A SHERIFF IN PENNSYLVANIA
AND TWO CITY POLICE OFFICERS IN ILLINOIS.

CONSIDERED ARMED AND EXTREMELY DANGEROUS

IF YOU HAVE ANY INFORMATION CONCERNING
THIS PERSON, PLEASE CONTACT YOUR LOCAL
FBI OFFICE OR THE NEAREST U.S. EMBASSY OR
CONSULATE.

REWARD

The FBI is offering a reward of up to
$I00,000 for information leading directly
to the arrest of Dominick Clarke Sawyer.

Dominick blinked. When he closed his eyes, the wanted paper ceased to exist. But it burned back to life when his eyelids opened. It shook in his hands. Benny Ward and Dominick had tented together. They'd been responsible for each other's lives. They'd dug into the sand and watched tracer rounds arc into the night. Was this what all that had come to be balanced against? He couldn't believe it. He paced the rooms. He thought he was lucky to love all of them the way that he did. His wife and children. Benny, too. Because of them, he was more than just the poor assemblage of himself. They were living prostheses. Did he deserve them? He knew he didn't. All great things come without being earned.

He waited out the dark until he couldn't wait any longer. Then he went to find Clarke. He pounded on the cabin door until Clarke rose to walk the property line with his father. Neither of them could see anything in front of them. The air was humid and warming up and the night pushed against them wet and black. It was almost funny, the slow shuffle of their feet. Their arms extended in front of them into unknown spaces. Their forward movement might have been useless.

Clarke heard his father's footsteps stop ahead of him. The ground beneath his feet was soft and springy. When his body bumped into his father's, he felt he'd run up against something huge and immovable. He heard his father draw in a breath and then hold quiet, waiting for some unknown signal before he'd speak.

Clarke waited it out. His eyes began to adjust, to filter out a dull grayscale world.

"Everything okay?" his father asked.

"It's fine," Clarke said.

"Fine how?"

"How do you get along with women?"

"You're asking me?" his father said.

"Who else, Dad?"

"Elsie, you mean? Are you listening to her?"

"Sometimes she doesn't make sense."

"I understand that," his father said. "But nobody makes sense."

"What do I do?"

"Are you listening to the way that she doesn't make sense?"

Before morning, the surf woke King from a thin film of sleep to her mother's tongue. Her mother's slow whispering sounded like sand pouring. King listened with her head cocked against the dark. Her mother's voice was a low susurrus through the screened window. The stars winked on and off like handfuls of thrown coins. King stood from her bed. The cold dimpled her bare skin. Her teeth cracked together. She listened hard. If her mother used words, King couldn't parse them, couldn't separate the edges of her phrases. Her mother's secrets, like the earth's, called for an interpreter.

Half asleep, King walked out of the house, the screen door flapping behind her. From the kitchen table, she had picked up her father's Wharncliffe knife. The handle was darkened, the blade deeply notched. She shivered but she didn't fully wake.

Wearing only underpants and a T-shirt, she walked across the yard and down the rocky trail that led past the bluff. She walked into the dark ocean and let herself settle to the bottom. Driving her palms into silt, she felt for bones. She wouldn't return to the surface until she found them. Her hands closed around soft branches, round stones, bits of glass, tin. Her lungs tore her insides. Bubbles escaped her mouth and rose toward the moonlight on the surface. Turning her head upward, she saw herself as a grown woman, a woman tied to a hollow pine by a red scarf. A woman whose neck would be throttled until it snapped. Holding her breath became worse than breathing water. She opened her mouth, let it rush in, surrendered and became her mother, Sarah Tower Sawyer. Her arms tied to the pine, her ring finger carved off by a knife, her body tossed into the river. Seizures wracked her chest and then she was free, crawling toward the light shining off the surface of the water, touching the skin of the water and watching the cloud of blood spread from her hands. Then the yank of her braid, and the screaming, and the fingers at her throat that held her head beneath water as her limbs flailed.

And as their body kicked upward from the sanded bottom, broke the surface, and breathed in the light, King saw the face that looked back into her mother's as the bones in her neck snapped and she drowned.

In their cabin, Clarke and Elsie woke early and rolled across the bed. What each of them wanted was to crawl inside the skin of the other. They clawed at one another with their fingernails. They left bruises on each other's arms and backs. Clarke pushed Elsie hard to the bed, and she arched her back and pulled him to her and dug her nails into the soft skin on his thick sides. She rolled up onto her knees, reached behind and hooked her finger inside his mouth. He crammed himself forward, and she pulled at his hips. They wanted boundaries to fall, to hurt one another in good faith.

"Can we stay together?" Elsie asked.

"I don't know," Clarke said.

"When will you know?"

"Maybe tomorrow."

At first light, Dominick shoved open the door to Benjamin Ward's bedroom. A splintered artifact of light pushed its way around the blinds. Benny's great body dented the mattress. His eyes blinked slowly as though the lashes were gummed.

Dominick pushed the paper holding his name in front of him. "What's this?" he said. For a moment, Benny's face went empty of all expression. "Did you call?" Dominick asked. "Tell me you didn't."

Neither said anything. Benny kept his head down. The downy hair of his forearms and the known smell of himself brought up all the other moments he'd buried his head against his arms and looked away from what confronted him. As a child, his father had read to Benny from books about round-bodied beasts with horns and beaks and Benny had wrapped his arms around his own head and howled and hidden his eyes. When his ex-wife had walked out of the house without looking back, the edges of her skin like an unlit match, he had wanted to start after her but he hadn't, he hadn't done anything—instead he'd sunk to his knees and his arms had come to rest in front of his eyes. Outside Fallujah, he'd walked in a line of men in the pitch dark until the ground in front of him had exploded with light, as though the fire had burst up from beneath the ground, and the bodies of the men ahead of him broke into pieces that hit the earth with sick, wet thumps and Benny had thrown himself on the ground and pressed his fire-blinded eyes into his fire-blackened arms.

They were quiet for a long time. Then Dominick said, "Benny?" His voice was like an old blanket. He reached around and touched the gun behind his belt. "Can I tell you something?"

"Okay," Benny said.

Dominick told him how it had all started. How the first deputy had come to the door of the A-frame. How he'd watched from a window when the deputy, a young man, a boy really in a gray-green uniform, had scuffed his feet on the welcome mat. The boy stood stiffly and rapped on the door hard. Wind see-sawed between field and forest and the late-afternoon sun trespassed everywhere. The boy held a red scarf in one hand. One boot lifted and fell on the cement steps. His skin ruddied in the late light. He took off his hat. He knocked again.

Dominick stepped out onto the porch, into a wash of light only strong enough to warm the surface of things. The porch boards creaked. A distant burn bin smelled of burned rubber.

"Afternoon," said the deputy. There was something in his voice, a false note of relaxation that hid a bit of nervousness, some small indefinite concern.

"Something wrong?" Dominick asked. His body's frame filled the frame of the door.

"I'm Deputy Donny Boyer," the boy said. He held out his empty hand. The irregular patter of rifle fire echoed across the top of the western ridge and down into the valley. Someone practicing with paper targets or pie tins hung on strings.

"You been a deputy long?"

"Not long," Donny Boyer said, "still in my first year." He held up the scarf. "You seen this before?"

"Not sure," Dominick said. "My wife had a red one." His stomach muscles knotted. "You think that scarf is my wife's?"

"That's what I come to ask you," Donny said. "It's made of alpaca wool. It's an unusual knit." He lifted the scarf toward Dominick.

A neighbor's distant lawn mower was the small whining engine of a Predator drone. "I can't tell if it's hers," Dominick said. "How'd you come by it?"

"Some kids dumped a stolen bike in the river," said Donny Boyer. "South of here, outside Liverpool. I waded in there and pulled the bike out through the cattails at the bank. That's when I found the scarf. Knew it was alpaca wool straightaway. My aunt raises alpaca."

"All the way over by Liverpool?" Dominick said, a coarse fear boiling up past his stomach to touch his esophagus. It caught in his throat, hung there choking him, a partially digested mass of all the times he'd been afraid before, causing his eyes to water. His heart began to jump in his chest. His palms to sweat.

"That's right," Donny Boyer said. "It's a nice scarf, too. I figured somebody would like to have it back. So I rode over to Patchwork Farms. That's in Kantz pretty near here. They got an alpaca store. You know Mrs. Yoder? She runs the place. I walk in there and make some small talk. Then I hold the scarf and say, 'You know anything about this?' and she took it off me and felt the knit. Mrs. Yoder said she made that scarf for Sarah Sawyer. Gave it to her, she said, as a Christmas present. Right away when I heard your wife's name I remembered the missing-person report. That's why I come by."

Deputy Donny Boyer looked at Dominick, took a step back, shifted his hand closer to his gun belt. "Hey?" he said. "Hey, you okay?"

The arms that reached out to overwhelm the boy were not Dom's own. The eyes that saw all the things he had seen should never have belonged to him. He could never do the things that he did next. He couldn't feel the body shake beneath his arms. He couldn't listen to its smothered voice. He closed his eyes and squeezed and squeezed, and when the deputy no longer moved, Dominick wrapped what was left in black plastic, dragged it to the river, and threw it in.

Inside the main house, King was white as a ghost. She shivered. Her small angular reflection passed across the glass of the French doors. She heard her father's voice in Benjamin Ward's room. She dropped her father's Wharncliffe knife on the table and took the canister of salt from the cabinet. She walked on the tips of her toes. Her feet left moist prints on the floor that evaporated after her weight was gone. She knelt on the wood floor outside her father's room and ran her fingers over the seams between strips of wood. Her head bowed. In her hands, the container tipped and salt spilled into words.

Murder, wrote King, *Renascence, Miracle.*

CHARLIE BASIN HAD them now. The black Chevy Suburban felt heavy against the road. It had weight. He was being followed by a line of police cruisers and the up-armored Humvee of Seattle's SWAT team. He had banned sirens and lights. A single phone call and the Sawyers' location, so hard to determine, was illuminated like a point on a light-up map. His body felt electrified. This was beautiful country out here. The hills mounded like the backs of petrified beasts. The mist rose off the green ground. Everything seemed so alive. He pulled his Glock 23 from its holster and set it on the seat. He pushed the brake, pulled into the long gravel driveway that led to Benjamin Ward's house, and pushed the gas hard enough that the Suburban's engine barked and jumped forward.

◄⋅⋅ The gun in Dominick's hands was the final and definitive truth. He pointed it at Benjamin Ward. The barrel did not waver. "Go ahead," Benny said. "You ought to shoot." He pulled the green sheet up so that it covered his chest.

"What the hell, Benny?" Dominick said. His hands shook, just once, around the handle of the gun.

"I can't explain it, Dom," Benny said. "It hasn't been good

since we came back. I got nothing. I got dark thoughts about my wife. She said she left because of money."

"We've been like brothers," Dominick said.

"Not for a while."

The truth left them both quiet for a minute. Outside sounds crowded in. The distant snarl of a heavy engine. The whistled yelp of a white-tailed kite. The crunch and spit of tires against loose stones.

"Somebody coming over?" Dominick asked.

Benny pushed himself up with his hands so that the sheet fell away and exposed the corded muscle of his arms and chest. "I think they're here," Benny said. "Dom, I talked to the FBI."

Dominick backed toward the door. He stopped at the entrance of the hallway with the gun rack behind him, raised the pistol toward the ceiling, and fired.

The tendons pulled across Benny's throat as he called, "I'm sorry, Dom, I'm sorry!"

In the hallway, King paid no attention to the gunshot, nor to the swollen voices of Benjamin Ward and her father. She walked out of the house carrying the canister in one hand. Salt spilled behind her in a thin trail. She wore no shoes. Her skin was pale against the mossed rocks. She stumbled across the dewed grass and over a mound of earth covered with clovers. The morning sky was shaking with anxiety. She moved into a half-round of giant trees and soft dripping sounds. The arch of trees cupped oversized ferns and Canterbury bells. The red sun erupted in the sky. She felt unsteady. She felt uneven. She pushed at the flowers with her hands and tried to look at them, at bell and stamen and pistil, but her vision splintered into circling patches of light. Each frond was a cataract of blue blossoms. Her ears rang. She was going to faint, she knew that. She held herself up, wavering, until the sky moved down unilaterally, like a great obliterating fog.

Charlie Basin had his window down. The Suburban bucked and jumped over potholes and hills. The pitted drive was nearly a mile long and the police convoy had covered half the distance. Charlie could smell something in the air, lavender and salt and ash. When the single gunshot rang out, it sounded distant and contained. Small-arms fire. Probably indoors. He couldn't see the house that he knew lay ahead. To his left, he spotted a Volvo station wagon parked behind a pile of logs, half covered by a blue tarp. He stuck his arm out of his window and motioned the SWAT team forward. The Humvee glittered like a beetle and crashed through the bushes alongside the driveway and pulled forward with a great turn of wheels and Charlie Basin knew that this was out of his hands, whatever might happen now. He had put these kids, who were so much like his kids, in danger. Charlie Basin could have been this man, this Dominick, whose voice he had never heard and whose face he had never seen, if just a few unidentifiable moments of his life had tipped against him.

◄⁒ The single crack of a pistol shot returned Clarke and Elsie to their own skins. They became aware of their nakedness, of their grotesque angles, of the blood between them. They looked at one another, really looked. Between them there was something as fragile as a rope of spit between two lips. They slipped apart, wiped fluids on the sheets, and rooted around for clothes, reeling themselves back together.

Dominick went through the hall and past the rack of guns in two great steps. He took the turn hard enough that his shoulder dented the drywall and he spun and reached for the door to King's temporary room. He pushed it open with such force that the screws pulled from the top hinge. Empty space. A rumpled sheet on a bed. The door tipped forward until it hung precariously in the air, pulling against the single bottom hinge. Dominick stepped to his room over the _Murder, Renascence, Miracle_ on the threshold.

He picked up the two bags that lay packed on the made bed and went back fast, past the salt. He pushed out the rear door hard enough that it slammed into the siding with the sound of a hand clapped on water. When he leapt over the porch, the green duffel bags flapped like tumorous wings. He hit the blue door to Clarke and Elsie's cabin still running and his shoulder pressed the wood until it snapped.

Clarke flinched when the door exploded inward. Solid wood broke along the bevel. The panels cracked into pieces and gave way to a splintered vision of Dominick's flesh. Elsie and Clarke were beside the bed, bits of clothing in their hands. Dominick didn't stop moving but gathered Clarke's T-shirt and Elsie's pants from a chair and tossed them at them. Clarke thought of giving up, of waiting here beside Elsie in the soft bed, of embracing what might come. Then he thought of his sister left alone.

His father kicked his shoes toward him. He had a handgun in the holster under his belt and he looked as purposeful as steel. He stopped in front of Clarke and Elsie and put a hand on each of their shoulders. "Are you ready?" he asked.

"I'm ready," Clarke said and hitched his shoulders.

Dominick herded Clarke and Elsie before him, pushing them out of the cabin and toward a dark cavelike break in the line of trees to the south. He kept the buildings between them and the sounds of engines and brakes and then the voices crackling on radios. Over the bluff, the sea shone with light. Elsie stumbled and breathed hard. Her eyes were wide.

"Where's King?" Clarke grunted.

"We don't have time," Dominick said.

"She's ours," said Clarke.

"First we disappear, then we find her," Dominick said. "We don't leave anybody behind."

On the slight hill that led into the break in the trees, Elsie tripped. She saw the white clovers among the grass. Her hands extended forward to break her fall but then her body slowed and jerked backward, and she felt Clarke's huge, warm hand wrapped around her upper arm, and she saw his face, tanned and sweating and anxious and darkly beautiful. The dim clutch of trees waved them forward. Clarke set Elsie on her feet and gave her half a smile. Just ahead, Dominick waved them both forward with the same hand that loosely held the pistol. Tree roots wound through the dirt like the carcasses of great worms. Moss ran up the red bark of the trunks. Ferns fluttered like tattered wings. Dark birds scattered before them, winging upward and shrieking warning to one another.

Elsie felt a sense of impending grace, of deep satisfaction that this urgency was hers and that this boy, this man, who pulled her forward wanted her enough that they'd run forward together. A cold wind blew from beneath the canopy of the trees and her eyes watered.

Charlie Basin stood by the Suburban. The SWAT team and the police officers fanned across the property. They pushed into the buildings. He heard things topple inside. He heard things smash. Charlie had his gun drawn but it felt like a formality. The bulletproof vest under his jacket irritated his armpits. He glanced behind him at the clovered mound of earth and the semicircle of old trees cupped around hundreds of bluebell-shaped flowers. What was that he smelled? What was that thin white line on the ground that trailed from the cabin? He bent and touched the line with his finger. Salt? Then, up the hill where the white trail led, he saw something skin-colored and thin among the flowers. A foot? He stepped forward, holding his gun before him with both hands. His legs scissored as he pressed among the blossoms. His focus cleared and his angle of vision widened and the sole of the foot became callused. The foot was attached to a leg, the leg to the body of a small girl. Black-haired and loose-faced. The girl convulsed once and then her body relaxed. The bells bobbed around them. He holstered his gun and plucked the kid from the ground. She felt no heavier than a cat. Her limbs were so thin, like bones beneath paper. Charlie carried her back down the hill, her head resting against his shoulder. Her mouth drooled on his shirt and the moment doubled up and became overlaid with hundreds of other times that Charlie had carried his children. Oswell draped against his shoulder when he'd pulled the boy from the car seat and walked him inside and up the stairs and settled him into bed. Charlene, who'd once cut her hand and passed out on the tiled floor of the kitchen, bloody and unconscious, and Charlie had come on her like that and, as he'd done so many times before, he'd lifted her up. All the scraped knees and bicycle falls and the heft of his kids and the comfort that passed both ways when he held them to his chest.

Dominick and Clarke and Elsie climbed into the hills. Miles passed beneath their feet. Their legs burned as they jogged to the peaks and caught glimpses of a distant settlement before they trotted down into brief valleys. They followed the coastline. They tromped into a wet forest with Dominick urging them wordlessly forward. A cold fog settled over the hills and crept inside their clothes and then a light rain began and night settled over them. They huddled together. From a bag, Dominick pulled a tarp and a blanket and they sat close

together. The moon was full. The craggy silhouettes of firs circled around them. Clarke's stomach rumbled.

"We've got no food," Dominick said.

"We don't?" Elsie's face collapsed.

"There wasn't time."

"I'm hungry," she said.

Dominick pointed through a break in the trees over a cliff,
where they could just make out a long gray wharf extending
into the ocean. "We'll find something soon."

DOES THE UNCONSCIOUS child dream? Is her skin fevered? Does the daylight perform beneath her closed eyelids? Is the flicker of light a love story? Does her family come to act out parts better left untended? Will she one day reenact each role herself? Will she come to know herself only by inhabiting another? Does her body shiver? Does it convulse? Does it bite its own tongue? Does the palsy of the dream echo in flesh? Does it choke on blood? Does it knock her head against rocky earth? Will it lie still again? Is she trapped inside? Will her body come back to her? Will her eyes stay closed longer than demanded by her unseen wounds? Will she have wet herself? Does she already feel the bottomless fear she will wake to? Does she lie there taking comfort in the dark? Is she already awake?

CHARLIE BASIN DROVE to St. Joseph's Hospital in Bellingham, the girl's head resting in his lap. Her pulse was strong. She breathed evenly. She was going to be okay.

They had found Benjamin Ward but not the others. Ward had lain in his bed, eyes wide and open. He put his hands over his head. He had nothing useful to say. Dominick and the older kids had slipped into the woods. The forests in the Pacific Northwest were dark and mushroomed and wet. Charlie had called Andrew Fry and asked him to pressure the locals for more manpower. Let the young guys handle the legwork. The police and the SWAT team were even now spreading out across the property in a great human net.

The traffic curled around overpasses and over bridges and the sea glittered to the west and the sky was a giddy unrealistic blue. Charlie looked at King's bare feet. There was dirt embedded in her skin's shallow creases, a hangnail on her left big toe.

He telephoned the SWAT team leader to get an update. They'd lost the trail in the woods but hounds were on the way. He put the phone back in the breast pocket of his coat. What had he once enjoyed about this job?

The wheels hummed against the blacktop. He straightened a

lock of the girl's black hair. She smelled unwashed. Why hadn't he just called an ambulance? Or he could have sent one of the uniformed police officers. Why take her to the hospital himself? The girl curled into a fetal position. What had he missed at his home while he'd been hunting men?

DOMINICK WALKED ONTO the wooden wharf past two men carrying a blue plastic cooler, their backs bent like fishhooks. Two teenagers hung their bare feet in the water. Dominick's feet knocked on the wood. He looked purposeful. He looked like he belonged where he was. Clarke and Elsie followed, holding hands. The wharf was lined with jet boats and cabin cruisers and yachts of polished teak. Near the end of the dock, seals rolled among the pilings. Kelp bulbs bobbed on the water's surface. The surf sounded like someone whispering. Dominick dropped his duffel bags on the white vinyl seating of a speedboat. "Hop in," he said. He sounded like a father impatient to show his kids the vagaries of the sea. He wiped his hand across his brow. He unzipped one bag. He put his back between the steering wheel and the wharf. When the engine stuttered to life, he said, "You two ought to sit down." He motored slowly beside the wharf, maneuvering past the buoys, pointing the bow toward the distant ferries and scows and barges and the white-sailed schooners. He pushed the throttle forward and the seagulls drifted behind them as they moved through Bellingham Bay and out into the Puget Sound.

Dominick turned the boat to the south. Coins of light dappled the water. To their left sat the mainland and to the right the lumped excrescences of the San Juan Islands. The name *Sainte-Marie* curled in thin black letters on the hull of the speedboat. Water spat behind the motor. The bow rose. Elsie's hair whipped behind her head and one dark strand caught on her cheek. They passed through the wake of a garbage barge, leaping from the peaks of the waves and hammering, flat-bottomed, into the troughs. Inside them, their organs shook.

Clarke shouted, "Where will they take her?" He had to scream to be heard over the wind and the engine. He looked tense, like a figure carved of wood.

Dominick shouted, "I don't know." He stood at the wheel and steered with smooth gestures.

Clarke's head was lowered. Elsie held his forearm tightly as if she was afraid one of them would fall off the boat. They pressed their backs into the cream-colored seats. Clarke shouted at his father, "How're we going to find her?"

Dominick opened his mouth and his larynx worked and the muscles of his voice box pinched together but the wind curled inside the cave of his mouth and stripped his voice and left the sound back behind them, disowned.

Elsie first pointed at the whales. Tall dorsal fins cut near the sides of the boat. White bellies and saddle patches. The black hulking rise of skin. The orca pod moved faster than the *Sainte-Marie*; Dominick cut the engine and the boat slowed to a halt. Elsie grabbed Clarke and said, "What're those?"

"Killer whales?"

Twenty yards out, a giant male breached the surface and water poured from his fins as he half turned in the air and his white belly caught the sun. The splash when he belly flopped was so great that drops of water scattered across their faces. Dominick touched the spray and put his salty fingers to his mouth. He restarted the speedboat's engine.

A mother and two calves spy-hopped their heads from the water and their dark eyes ogled the thin land creatures standing in the half egg.

Dominick pushed the throttle and the boat sped forward again. Clarke stood on uneven sea legs and shouted, "King's scared." He gripped his father's shoulder too hard. "We have to turn back! She thinks we're coming!"

His father put his mouth near Clarke's ear and said, "We are."

KING OPENED HER eyes to a white ceiling and white walls. She wore a light blue gown. She lay on a bed. There was an IV in her arm. A light-skinned man with sharp eyes sat in the chair beside her. He was not her father. He was smaller than her father, neither as tall nor as broad. He looked comfortable in his blue suit.

King said, "Who're you?"

The man stood and held out his hand. "I'm Charlie Basin."

"I'm King Sawyer," she said. They shook hands. "Are you looking for my dad?"

"That's right," said Charlie.

"I want to go home," King said. Her hand had touched the cuff of Charlie's jacket and the wool felt thin. The hospital light was bluish and harsh. Outside the room, a voice floated over the intercom.

"Are you thirsty, kiddo?" Charlie asked. "You want anything? A 7-Up? A popsicle?"

Charlie went out for a while. He sat in a waiting room and took his phone out of his pocket, glanced at it in his hand, and called Charlene. She didn't answer. Her voice prompted him to leave a message, then there was a mechanical chirp. He let the buzzing quiet go on too long. She wouldn't listen to so much silence, would she? What would she hear? Heels walking tiled corridors? A distant intercom? A throat being cleared? He hung up and dialed again. This time he left a message.

"Guess where I am right now? I'm in a hospital with somebody else's daughter. Her name is King. She's eleven years old. She's been unconscious but she just woke up. I feel a little shaky. I need to know that you're going to be okay, Charlene."

He sat in the waiting room for a few minutes, then he went back into the kid's room. She was sitting up in bed. She looked good. Skinny but ruddy with health. She had eaten most of her lunch. Roast beef. Corn. Broccoli. A roll. Milk. Butterscotch pudding. Charlie stood by the door. He asked, "What do you mean you want to go home?"

"I want to go back to Pennsylvania," King said. Sharp hills rose outside the window. She said, "I want you to take me."

"There's nobody there, King."

"Our neighbor found something of my mom's."

"A neighbor? Jon Howland?"

"Uh-huh," King said. "I talked to him on a pay phone."

"What did he say?"

"I told you already. He found something of my mom's."

"What did he find?"

"I can't tell you till I'm home."

A nurse walked by the doorway, holding a syringe. Charlie moved into the room and sat in a chair beside the bed. King pulled a blue blanket up so that it covered her to the neck. She said, "Will you take me back?"

"Like your dad," Charlie said, "I have two children. A boy and a girl."

"Who's older?" King said.

"The boy, Oswell."

"Oswell?"

"It's my grandfather's name."

"My dad and me aren't getting along," King said.

"Does he know that?"

"Not yet," said King. She wrinkled her nose. "You get along with your daughter?"

"Not very well right now."

"What did you do wrong?" King asked.

Charlie stood up. He straightened his pressed pants. "I'm going to get myself some lunch, King," he said. "You want anything?"

She looked down at her long dirty nails, her palms, the veins beneath the skin looked like worms. Her black hair fell across her face.

Charlie waited, then spoke. "We can talk about me taking you back home," he said. "Let me give Jon Howland a call, see what he says."

"If you take me back," King said, "I'll help you find my dad."

◄⋅⋅ A long-faced doctor at St. Joseph's Hospital observed King for two nights. Charlie spent time inside the hospital room and time outside the hospital room. He spoke with the Bellingham police chief and the SWAT team leader. The search party dead-ended on a wharf south of Bellingham, a boat had been stolen but had not yet been found. Charlie called Andy Fry.

"This guy is capable," Andy said. "You knew that."

"It wasn't all a loss. We got something he wants."

"You think we can get to Sawyer through his daughter?"

"That's right," Charlie said. "I think he's desperate."

"Do it, then."

With a few phone calls, Assistant Director Andrew C. Fry had King released into the custody of Charles Basin. King put on her tattered jeans and the threadbare Spiderman T-shirt that Charlie had retrieved from Benny Ward's house, then she sat on the edge of the bed. Her belly pushed out over the top of her pants. When she pulled her socks on, Charlie said, "Okay."

The kid looked up. "Okay what?" she said. She had a face straight out of a parenting magazine, only a little too thin and pale.

"Okay," Charlie said, "I'll take you home."

They stopped at a department store and bought a package of polka-dotted children's underwear, a few pairs of jeans, and three T-shirts. King trailed after Charlie Basin, just at his heels. By the rack of shirts, King said, "Can I pick the colors?" She took her time. She picked yellow, orange, and blue. She tried them on in a changing room with Charlie sitting on a chair beside the door. King said, "Everything fits okay." She said, "Thanks."

On the hourlong drive to Sea-Tac airport, Charlie Basin decided that she didn't talk enough for an eleven-year-old. He tried to get her going. "You don't talk a whole lot?"

"I don't really know you," she said. "Did your kids talk a lot more?"

"I think so," Charlie said. "It's hard to remember."

He didn't ask hard questions, nothing about her mother or her father, or about the flight to Washington, D.C., or the secret of what Jon Howland had found. Instead he asked if she was comfortable and turned on the air conditioning. He asked if the blue T-shirt she was wearing was too big. He glanced at her shaggy black hair. He remembered how infrequently he'd spoken to Charlene during their trips in the car. He'd tuned out. He'd thought of other things. He'd always thought of himself as too busy.

"You been in an airplane before, King?"

"No."

"Are you excited?"

"Not really."

"You hungry? You want to stop for something?"

"No."

"It's going to be okay, kid." He didn't know what else to say. There wasn't room for small talk.

King's eyes were wrinkled and skeptical. "You really think so?"

She was right, it had been a dumb thing to say.

With Charlie's federal ID they passed briskly through security at Sea-Tac. They walked beside one another. Polished glass threw their image back at them, a faceless man beside a faceless child. At the noisy terminal, they waited for the departure. Charlie sat in a chair. King pressed against the glass and looked out at the great dark stretches of tarmac. Her clothes looked new but her face looked old, like a carving in ivory or bone. Charlie thought, What awful human power can age a child? What happens to a kid who loses her father?

THE SAINTE-MARIE SLID onto the beach out-
side the ferry town of Anacortes. The hull grated to a halt on the
sand, the sound like something old being worn away. A mass of
heavy-bellied clouds hung overhead. Dominick jumped from
the bow. His legs bent—great anonymous hollows pressed into
the sand. Elsie jumped overboard and Clarke slung the duffels
full of guns to his father.

They walked up the beach until the sand ended and they
scrambled over head-sized stones and driftwood. The air was
cool and moist. The beach gave way to a line of scrappy trees
and then to a boat storage warehouse sided with red corrugated
metal. They walked into residential Anacortes. Among small
brightly painted ranch houses, they split up. Dominick to find
a car. Clarke and Elsie to find a pay phone.

Walking toward town, Clarke and Elsie could see a clock
tower rising above the roofs of the squat houses. They found
a phone in the parking lot of a dingy grocery store. The
sun had just begun to set and neon signs for FISH and BEER
blinked brightly in the windows. Clarke wore a tattered
blue sweatshirt. He looked at Elsie, her pale pink shirt and
grungy wool sweater. She had a smudge of something dark
and greasy on the underside of her jaw. He licked his thumb

and tried to rub it off. He nodded. She looked like any other teenaged urchin.

He made change in the grocery store and called his Aunt Annie.

"Clarke, Clarke!" Annie said. "Are you okay?"

"We're okay," Clarke said. "I only have a minute. Have you seen King? Heard from her?"

"What do you mean have I seen King? You've lost King? Oh, my God!"

"We're trying to find her."

"Listen to me, Clarke," Annie said, "you need to get away from your father."

"I don't think so," Clarke said. "I'm committed. I don't want to get away from him anymore." He paused. "We'll get King back. I promise."

When Clarke hung up, he put his hands on his knees. His vision seemed unstable for a minute, as if the grocery store and clock tower were trying to corkscrew around him. He thought about where King would want to go. Home. King would want to go home. He dialed Jon Howland's phone number and listened to the static between each ring.

"Hello?" Jon Howland said.

"Jon, it's Clarke."

"Hey, boyo, I've got news."

"You talked to King?"

"Not King, no. The FBI. They say she's with them."

"Is she okay?"

"I think so. Here's the thing. They're coming back this way."

Dominick pulled up in a Lincoln Continental. Clarke placed the phone gently in its cradle. He and Elsie opened the doors of the stolen car.

The leather seats felt smooth and cold. They took turns behind the driver's seat as the miles ahead of them blurred into the miles behind. In the night theirs was the only vehicle on the road, and each driver's mind fumbled with sleep and wove over the center line, and the car shivered over the rumble strips. They bought plastic-wrapped crackers and shared gallons of milk. They stopped beneath cones of light and pumped gas and looked up at the pale moths circling the bulbs. Coyotes called beyond the periphery of the light and farther out they could sense the great voided darkness.

They consulted an atlas. Straight through, the drive would take over forty hours. They would sleep in shifts. Before they left the gas station, Elsie slid behind the wheel. She turned the ignition. The car trembled beneath them, its frame an untuned percussion instrument. She pushed the accelerator, and wheeled the steering wheel, and asked, "Is this trip coming to an end?"

"No," Dominick said, "it's not."

"We're screwed," Elsie said.

Clarke said, "I don't know." His eyelids were like weights. He was so tired he couldn't summon the appropriate fear.

Dominick reached from the backseat and awkwardly patted Elsie's shoulder. "We can drop you back in Illinois," he said. He spoke kindly, without threat.

"No," she said. "There's nothing there. I don't want to go back."

To pass the time, they counted cows and cemeteries. They called out the letters of the alphabet as found in road signs. Sometimes they drove in silence. They shifted around the shabby interior. Each of them felt that something about them had shrunk. Their skins were a size too small. They felt delirious. Sometimes one of them would begin to shake with cold or sleeplessness or fear or hunger and they'd turn up the heat or close their eyes or speak in calming tones or pull into convenience stores and out again with small bags of corn chips and green soda bottles and dried beef. They drove the main road, I-90, and they drove fast. They were reckless, crossing the states in a blur. Clarke slept through the state of South Dakota. Elsie slept through Minnesota and Wisconsin. Dominick didn't sleep at all.

THE AIRPLANE PASSENGERS were rolled inside a thin cylinder of steel. King's eyes were closed. Her thin arms were goose bumped. This man beside her smelled of breath mints and fabric softener and soap but beneath there was sawdust and sweat and, when he bent in close to say something, indigestion. King turned to Charlie. She pushed against his arm. She asked him, "Is my father a bad man?" She looked serious.

"Bad is complicated," Charlie said.

"No, it's not." King leaned across Charlie's lap and closed the small oval shade so that she couldn't see the wisps of clouds and the contoured map of land. She pushed a button on the arm of her seat so that it reclined. She closed her eyes. She felt Charlie cover her with a small blanket. Her ears hurt a little. She listened to the roaring noise of the engines, a noise like the unfolding of thousands of small wings.

The plane landed in D.C. and Charlie drove King to his suburban home. He parked against the curb, cut the engine, and turned toward her. She hung her head and her black hair covered most of her face. She didn't speak. What had he done with Charlene when she was this age? How had he talked to her? In what tone? How had he gotten her to smile? "Hey," he said, "are you hungry?"

"I guess."

"You want to come inside for dinner? Meet my wife? Her name is Rosamund."

"I don't know."

"Come on," Charlie said, "I'm tired. I promise to drive you home first thing in the morning."

"Okay."

King trailed a few feet behind Charlie. He held the door open. The oak floors were bright and his house had never felt so spacious and wide open. The kitchen smelled of basil and garlic and oil. Sliced tomatoes piled on a cutting board. Rosamund wiped her hands on her apron. Her graying hair curled behind her ears. "Oh my goodness," she said, "what a beautiful girl!"

Charlie and King stood at the entranceway to the kitchen. "King," Charlie said, "this is my wife, Rosamund." King raised a hand to signal hello. To their right, down the hallway, feet knocked against the wooden stairs on the back staircase. A slight foot. Charlie's daughter in the hallway, wearing an old sweatshirt, her hair pulled into a braid.

Rosamund pushed a strand of her hair away from her lip. She turned toward Charlie. "Charlene's here," she said.

"I see that," Charlie said.

"She's making supper," Rosamund said. "I'm just the help. Isn't that right?"

"I guess," Charlene said. The muscles in her face twitched, as volatile as boiled water. She looked from her father to the little girl standing beside him.

"Hey, Charlene," Charlie said, "this is King."

Charlene held still. She didn't answer.

"Charlene?" Charlie said.

Again she didn't answer. Her brow lifted, her teeth gritted, then her eyes fell. She came forward, took King by the shoulders, and pulled her under the bright lights that hovered above the tiled island. Holding a paring knife out to King, she said, "Would you mind giving me a hand?" She handed King a green pepper and an onion. "You know how to dice?"

"Yes," said King.

"Charlie, can I speak with you for a minute?" Rosamund pointed toward the swinging door and they faded from the room.

King lost herself in the movement of the knife. She piled the vegetables into shallow bowls. Somber string music began to play elsewhere in the house. Charlene went to the refrigerator and, without asking, poured King a glass of orange juice and set it beside her. The first drink bit King's throat enough to hurt. She turned to Charlene. "Is your family always like this?" she asked.

"Like what?"

"I don't know," King said. "So calm."

"No," Charlene said, "not always." Her lips fluttered upward at their edges. She washed her hands at the sink. "You think this is calm?"

"I guess," King said.

"I don't understand the situation you're in at all. It must be hard. You're on the run?"

"Not anymore."

"My dad," Charlene said, "has he been talking to you much?"

"Sometimes."

"What does he say?"

"He asked a lot of questions about my dad." King sliced a red pepper in half. "He told me about you."

"He did?"

"Uh-huh."

Charlene lifted a hand to smooth the hair that had escaped from her braid. "You know where your dad is right now?"

"No."

"Why's my dad looking for him?" Charlene asked. "What's he done?"

"He hurts people."

"Lots of people?"

"I don't know how many."

Outside, a weeping spruce bent over like a thick-bodied man straining to touch his toes. Something small and windblown struck a windowpane. Steam rose from a copper pot on the stove and, underneath, blue flames roared quietly. Charlie and Rosamund pushed through the swinging door and Rosamund turned to a cabinet and put her hands on the blue-flowered bone china. She said, "King, would you help me set the table?" She set four plates in King's arms, lifted a flatware chest, and followed the girl back through the swinging door.

the people of the broken neck

In the kitchen, Charlie stood quietly for a minute. He opened the refrigerator door and then closed it again. Charlene stirred red pepper and garlic in oil. "I'm surprised you're here," Charlie said. He took a step closer to her, lifted his hands, then let them drop back to his sides. "That didn't come out right. I mean, it's a good surprise."

"I'm surprised you're here, too," Charlene said.

"Aren't you missing classes?"

"Aren't you, kind of literally, bringing work home with you?"

"I am. But I like her."

"I'm missing a lot of classes," Charlene said.

Charlie took another step closer to her. "You shouldn't worry about your classes right now."

Charlene's eyes were half closed. Her hands froze above the stove. "I'm dropping out," she said. She did not look at him.

Charlie opened his mouth to speak and closed it again. His brow furrowed and settled. One hand clenched. He leaned against the counter. "You think," he asked, "you think that's the best thing to do?"

"No. But I'm doing it."

"Okay," Charlie said. "Okay." He tried to stop himself from nodding too much. "You're dropping out. Where are you thinking about going? Are you going to come live with us?"

"WE'RE HERE." CLARKE said and the warm grace of being home spread through him like a stolen sip of whiskey. Dominick drove slowly as if there was no hurry. The Pennsylvania hills were heavily treed. Creeks trickled in barely visible gullies. The day was temperate. The sun burned hot but the cool breeze could goose bump skin in the shade.

In the backseat, Elsie slid closer to Clarke. Her hand whispered up his leg toward his crotch. Her lips brushed his ear. She whispered, "I don't know about this."

"About what?" Clarke whispered back.

"What sense does this make?" Elsie asked.

"She's my sister."

"Even if she's really here," Elsie said, "how will we get her back?"

"I don't know. We just will."

"And then what?" Elsie said. "What do we do? Where would we go?"

Clarke shrugged. They would figure it out when they were all together again. He looked at the back of his father's head. The dark bristling hair, the rough beard visible on one cheek. Clarke admired the way his father focused on what was just ahead of them.

Elsie pushed her head against Clarke's shoulder. He rubbed his mouth on her scalp and a strand of her dark hair tickled his nose. She smelled like some flowered and earthy weed like dandelion or clover.

They moved among the roads that Clarke remembered. A macadam lane arched over with horse chestnut trees. Flint Valley Road. They would be home too soon. There were few vehicles on the road besides theirs. A short-nosed school bus. Black Mennonite buggies pulled by teams of horses. A rust-colored van that backfired. At a crossroads, a dark Suburban traveled in their direction. Clarke closed his eyes. He imagined frozen water. Spit hanging in the air like a dragonfly. Idle cars on eternal country roads. Mouths hanging wide open. Stilled tongues not moving, not moving at all.

In the morning, Charlie Basin drove King home. When the hill country began to look familiar, King rolled down the window. Air lisped around the glass. A long sedan pulled through the crossroads ahead of them. Flint Valley Road. King drew a low breath. In that sedan, she recognized the profile of her father's oversized sharp-angled skull. Charlie Basin was looking out the side window, braking so that the Suburban slowed gently. Beside them, a bonneted woman hung plain black dresses on a clothesline. One of King's hands squeezed her other hand. She watched Charlie Basin study the heavy beams of the farm at the crossroads. They came to a full stop. The scoliotic stop sign was pocked with birdshot. The old barn at the crossroads had long been unpainted, its shiplap siding grayed and bored by insects. Its tin roof had rusted through. On the hill behind the ruined house, he could see another small farm. A half-dozen skinny cows. A rutted lane. A dying landscape.

A half-mile from the home he'd built, Dominick pulled the Continental onto an old logging road and stopped. He yanked the duffel bags from the car and walked with his son and Elsie back to Flint Valley Road. Loosestrife trailed along the roadside. They stepped on dark green shoots and smelled wild onion. From the road, Dominick looked back to see that the Lincoln was fully hidden, and then they moved through the shadowed woods and followed the splintered deer trails toward the A-frame.

Dominick slowed when the trees thinned, the cabin just visible beyond the crush of trunks. He set the duffels on the ground and knelt beside them. Low black mushrooms crushed under his knees and dark clouds of spores drifted. He pulled out the Springfield Armory rifle and the Beretta pistol. He slipped into the tactical vest.

Clarke watched him. Elsie touched the small of Clarke's back with the palm of her hand.

"I'll take a gun," Clarke said to his father.

"No, you won't."

"I'm going to get her back, Dad."

"I know you are," Dominick said. "But way before you made

that commitment, I made one to you." He dropped the duffel and moved forward and wedged himself behind a mossy boulder. "I won't see you hurt." Light slanted against the A-frame. The red tulips his wife had planted were in bloom beneath the conifers. He studied the house, the doorway, the woodpile and the gravel drive, and the darkened empty woods. "They're not here yet," he said.

"This was your house?" Elsie whispered.

"Dad built it."

"Maybe they're not coming," Elsie said. "Maybe we should get out of here."

Dominick balanced the rifle in one hand. He glanced up at the boughs of the trees curled protectively over them. He sighted the rifle over the boulder toward his own house. "We wait here," he said. "We stay quiet."

"That's all we do?" Clarke asked.

"When they come, I'll get King back."

"What about us?" Clarke said.

"You stay here. You stay safe."

Charlie Basin stood just behind King as she knocked on Jon Howland's door. The girl's knuckles were small and indented and reddish. The wood door sounded solid. When it opened, they smelled mildew and old leather. Jon Howland wore a red shirt with three buttons at the neck. He put a hand to his kind low-slung face, the skin falling in curves as gentle as melted wax. Then he said, "Hey, girl. Didn't expect you back so soon."

"This is Charlie." King pointed with her thumb. "He brought me."

"Was that nice of him?"

"I asked him to."

The wind blew and the long grass behind them bent over and then straightened. Howland said, "You want to come in?" He looked at the suited man with his lean face and deep wrinkles beside his mouth.

"I don't think so," King said. "Can I have the stuff you got from the woodpile?"

"Sure, sure," said Howland. "Hold on."

Howland came back with a glass perfume vial, a red-beaded crucifix, a photo of King and her mother and a box turtle, and a linen handkerchief. He passed them to King. Charlie Basin stepped up to see.

King unscrewed the glass vial of perfume and put her nose near the tip. Her mom touched the back of her neck and called her pumpkin. King put the crucifix and the photo into the pockets of her jeans. Then she unfolded the handkerchief. White going on yellow. It had something written on it. She looked at the pale marks she saw on the linen. A rough map of their property took shape—the kind of thing her mother used in treasure hunts. There was the hollow pine. The cabin and the woodpile. The field and the river. A small star beside the plum tree.

Howland put his hand on King's shoulder. He asked, "Is it worth anything to you?"

King turned her face up toward Jon Howland and something passed between them, some silent commiseration. An amalgamated memory of King standing before Howland on that same threshold in a hundred other moments, a figure on a smaller scale. Sometimes towing a sled and wearing a tasseled wool hat. Sometimes in a raincoat and galoshes, swallows wheeling in the air behind her. Sometimes there of her own volition, sometimes sent by her mother and clutching a plastic-wrapped loaf of zucchini bread or raspberry cobbler whose feel and smell traveled along the corkscrew of time until it found Jon Howland and King together again on the stoop, carrying a waft of sadness so heavy that both of them blinked their eyes to clear the blur.

"I'm ready to go," King said to Charlie Basin. "Will you take me to my house now?"

Behind the boulder in the wood, Elsie wrapped her arms around her chest. Her feet would not stay still. She looked from Clarke to Dominick and to Clarke again. "I can't do this," she said. "I've got to leave."

From behind the boulder, Dominick watched his house. He heard the engine first, the low even rumble of a V8. A dark car with darkened windows. Sunlight fracturing off chrome hubcaps and wing mirrors. Dominick couldn't make out much past the windows but pale shadows, a dark human smear in the driver's seat. He believed his daughter was the sense of movement in the rear. He felt the others stir beside him. "Stay down," he said, motioning with a flat palm. "Don't move." The black truck ground against the gravel drive that led to the east side of the A-frame. The sky was an overheated almost rabid color of blue. Dominick's chest tightened. The A-frame shivered. Something dark massed in the windows, something that gathered, then poured through like syrup and withered the hyacinths in their beds and sank into the ground and bled outward toward him, running underground in the bedrock, until he felt it move upward through the soles of his feet and sweep into his capillaries and veins and intestines and heart. Dominick breathed deeply and his chest pulled taut beneath the tactical vest. He knew that this was his daughter come home. He knew that, in a flickering moment, they'd be together again and that there was nothing at all that could not be forgiven.

The gravel crunched under the Suburban's wheels like sand between teeth. Charlie Basin pushed the brake pedal and the truck pulled to a stop. He slung one arm over the leather passenger seat and turned back toward King. "You're home," he said. "How's it feel? Good?"

"No."

"I'm sorry, kid."

"It's okay."

Charlie killed the ignition and the car shuddered once and stilled. The air conditioner cut out and the fan spun a moment longer. The sun cut in hot rectangles through the windows, making shapes in their laps.

"How're you going to help me find your father?" Charlie asked.

"It's going to be easy."

"How so?"

"He's already here."

◄⁝⁃ Clarke hunkered behind the boulder with one arm around Elsie. Blades of grass sprouted in patches around his shoes. Why were there little holes in the dirt? What lived in there? What was his father doing above him? Why was he always, always below? And why did the thought of losing Elsie pale next to the thought of losing his sister? He heard a metallic click. His father's gun against rock? Elsie hunched beside him, her spine curled forward, her cheeks wet. She was looking at him. Something wet hung from her rounded nose. Her hair shone in the overly bright light.

From near the house, he heard a car door creak open and then slam shut. His father shifted above him, standing so that his head rose just above the top of the rock. Looking up, Clarke could see the length of his father's blue jeans and the long black tactical vest and the bottom of his father's beard and the sharp underside of his nose. His father's leg pressed against him, heavy and solid and muscled, and then pulled away.

◄⁝⁃ "No," Charlie Basin said, "he can't be here. No." He scanned the house as he spoke, the field, the line of trees. He pulled his phone from his pocket and called the field office for backup. Then he opened the door and stepped out into the sheer white light. He stood behind the door and shaded his eyes with one hand. Right away he started to sweat. He reached up and pulled his tie loose. He was conscious of the weight of his pistol on his hip. He surveyed the grassy field and the derelict apple orchard and the single plum tree. Deciduous trees mixed with great chunks of stone. There's no one here, he thought. No one. The girl hadn't moved from the backseat. Charlie put his hand near his gun, cocked his head to one side, and listened. The wind pushed warm air. A grackle scrambled out of a nest in the cabin's eave. The spring peepers sounded like sleigh bells. A very distant gunshot, small-bore, probably a hunting rifle. The crack and squeal of the rear door of the Suburban.

Charlie turned back. The girl slid out of the seat backward, stepped onto the running board and then to white gravel. Skinny, doe-eyed little kid. Her dyed hair so dark. What could he offer? What could he say to make any of this better?

King's eyes darted up his legs and past his right hip, away toward the low dark wood and the boulders among them. Her eyelids did not widen. Her eyebrows stayed flat. One cheek crinkled upward so that her left eye squinted and Charlie Basin heard it then, or felt it, a rhythmic thud. Something heavy pounding the earth. He spun on one heel and his hand slid down to his belt, to the worn familiar FBI-cant holster that cradled his gun.

When the Suburban's rear door opened and the dark-suited FBI agent turned toward King, Dominick slung the rifle over his shoulder and ran forward. He hadn't wanted to take the shot. Why not? Because he needed to spare his children's eyes? Because he wanted the chase to end? Because he wanted to be as close to this as he could? Regardless of reason, his feet hit the ground hard. Each step was an explosion that propelled him forward and sent tufted grass and dirt and dangling white root arcing back toward his older son. King stood on the gravel. She wore dark unfaded blue jeans and an orange shirt. The FBI man turned too quickly, reached for his gun with a smooth unfumbling hand, and began levering it up to level. Dominick knew it wouldn't matter. He could feel it. He'd thrown himself forward too hard to be cut off now. Who was this man who had bought his daughter new clothes? There were only ten yards between them. The FBI agent did not waver. The gun was up, flat between then, so that they were connected and the muzzle yawned and spat fire. Dominick felt the soft bite low against the vest, and he didn't even slow.

KING HEARD THE gunshot. Her eyes were watering hard enough that the dark suit in front of her was a blur. She held on to the cold metal of the car door. She wanted to hurt her father for his sins, she also wanted to save him. She tucked herself into a ball and hurled herself against the back of Charlie Basin's knees. A dark marble of a girl who rolled across the gravel and disassembled into a torso and a pile of limbs. Charlie folded at the knees and rose again.

But her father was there, a human avalanche hitting Charlie head-on, knocking him sprawling. Her father pressed forward against the falling man, reached out and hauled him up by the arm and throat and tossed him against the log house so that the frame trembled.

Charlie slid down the logs like a child's doll. Overhead, a flock of migratory birds. The thinnest wisps of clouds like cotton batting stretched to webbing. The wide arc of sky a painfully bright blue. Is this what it was to die? To hear your blood like a great cataract? To have lost authority over the vessel of your limbs? To have your diaphragm spasm, your mouth gasp like a dying fish? To feel the earth rise up and gently cup your back? Charlie struggled to breathe. He saw the woods and the fields. King running through tall grass toward a plum tree.

The great backlit figure of a giant man reaching down for him, slapping his face, putting his wet lips too close to his ear.

"Get up!" Dominick said. "Get the hell up, you're still alive."

King ran and the field grass was green at the base and brown at the tip and it whispered against the denim of her jeans. She sprawled under the plum. The roots, white like thin fingers, curled up from underground. She pulled herself to the tree with her arms, dragging herself across dirt, digging with her hands, searching for what she did not want to find. A star on a map drawn on a linen napkin. Nestled by the roots, a single fieldstone. She pried her fingers around the rock's edges. She pulled and when the earth gave up its grip, she reached into the hollow left behind. She found three small white finger bones held together by grayish wormlike ligaments.

Sweat beaded on King's skin. She was spotted with the shadows of leaves. She shivered. She closed her eyes. There was grit in her mouth. Reddish lights played behind her eyelids in shapes that looked like foreign words.

Dominick set Charlie Basin in a lawn chair and tied him to it with old cattle ropes pulled from a tin on the porch. Charlie's suit was torn at the lapel and the shoulder. Dominick threaded a rope around his neck. Clarke and Elsie walked out from behind the boulder in the woods, their legs like ribbons tied into a bow, their mouths huddled close.

When Charlie's wits returned, he angled his neck toward Dominick. "You don't want to do this."

"No kidding," Dominick said. He pulled a rope tight around Charlie's feet. "When did I get what I wanted?"

"You complaining?" Charlie Basin asked. "You think you're not responsible?"

"Nope," Dominick said. "That's not what I think."

"Your children are going to get hurt."

"Not by my hand."

A deep foreign intimacy exists in the relationship between the man who ties the ropes and the man who is tied by them. Charlie shifted in the lawn chair. He said, "You could just let me go."

"I don't see how," Dominick said.

"I called for backup," Charlie said.

"It doesn't surprise me."

"Turn yourself in, Sawyer."

"I don't know," Dominick said. "I'm pretty tired."

"Jesus," Charlie said, "I'm glad you didn't shoot me."

"It wasn't you. I don't give a shit about you."

The sun fell strongly enough that Charlie could feel his face burn. He twisted against the ropes. He inhaled and caught the faint smell of manure and gasoline. He said, "Can I tell you something?"

"If you want to," Dominick said.

"I like King. She's a good kid."

◂᠁ In the field, when Elsie put her head under Clarke's chin and leaned against him, he knew it was over. Their hearts beat at different rates. The sky was wide and open and empty. Elsie's hands held him tight enough to leave an imprint of her fingers on his arms. It felt good to be bound up like that, to be contained by her idea of who he was. The sun was a pinprick of heat and light. Clarke let his head fall so that his lips rested against her dark hair. She spoke in a whisper against his throat. She said, "It's time for us to go."

She said, "Let's get out of this together."

Clarke lifted his mouth from her head and felt the individual hairs pasted to his lips. His voice was muffled. "I can't leave," he said.

Elsie said, "I'm going."

Already, Clarke was looking out beyond the two of them, at his father kneeling beside the FBI agent, his head down as if in penitence. The dandelions that his mother would once have rooted from the grass. The A-frame cabin was lit like a lantern from the inside and a thick dark smoke trailed from the chimney.

"Dad," Clarke's voice was nearly a yell, "what's that?" He pointed toward the cabin's glaring windows.

Charlie Basin strained against the rope to look toward the A-frame. He jutted his chin toward the southern window. Beyond the glass, a lean girlish figure did not move away from the fire's quick advance. "King!" Charlie called. A bedroom window blew outward and a tongue of flame licked through the glass-toothed hollow. The quick soundless explosion of a whole house taking fire. Harsh light flickered outward around the house in a wave. Dominick and Clarke's shoulders collided as they moved forward at the same time. The door in front of them snapped like kindling and smoke poured out, hot and dark as tar.

⟵ Flames ran up the drapes and across the floor. King stood in the middle of the living room over a gas can. She breathed and the smoke burned her lungs. She held her mother's ring finger in her hand. Fire lapped at the carpet by her feet and burst upward and raced around her, chasing the scent of gasoline. Something in the dark snapped and the great lumped figures of her father and brother gasped and choked and small dark clouds flew out of their mouths and rose to pool with the swirling mass on the ceiling. Then one of them had her by the arms and she was lifted and turned and swept back through the darkness and the heat, and her skin stung and her eyes bleared. And they were outside. They were free. Their throats raw and choking. Their skins blackened. Coughing to let the clear air fill their lungs. Knuckling the heat in their eyes until they could see again.

A single siren began to well over the hills.

Holes, rimmed with fire, bloomed like flowers in his children's T-shirts, and Dominick slapped at them with his hands. He shushed though his kids made no sounds. The last plum blossoms brushed through the air. Charlie Basin had flipped over in the blue aluminum lawn chair and lay with his chest against the grass, his brow furrowed, his gaze on them unwavering. Above the cabin, smoke massed into a great head. Blacker eyes against a black face. A vision that summed up what was left and found it wanting.

Elsie walked down the white rock lane. Clarke watched as she slipped. One ankle bent outward. She wobbled and caught herself with one hand against the ground but she did not look back.

The sirens multiplied into a chorus and the Sawyers filed through the grass behind the house and past the plum tree and down the hill toward the river. Dominick walked between his two children. They passed through rectangular fields, past lines of trees. The sirens behind them rose and fell over hills. A plume of black smoke rose into the sky. Dominick hitched the rifle higher on his shoulder. They were together and, whatever else, he felt that this at least was right.

Clarke's hands caught at his pockets and buried themselves. He felt his chest expanding and shrinking. He watched King and wondered what had come over her. She'd burned down their house? Was she okay? Why didn't she speak?

King clutched her mother's finger. Her mind held to words so hard that her mouth could not form them. Farmhouses lumped in the distance. Red barns canted to one side. Wind passed through hollow corncribs. King made small noises, the starting ends of words that her father and brother did not have time to address. She wanted to hold the finger in front of her father's face. She wanted to accuse him. She wanted to ask for her mother's ring back. She slowed and stumbled over an old stone wall and her father swept her into his arms and moved forward. King liked the feeling of having her weight borne and she felt bad that she liked it. She opened her hand. Grayish bits of skin and gristle and thin white bone. Her father's eyes were empty and King's hand rose as of its own accord and touched the dead finger to her father's lips.

Dominick recoiled. His mouth drew into a thin line. He held his wife's child tight and looked at her. Tall grass shivered at his feet. The sun lit them heavily and cast long shadows ahead of them. His daughter weighed no more than a loaf of bread. Must the failing light prefigure some coming fall? What parts of him would his son and daughter carry forward?

"Dad," King asked, "what've you done?"

HIS WIFE HAD once said, "Why didn't you die in the war?" and Dominick's insides had quivered like a struck bell. He'd gagged on the anger that rose in his throat. She wished he'd died? He *had* died. He'd been dead for a while now. He took a step toward her. He was going to show her just what death could do.

Then he squashed the thought, tried to hold his insides still. He got a wool blanket from the bedroom closet, went to sleep on the couch. In the morning, his insides still quivered. He wanted to curse and spit on the floor. Instead he poured bowls of cereal for his children. He poured them milk. He watched them chew. He couldn't look at his wife. He couldn't speak. He willed the war to come back and it did, in short flashes of pleasure. For three days, he walked around in a kind of fog, his insides ringing. When she confronted him again, her face was like a dishrag. It was night. Her teeth were sharp. She yelled a lot of things at him. He didn't yell back. She shoved him, he thought she shoved him. Didn't she? Everything was mixed up.

The night went on a long time. She followed him around, telling him things about himself that were true but weren't good. He tried not to listen. Instead, he tried to hold it all inside him, the ringing bell, the war, all the things he had done and seen, the fear and the rage, which maybe were the same thing. He held in the good things, too. The hills and rivers of Pennsylvania, and how he'd once known that his home had been built by his own hands, and the way he loved his kids as deeply as heartwood.

He could feel how everything good was being squeezed out of him.

She pushed his shoulder. Her mouth contorted into a flat line. He tried not to hear her. He watched her lips. "What's wrong with you?" she demanded.

He felt himself slip, a tear in some seam inside him. Visions slipped out through the hole. A finger in the dirt. The quivering on the inside moved out into his arms, then his fingers. It felt cold. He looked down at his hands, shaking. His wife's eyes widened, her hair curled at her throat. She stopped talking.

The warm rage coursed through his veins, running out through his shoulders, down his arms. For a moment, it burned out the fear. He watched his hands stop shaking, his whole body come dead still.

It was so easy this way. He reached and picked her up and tossed her through the front door of the house. She spun like a daisy wheel, landed on the grass. Bees rose and fell like confetti. He grabbed the red scarf from the coatrack, pulled her off the ground, dragged her to the hollow pine, and tied her there. She coughed and spat and pleaded and he went back into the house. He came out holding his Wharncliffe knife. She had worked free of the scarf that bound her hands and he felt he both was her husband and wasn't. She darted toward the red-blossomed plum. She seemed purposeful but he didn't care. Purpose had ceased to matter. He caught her before she reached the tree, just to show her how easy this was, and held her down in the grass.

He carved off her ring finger with his knife. Blood ran over her hand and dripped. She screamed and kicked at his face with her heels, her feet hitting his head solidly. His grip loosened as she slickened with blood. She turned and they scrabbled over her finger in the dirt. She wasn't going to let him have the smallest piece of her. His hand closed on her wedding ring but, with her good hand, his wife grabbed her finger out of the grass. Dominick held the ring up and looked at it, at the space it contained. His wife's feet caught against the ground and she ran, once again toward the plum tree. She held the red scarf in her damaged hand. Her dress flapped around her. She was bleeding. She was hurt. There wasn't anywhere for her to go. She threw herself on the ground beneath the plum tree and began scrambling in the dirt. Dominick came up behind her slowly. She glanced at him once, then she turned down the hill toward the river and ran. She ran. She ran.

He followed. It was easy. He'd done this before. He let the rage inside him follow her. It wasn't really he who let her get as far as the riverbank, or broke her neck, or weighted her body with stones.

BEHIND THEM. **AT** the top of the hill, police cars rolled onto the gravel in a line and the officers spread out across the grass. The fire had climbed out the windows of the house, scaled the log walls, and rejoined the flames that burst through the roof. From forty feet away, Charlie could feel the heat. Charlie unloaded his rifle from the cargo area in the rear of the Suburban. The police opened the cars' deep trunks and pulled out weapons and vests and gathered around Charlie Basin. He put his mouth near the ear of the bearded officer in charge and pointed out the path the Sawyers had taken. The officer in charge barked orders and everyone began to move.

Behind the line of trees at the bank of the Susquehanna, Dominick stopped. He set King on a tuft of soft grass. Their feet nestled among tiny bluebells and giant-leafed skunk cabbage. Clarke, straight-backed and tense, stood beside a fallen log. He held still but looked like a person about to take a step forward. The riverbank was littered with bone-white branches and hand-sized stones. Cattails leaned out toward the water that was flat and broad and shallow.

It was at the edge of the Susquehanna that Clarke and King

began to separate, the fraternity of their minds to break, their memories to diverge. Later they would begin the long process of not thinking about the past. They would grow older. They would live far from one another. Infrequently, they would turn backward and face the currents of time that pushed them forward and briefly remember what lay behind. These moments would be rare, but in them they would recall two separate versions of their father on the riverbank.

Clarke and King would agree that he grabbed hold of both of them. They would agree that his voice sounded like pressed gravel. They agreed that he said, "Listen here, I've done something wrong," and that it was Clarke who in a trembling voice asked, "What?"

But then the moment cleaved. A watershed. For Clarke, their father said, "I can't stomach telling you." But King already knew.

None of them watched the hills where the police officers threaded through the grass. Or the river otter that glided through the shallows. Or the birds that swooped and flapped and dove. Dominick swung the rifle from his back and put the stock to his shoulder. He looked away from his children, past the barrel of the rifle, past the thin trees, toward the thick living bodies coming after his kids. He sighted the first among them. "Listen," he said, "all flesh is grass." He pushed the safety off. He stiffened. He fired and turned, and fired and turned, and fired.

THROUGHOUT OUR LIVES, time wilts and curls like a cut flower.

AHEAD OF CHARLIE Basin, blood arched from the rear of an officer's head. His body hit the ground with a softened thump. Charlie lay flat near the top of the hill. He inched his rifle forward, braced the stock against his shoulder. To his left and right, officers fell. Others scattered and hid. Blood pattered behind them like rain. Charlie burrowed into the dirt. He breathed slowly and smelled mildew and worms and wet earth tinged with manure. He watched a deer tick crawl across the back of his hand. He let his eye run down the stock and through the glass sight and then the riverbank leapt toward him, the distant tree trunks suddenly close enough to see the variegated bark, the broad leaves like spread hands, the burned and filthy children, the giant man half behind a tree with his rifle raised. A burst of fire from the barrel. A gunshot and a scream to Charlie's right. He drew in a deep breath. His finger touched the trigger. He had shot men before but never before had he felt like he was about to shoot himself.

Down by the riverbank, the two kids watched their father stumble backward into the water. A puff at his chest, the black fabric evaporating. The armor-piercing shell swiveled through the vest. The sound of the single gunshot as distant and untenable as a stranger's life.

Their father caught himself with a palm against an adolescent elm. The leaves trembled on the thinnest branches. His skin had opened above his sternum and his organs accepted the bullet as though they had been waiting for such an intrusion all along. Their father let go of his rifle and pressed a hand against the rising blood. One of his feet slipped in the mud. He looked from his children out to the river. Something fast and blurred and winged dropped from the sky and skimmed the surface of the water. Sap blew from the trees. Dominick felt his weight shifting strangely beneath him. He stumbled, impatient with the bounds between his life and another. Water soaked into his shoes and socks. Mud sucked at his feet. And so Dominick let his children go.

On the hill, police officers rose from the ground and rushed over to those who had not risen. Voices chopped against radio static. Charlie pressed himself to his knees, still watching. Eye pressed to the rifle's sight, he watched Dominick stumble, catch himself, and, it seemed, face his children. The edges of his skin looked like a sun-heated shoal. He seemed to shrug his shoulders in some inestimable gesture of doubt, or purposelessness, or distaste, or discomfort beneath an unbearable weight. He moved backward, the water rising past his knees, his waist. The blood turned the river a living pink. When Dominick went under, Charlie Basin couldn't tell if he had awkwardly dived or if he'd fallen.

◀˙ˑ He was borne on the flood of the river. His body flowed around stones, rose toward the surface, toward the yellow light and the hundreds of paper wasps that blurred in the air, only to be swept toward the silt and rock bottom. He slowed here, caught against a tire, against stone, against the tongues of yellow-green riverweeds. Hand-sized perch scattered at his approach. His pants caught on a branch and he hung there, one leg rising to break the surface, as the current pressed and tickled and worried the Wharncliffe knife from his belt, the few bubbles from his mouth, and then the pants tore and he flowed. Above him, the skin of the water flickered with light. One hand, dragging along the river bottom, raised a slowly expanding trail of silt.

◀˙ˑ Charlie had taken his eye from the gun sight. He waved off the officers who came to shake his hand, to compliment his shooting. Their voices were faded and distant. He put his fingers to his sternum, felt the fierce drum of his heart, fingered the bullet hole that was not there. The officers rushed down the hill toward the riverbank and the children and the man in the water. They swept forward as one, the grass bending before them. They called back and forth to each other as though they were the limbs of a single body. The line of trees on the riverbank sheltered the sound of bootfall. They caught glimpses of the gleaming river between mossy trunks, the rotted dock hung on failing pilings, the two lost and filthy kids standing in the water among the cattails and muddy footprints and anger, and the paper wasps that swarmed from the willows.

Near the shallows, Clarke was silent. His throat clutched his tongue. Standing beside him, King yelled for her father. Her voice warbled. She remembered overlooking the Grand Coulee Dam, and the water pooled beneath, and the way she had called her father's name quietly, and how he had come to stand beside her. She was torn by memory, and the images came at her doubled up and overlaid. Within the ark of her remembrance came the resurrection of a hundred other times she had called for her father. She remembered standing beside him, their pants rolled high and poles in hand, along the edgewaters of the Susquehanna. Their skins smeared with dirt. Their toes curled in mud or silt. The water lapping at their calves. She remembered, too, the cold shock of the ocean in Maine, and the dark, and her father's deep laughter, and his warm hands.

Somewhere, her brother Clarke had found an emergency blanket and put it over her shoulders. With shaking hands, he held her, and together they watched the searchlights.

King remembered inflating inner tubes with her father and walking past her mother lying on a towel beneath the plum tree. She remembered a mist of bees rising from the ground as she walked down through soy and alfalfa and winter wheat to float in the river and yell out to her father behind her. With

the people of the broken neck

Clarke holding her steady, she called out now. She called him
back, her father. In this place, she had many mouths and her
cries echoed across the water. Raising all her faces and working
her many lungs, she called him, then called him again. And,
carrying both promise and pestilence, he came.